PIERS' DESIRE

PIERS' DESIRE

MARIANNE ACKERMAN

a novel

McArthur & Company
Toronto

First published in 2010 by
McArthur & Company
322 King Street West, Suite 402
Toronto, Ontario
M5V 1J2
www.mcarthur-co.com

Library and Archives Canada Cataloguing in Publication

Ackerman, Marianne
Piers' desire / Marianne Ackerman.

ISBN 978-1-55278-850-9

I. Title.

PS8551.C33P54 2010   C813'.54   C2010-901119-8

The publisher would like to acknowledge the financial support of
the Government of Canada through the Canada Book Fund and the
Canada Council for our publishing activities. The publisher further
wishes to acknowledge the financial support of the Ontario Arts
Council and the OMDC for our publishing program.

Design and composition by Tania Craan
Cover image © Wessel Wessels / arcangel-images.com
Copyediting by Pamela Erlichman

Printed in Canada by Transcontinental Printing

10 9 8 7 6 5 4 3 2 1

To the memory of my mother, Susan Kathleen,
and all our unfinished conversations.

ONE

....

RUE DES GRIFFONS is a single crooked block of stone facades protected from the wind and always in the shade. A street built with mules and monks in mind, the narrow end meets an alley no wider than a footpath. The other leads into rue de la Bonneterie and on to the Papal Palace, a medieval fortress in the heart of Avignon.

For a few years at the end of the century, Piers Le Gris lived at number 9. His room was on the second floor. A large cracked cube with high ceilings and water-stained walls, it was lit by a chandelier and French windows that opened onto a walled garden. A threadbare rug covered terracotta tiles. Stacks of newspapers and piles of stray books leaned against a massive armoire and spilled out of crowded bookcases. In one corner was a sink. A door beside the bed led into a smaller room, empty except for suitcases and a clock radio whose plug fit none of the wobbly outlets. Sometimes he felt belittled by the room's steadfast grandeur in the midst of decay; more often he was grateful for the refuge. Inside these walls Piers lived a solitary rule of his own invention. His correspondence with the outside world was sporadic, his life on rue des Griffons one of solace, simplicity and almost complete deception.

On the night it all began to crumble like so much weary plaster, midnight found him slumped in a horsehair recliner, drifting between muddled dreams and routine anxieties. The alarm clock rang as usual. He set the espresso machine to gurgle and began the ritual assembly of his tools: notebooks filled with scrawls, research clippings, files, a bag of hard candy in the pocket of his bathrobe.

A sudden gust of wind rattled the windows. A mistral had risen in midmorning and bore down hard by sunset, relentless blasts of cold from the north followed by gulps of silence. He drew back the curtains and stood looking out on a dense tangle of late-summer growth, watching the drama of shadows tossed by clouds, gathering strength. Relentless, exhausting, at least two more days to go: the mistral blows in three, or so the ancients claimed. A malevolent spirit, it was known to bring on trouble. Reaching out the window he swung the shutters closed and secured them with a stiff metal arm. Thus battened down, the house resembled a ship.

The first taste of coffee made him wince. He studied a swathe of brown paper taped above the sink, the outline of his work-in-progress, *The Lethal Guitar*, vintage Piers Le Gris. Lean page-turners full of victims maimed or killed, criminals jailed or shot point blank, feverish descriptions of women putting out and men taken in, they sold like stout at closing time. Fifteen hundred words a night, six nights a week (allowing for the occasional diversion and a fortnight for revision), in three months he could post a manuscript to London and begin again. A good living, but an old life laid claim, reduced his existence to a monkish grind.

This one was set in Marseille amid the drug trade. The structure was tight, the opening chapters flew. So far he'd killed off a voluptuous blonde and mailed her to New York, though how she made it through customs remained a problem to be solved. He yawned. The bed was tempting. Once his fingers touched the keyboard the flow would take over and he would lose himself in a blaze of typing. The hardest part was sitting down.

He got as far as placing a hand on the swivel chair when a sound stopped him. A dull thump, followed by a groan. Then another thump, another groan, sounds coming from behind the wall that separated his room from another room he'd thought was empty. He stood up, went over to the wall, leaned into the sounds.

Clunk-clunk, clunk-clunk, clunk-clunk — something or someone pushing hard against a heavy object or being pushed, a muscular rhythm punctuated by moans rising into short, high-pitched yelps, cries and thuds merging into a steadfast stream. A halo of perspiration formed on his brow. He wondered if the ancient floorboards could tolerate such an assault. Finally, the crescendo — a female roar beyond gratitude and necessity, a delirious unembarrassed theatrical Ohhhhhhuuuuu!

He set his coffee cup on the side of the table. It missed the edge and fell. While a tepid stain soaked through his slippers, the meaning of this interruption drenched his neck with sweat: a woman had moved into the room next door, broken the house rule and brought a man upstairs to be duped by cries of ecstasy. False, he was certain. A phoney blast of opera staged for the benefit of—?

Piers loathed exaggeration. His work was a testament to the efficacy of verbs and nouns. The work of words (his only defence against the abiding temptations of sloth and drink) lit the empty hours between midnight and dawn. He could no more type by day than a painter could paint by candlelight though he knew of some who claimed they did.

Stepping out of damp slippers, he dropped a newspaper onto the spill and padded across the room to
make another cup of coffee, wondering as he did
whether Madame Reboul in her near-sighted inno-
cence might not have taken in a whore.

He pressed an ear against the partition. Nothing.

He knew the inside of that room, watery mirror
in a garish frame hung low to hide cracks in the
plaster, spindly desk, stiff-backed chair, sagging double bed and pink walls, the colour of overripe
plums. He had chosen instead the avocado room
with a narrow cot and massive oak table on which
his life of papers lay spread out and waiting.

He sat down, placed his fingers on the keyboard,
tried to summon concentration but it was no use,
the night was ruined. Sure that every new word he
typed would contaminate the older words, he
stretched out on the bed, prepared to wait for dawn.
Sometime on the edge of light, he fell into a fitful
sleep and woke to the clap of dreams that fled like
thieves, leaving no stories to decipher.

A habit of frugality dating from the war had led
Nelly Reboul to leave the house largely untouched
after mourning her husband's death. She had no
need of an income. She let out rooms for the company to a string of temporary boarders, each leaving

something to talk about with the next. But after Piers arrived, she had turned down further requests until finally the agency stopped calling. A writer, she explained, her telephone voice dropping to a whisper, must have quiet.

She lit a flame under the kettle and set the breakfast tray with two cups, fresh croissants and marmalade. Tea is how an English author's day begins, Nelly was sure, just as she was sure that Piers Le Gris was English. He said something once about Montreal, but his books were published in London. (Nine leather-bound volumes personally inscribed occupied a prominent place on her mantle, waiting to be read.) She had taken to drinking tea herself and mastered the method from a book on English cookery: splash boiling water in the pot, swirl it around to heat the sides, empty, add a metal ball packed with leaves and fill the vessel to the brim.

The clack of footsteps in the hallway, Piers at the bottom of the stairs, dressed for the street in a dark suit. Tall and slim with fine, sharp features, he carried his forty-four years gracefully, as though he'd seen the world and been unimpressed.

It was a ritual of long-standing, three kisses on the cheeks. She closed her eyes, inhaled the mixture of freshly shaven skin and olive soap.

Madame!

Bonjour Monsieur. Avez-vous bien travaillé?
Mais oui, merci. Et vous? J'espère que vous avez dormi?

His crisp bookish French delivered in a mesmerizing baritone sometimes made her forget to follow the words. Passing by his door one night she had heard him on the phone, the flat contrition of English, and thought it was a stranger. The whistling kettle called from the kitchen. She excused herself to make the tea.

He saw her in profile first, bathed in morning sunlight, dark hair falling over bare arms tanned rose like the stones of Avignon. She was sitting in his place at the table, bent over his newspaper. He slid into the chair reserved for guests and said, *bonjour*. She shot him a cursory nod and returned the word, simultaneously dipping a croissant into hot chocolate, drops and flakes landing on the newsprint as she leaned forward to take a bite. A gesture in slow time, it drew him in and pushed him away to the furthest corners of the room.

Remembering the moment later, he would think of swans.

An ancient black Labrador named for the hero of his century, The General followed Nelly down the hall. Age had rendered him suspicious of change. A steady stream of drool from the corner of his mouth left glistening drops on the tiles. Paws clicking, nose to the floor, he sniffed his way through the gloom. Strange body odours made him nervous. Unfamiliar voices set his teeth on edge. He could hardly see but his instincts remained sharp.

Holding the tray against her chest, Nelly swung the dining-room door open and stepped over the threshold. A sudden flood of sunlight. For a moment she could not comprehend what was wrong. Everything was wrong. Piers was sitting in the place reserved for guests. He looked up at her and quickly looked away.

Guilty. But of what? Of sitting in the wrong place?

"Magali!" A shriek, as if someone other than herself had shouted. She reeled, stepped back, her heel landing on the dog's paw.

Certain now the bad smells were out for him, The General yelped and sank his teeth into her ankle — couldn't help it, an impulse, only a nick, hardly any blood but she howled and the breakfast tray slipped, teapot landing first, a cacophony of broken china and scalding liquid. A burst of barking to cover his tracks, The General tried to get away but Nelly pulled him back. Piers leapt up to clear away the shards and fetch a mop.

A mumbled goodbye, Magali gathered up her bookbag and slipped out the front door. Two mornings in a row, she had overslept and just missed catching sight of the man Nelly described as a famous Author. Later, when Nelly wasn't looking, she'd taken down one of his leather-bound books, read a few pages and decided he was not at all the great literary genius her aunt had claimed. She'd imagined a small, greasy man, unkempt, pale and out of shape, the sort who leers and keeps sexy magazines under his bed. Twice she'd been woken at midnight by the sound of his alarm going off, the clatter and hiss of strange rituals, coughs and humming. Last night she had tucked into her nightly exercise routine with gusto, and knowing he could hear, had let herself go like the women in his books. A steamy fake orgasm for the benefit of a stranger she'd decided must be weird.

But the man who came down to breakfast was someone else. Tall and straight-shouldered, dressed in a suit. A voice as thick as wood smoke. He didn't leer, he glanced her way once, maybe twice, seeming to look straight through her as though everything hidden was easily on display and not very interesting. He made her blush and blushing made her angry. She was glad to escape.

TWO

....

PIERS LEFT RUE DES GRIFFONS shortly after nine. A purposeful stride to the post office, a parcel dispatched to London by registered mail, four chapters and a perfect excuse for delay: his wounded dog (not literally his, yet wounded, at least limping) and a promise of more to follow. Naturally, his editor would object. He hoped she'd have bigger fish to fry. Settling into his regular table at the Café du Forum, he opened his copy of *La Provence*, still unread.

Though resolutely closed to world events, Piers took an avid interest in the rise and fall of small-town politicians. He marvelled at the endless social obligations they were prepared to fulfil, all for the joy of being re-elected. He wondered what force drove them. A higher goal? Pure ambition? Or was obligation itself the prize? Did men seek public office to avoid the burden of inventing lives of their own? Outside the conventions of fiction, Piers had no idea what made other men tick, why their lives unfolded naturally, one day connected to the next in a steady flow, while his was an effort of perpetual improvisation.

Glancing at the sports page, he saw the wrong teams were winning, the best players out, though the season had hardly begun. The waiter brought an espresso with a square of chocolate. As it melted on his tongue, his attention drifted back to breakfast. Magali, rhymes with jubilee. Barely more than a child, not at all what he'd expected. And a man in her room? How had a stranger slipped by Nelly's watchful gaze? Dry drops of chocolate milk stained the pages of his newspaper, flakes of croissant embedded in the creases. What had she found so absorbing? Which teams did she follow?

He tossed the newspaper aside, leaned back and closed his eyes. The wind had dropped, the furnace of summer was gone, tourists sparse. His thoughts drifted to her eyes. Cinnamon, set off by thick lashes and charcoal eyeliner. Far from confident, but not timid either, her gaze burned with judgement. The memory made his face tingle.

After the calamity of broken china, an exaggerated calm had settled in. Nelly made a fresh pot of tea, and rambled on about a crisis in the garden, how her regular man was down with his back, the new one knew nothing. Finally, she blurted out the girl's story. Magali's grandmother, Brigitte, and Nelly were first cousins and had grown up together in the village of Ste. Cécile les Vignes, as close as sisters. Brigitte died of cancer a year ago. Her son Paul moved in with a mistress of long-standing and his wife, Claire, took a job in Geneva, leaving their youngest to start university in Avignon alone. Nelly's brother, the self-appointed patriarch, had declared a crisis and called on her to help. All of this delivered as a brittle, high-pitched litany of facts, her fingers twirling a spoon. She said she hoped there wouldn't be distraction, meaning of course there would be distraction.

He began to walk, a familiar circuit through Place de l'Horloge and up a curved street that opened onto a vast square facing the Papal Palace, a monument from the Holy See's century in exile when Avignon had been the capital of Christendom. In the first months after arriving, he had immersed himself in the city's glorious past. Lyon, 1305, Bertrand de Got, the Bishop of Bordeaux, elected Pope Clement V. Declaring Rome was too danger-ous, he had chosen to remain in Avignon, a temporary exile that stretched into years. After his death another French bishop was handed the mitre — seven Avignon popes in all and two pretenders who fought for control after the Holy See reverted to Rome in 1377. The more Piers learned, the more he became convinced his unplanned stay was the work of destiny. He had come down from London for a rendezvous, been summoned to a meeting with an emissary from the past, spent all of one afternoon in the appointed café, but no one appeared. The waiter recalled seeing a small man in a brown robe. He'd arrived that morning, waited an hour and disappeared, leaving no message. Whose mistake? Piers had searched for the crucial letter, must have dropped it on the train. So he had stayed on, hoping for a sign, convinced the ghostly city contained a message. If he stopped asking questions, he would understand. Three years went by, a quiet life of waiting and writing.

The palace was scrubbed and mapped for tourists now, a cluster of buildings resembling a huddle of rugby players, their backs turned against the crowds. He continued up the stone staircase, around a bend in the path, past scholarly gardens and manicured clumps of greenery to the top of the hill, the Rocher des Doms. The Rhone hugged the walled city in a silver arc. On the other side was Villeneuve les Avignon with a medieval castle, slate roofs, suburban sprawl and vineyards in the distance. Breathing deeply, he filled his lungs with the clarity of clouds and sky. Sweet release from the cloistered atmosphere of stone and narrow streets, made all the more intense by the sudden presence of a girl. The sight of her churned up overlapping thoughts of past and present, the reason he had stayed away from other places. Something to do with a girl, another girl, flight from yearning — so many questions — his thoughts broke like electrical shorts whenever he thought of her. An old way of life predating Avignon, beckoning constantly. He wondered if last night's interruption could be a sign. Maybe it was time to leave.

Exile is either temporary, or it is fatal.

Nelly heard the front door open and waited for the sound of footsteps. When none came, she decided it must have been the wind. Reaching for the remote, she turned off the TV, realized she'd been drifting again, back into old conversations, ancient themes. The drug of recollection. Lately she preferred it to television or books or anything the doctor prescribed. An innocent association could set her off: Monsieur Le Gris at breakfast, strands of thin grey hair slicked back off his forehead. She had wanted to say, you'd look better with a trim and a manly hat. You're tall. You could carry it off. But she'd lacked the nerve.

The Limoges teapot had been a birthday gift from Adèle, a friend since childhood. She'd been standing beside her the first time Nelly heard herself called Madame. The fall of 1968, it happened at Le Mouret, a hat shop on rue des Marchands, the same day she fell head over heels for a brown fedora. Tilting the brim over one eye, she had admired the way it set off the curve of her jaw, but the salesgirl disapproved, hence the frosty, as you wish, *Madame.* Never one to miss an opportunity, Adèle had chided, Might as well marry now, your mademoiselle days are over.

As schoolgirls in the village of Ste. Cécile les Vignes, Adèle had admired Nelly's boldness, but marriage to a notary had given her airs. She hinted then warned outright that a mature woman without a husband was courting disaster. What disaster? Solitude? Poverty? Nelly had a good job and never lacked for company. Jealousy, she thought. Not the first time she'd noticed the perverse craving of tightly married people to see the whole world bound. A woman should act and dress her age, Adèle insisted, keep her hair short and live with grey instead of wasting money in salons to keep it dark. But Nelly liked the feel of long hair wound up like a silk chignon, let loose at night to be brushed a hundred strokes. She liked good shoes and neat skirts that showed off her legs. She made an effort to stay slim and well into middle age could still turn heads. But attention is not enough, according to Adèle. A woman needs more.

It all began with the fedora. On the eve of her fortieth birthday, Nelly met Alphonse Reboul, a solid man who sold typewriters (owned the company, Adèle pointed out) and played boules on Sunday (every Sunday, Nelly sighed). Adèle was ecstatic and attached herself to the cause of courtship. A few months later, the matter of Madame was settled with a ceremony at the Mairie followed by a banquet at the Hôtel d'Europe, the Salon Baroncelli. How strange that day had seemed. She floated like a guest at someone else's wedding. Alphonse, poor man — he took it all so seriously.

The clack of hard-soled shoes on the tiles interrupted her reverie. Expecting a knock, she stood up. Most nights Piers peeked in to say hello and if it was still early, share a glass of nut wine, but the footsteps went on by. Nudging the door open, she watched him disappear up the stairs taking two steps at a time. From now on everything will be different, she thought. He'll slip away.

She closed her eyes, tried to recall the wedding banquet, the attention of the room when they entered as man and wife, but the melody was gone. The day had worn her out, yet she knew sleep would not come on its own. Reaching for a bottle of tablets in the china cabinet, she thought of the teapot, indigo with gold trim, so expensive. Adèle's scolding voice insisting the pieces be glued back together. Climbing the stairs, she remembered: Adèle is gone. On her way past Piers' door she stopped, listening for the click of his fingers on the keyboard, a hopeful sign, the author at work. But the room was silent. Behind Magali's door, the faint throb of music. Somewhere in the dressing-table drawer was the photo of herself wearing that fedora. She had worn it the day she met Alphonse, at a reception hosted by the mayor. She'd noticed him looking, and walked away. He followed. After they were married, Alphonse took pains to praise a feminine look but she was sure it was the hat that had caught his eye.

Fair enough, Adèle would say. A man's desire is often at odds with his taste.

At seventeen, Magali was sure adults were little more than prisoners of their addictions, families and jobs, which is why they liked to lecture the young. Most of them had taken a wrong turn somewhere, or were convinced they had. Her parents were a prime example, getting divorced in middle age. Marc claimed they should have split up years ago. At Easter, she spent a week with her brother in Paris, just the two of them. They sat up all night talking. Though twelve years older, Marc was still her best friend, he didn't take their father's side in every argument. He understood why she wanted to live in Paris instead of being banished to Avignon, a town of interest to no one but tourists. A punishment, surely. But for what? For being born? Marc promised that if things turned out badly, he'd help her get away. Give it a year, he said. Stay open, and keep an eye on Aunt Nelly. She's a strange bird.

Of all the things her brother had said while they talked till sunrise, one bit of information stuck in her mind. She turned it over and over until his offhand remark came to dominate the memory of that night. He said their parents had been on the verge of divorce when she was conceived. An accident, but they took it for an omen, hoping a baby might fix the marriage. Seventeen years later, they realized they'd been wrong.

She might not have thought so much about what he'd said, but a few months after the visit, in the middle of summer, she was back in Paris at a private clinic with a mistake of her own. When it was over, she walked along the Seine wondering how long it would be until the feeling of emptiness went away. In the softest of tones, with no hint of accusation, Marc had urged her to embrace the future. Make something of your life, he'd said. Give it meaning through projects and goals. She'd listened quietly all the while thinking, a mistake does not ask the meaning of life. A mistake's life has only one goal: to have as good a time as possible and avoid causing pain — especially to herself.

Nearly midnight. She had dragged the lumpy mattress into the centre of the room and lay staring at the ceiling, waiting for sounds of the Author, his strange nocturnal ritual. Pulling the duvet over her head, she reached for earphones and turned up the music and drifted off to sleep.

A burst of hall light woke her up. A figure entered the room and quickly closed the door. Even in the gloom, she recognised the outline of his posture, sloped shoulders on a lithe frame, as light as air.

"Mouloud!" she whispered angrily.

He put a finger to his lips, crept across the floor and sank onto the mattress beside her. He smelled of gasoline, his eyes full of racing energy, as if he hadn't slept in days.

"What are you doing here?"

"I've come to look after you," he murmured.

"I told you, I don't want to be looked after. You're supposed to be in Toulouse, at university. Your father'll be furious."

He reached for her hand, began kissing her

knuckles, whispering her name. She tried to resist but he was holding tight. His boldness was annoying. Still, she was half glad to see this familiar face on the strange planet of rue des Griffons, half angry with herself for caring.

"Please, go," she whispered, pulling her hand away. "You can't stay here. My aunt's strict. I'll get in trouble. If you don't leave right now, I'll—"

She caught herself, remembering, Mouloud was the prince of threats. She would not be drawn into his game.

From the first time they smoked a cigarette behind a cabanon at Les Hirondelles, Mouloud had been sure they belonged together. The youngest child of Ahmed Mourabed, a Moroccan who had tended her grandfather's vineyards for thirty years, he spoke French like a native and earned top marks at school. Though they shared a common childhood landscape — the vineyards, gardens and ancient stone buildings of a domain near Ste. Cécile les Vignes, in the foothills of Les Dentelles — their paths had never crossed. Each year, by the time Magali arrived for summer, Mouloud had left for Tangiers with his mother, Fatiha, until last year. In midwinter she was run down by a careless driver, died instantly. Mouloud refused to go back to Morocco. He promised he'd help his father if he could stay behind, but mostly he played music and wrote songs and spent his money on first-rate hash. On hot summer nights they hid out in a cellar full of Gigondas, a dark, dewy place smelling of oak barrels and fermenting grape. Smoking and talking, they discovered parallel childhood memories. Mouloud swore he'd end up knowing everything about her, how she loved the nutty aroma of wine yet hated the taste. The smell of dope made her queasy but she adored the floating sensation that came from holding a breath to the count of ten.

Finally, one night he brought a stash of the finest and held back until, groggy and giggling, she let him slip off her jeans. An act of play, Mouloud sinking into her, whispering a prayer or a poem, she couldn't tell which. A litany in Arabic, his words tripped over each other and caught in his throat. Afterwards he swore, "There is nothing more to gain from life. I'm sure of it." The desperation of his voice had made her shiver.

A few weeks later, she told him she was pregnant. Mouloud went wild, started making wedding plans. He wouldn't understand how crazy it was. He followed her to Paris, begged for a chance to be a father and love them both. Nothing she said made the slightest bit of difference.

Pulling the duvet over her bare shoulders, she drew away.

"How did you get in?"

He shrugged.

"You have to go. You can't stay here. It isn't allowed."

"Hey! I've walked all day. Nobody picks up hitchhikers, at least not me. Just let me lie down, please, Magali, a few minutes, then I'll go."

Without waiting for an answer, he stretched out on the mattress and buried his head in the pillows. She saw a flash of brown belly. How thin he'd become. The belt was yanked to its last notch.

A new day broke lead grey and calm. In the distance a dog barked, persistent choking yaps of certainty that barking mattered. Piers sat back in his chair while the printer chugged through dozens of pages of type. Stretching knotted limbs, he gave his groin a friendly squeeze, threw off the bathrobe and began a series of warm-up exercises. Exhausted but too keyed-up to sleep, he looked forward to a run in the dawn light before traffic made the trip a hazard. Five kilometres around the walled city, dodging cars and slowing for intrusions. Even with shortcuts it could take the better part of an hour.

He took a final swig of water, opened the door and headed toward the staircase. A figure stood on the landing, poised to descend. A young male, slight of frame, stepped back into the shadows, as if to let

Piers go first. Momentarily unnerved, Piers obliged, but a few steps down, he turned around. The stranger on his heels leapt past and bolted for the front door. Sure he was a thief, Piers followed.

Outside, a burst of dawn. The intruder strode calmly down the street. Piers rushed up behind, grabbed his jacket and wheeled him around until they were face to face. So now the recipient of noisy passion had a face. Fine features, startlingly feminine, eyes as dark as his hair, not a trace of fear, at most a glimmer of surprise mixed with contempt. Surprised by the unconscious sovereignty of great beauty, Piers released his grip, letting fall a fistful of soft brown leather and murmured, *Pardon*. The word slipped out, sounded foolish. The youth spun on his heel and walked away, as if nothing had happened.

Piers leaned against the stone wall, winded, as though he'd already circled the city. Retracing his steps up the stairs, he resolved to insist Nelly take action. She made the rules, she would have to enforce them. If the house turned into a hotel or worse, he could not work, and if he could not work he could not pay the rent. It was as simple as that. He was about to knock on her door when he remembered it was barely dawn.

By the time he reached his room his hands were

shaking. Rummaging through the drawer in the table, he found a package of herbal cigarettes purchased ages ago when he'd set out to break the habit. He groped for a match, lit a dried fag and drew deeply, a sour, disappointing taste. Still, as his lungs filled up with smoke, the trembling eased. He was sweating though his hands were cold. He lay down on the bed and closed his eyes.

Dawn crept through the window casting a red glow along the border between sleep and consciousness. The image danced, surrounded by flames, a boy-man walking backwards, nothing solid under his feet, edging calmly toward some equally vague horizon. He turned and looked at Piers, his face twisted in a grin. Then Magali appeared, more real than the floating cipher, lovely and ineffably ripe and smiling as she leaned into the boy's embrace. Watching them, Piers was seized by the certainty of danger. The kid reached out to pull her away and the two of them began to run. Piers tried to call out but no words came. His body spread like sand.

THREE

AOUENNION. AVENION. AVENNIO, from the Celts or Ligurians, a word meaning city of the river or city of violent winds — both are true. The Rhone is a bridge facilitating arrival, tempting invasion; the mistral, a devious gale from the north that can blow for days and unleash madness.

Civilization advanced slowly: the Abbey St. Ruf was built in the fifth century, a synagogue in 1017. In the mid-1220s, pissing in the streets was declared illegal. The punishment for starting a tavern brawl or frequenting brothels was to be thrown over the walls, fully clothed, into the deepest part of the Rhone. In the high Middle Ages, Avignon was the property of the Queen of Naples, who fell on hard times and sold it to the Papal Court in 1349.

A mule-like pace of change until the fourteenth century, the arrival of the Pope, an explosion, somewhere between a gold rush and a miracle. An unsuspecting town was burgeoned with foreigners —

Italian bankers, Tuscan painters, French architects, Swiss guards, enough Germans to form a confraternity, lawyers and moneylenders, furriers, illuminators, bookbinders, booksellers, goldsmiths, bakers, butchers, pilgrims, prostitutes, diplomats, professors, soothsayers, midwives, and undertakers — a polyglot population eventually exceeding one hundred thousand. With the most sophisticated tax-collecting system since the Romans, Christendom's Provençal capital at its height surpassed any of Europe's secular courts in pageantry, luxury and intrigue. Property values soared, magistrates scrambled to keep the peace. No rogue talent languished for want of opportunity.

"A second Babylonian captivity," wrote the Florentine-born poet Petrarch. Having grown up in Provence where his father served the Papal court, he stayed on and became Avignon's most famous detractor.

Licence characterized the Papal years, but not to the exclusion of liberty. A community of Jews was given protection; a university welcomed thousands of students. The village landscape was transformed by convents, chapels, churches, cardinals' palaces and, towering over them all, the Papal Palace. Thirty years under construction, it reconciled contrary styles, blending the walled austerity of

introvert popes with the pomp and glitter of flamboyant spenders.

Piers never tired of expounding new details from
his ongoing research. Nelly listened dutifully. She'd
passed the Palace every day for years and never set
foot inside. She had no interest in the remnants of
ecclesiastical power or architecture designed to
impress the faithful. Scornful of religious fervour,
she dismissed the bargains of prayer as pitiful superstition.

  After training as a nurse in Carpentras, she had
moved to Avignon for a position in the recovery
ward at Ste. Marthe's Hospital, which is where
she'd heard there was a prison nearby, Ste. Anne's.
She had an inmate as a patient, nursed him through
gangrene. His leg came off in bits, first at the ankle
and then above the knee. Under the guise of delirious recovery he told his story, how he'd been
honour-bound to kill a man and would surely have
been pardoned if not for an excitable cur that got
in the way of a stray bullet. He'd known he was
doomed by the faces of the jury when the prosecu-
tion mentioned the dog. Twelve well-fed peasants,
they were sure that men fight other men naturally
and often for good reason, but a decent soul leaves
a dog alone.

The story took Nelly's breath away: a life sent reeling by a random act of fate. And yet he bore no grudge. A day, a week, a year, a decade — he seemed not to feel the difference, which is how she came to see that time is a fluid thing, immeasurable, elusive, somehow not quite real. Everything about the man had moved her. His pain, his humour dampened by resignation, yet underneath the performance, a keen desire for life. Most of all, she was captivated by the aura of mystery he constructed around himself. As the confession poured out, she could see he was watching for her response, savouring the tale's bitter twist, expecting a laugh. Later, when the fever had passed, he made her swear an oath of secrecy. She'd been puzzled, could only assume he hadn't told her everything.

Her first day at Ste. Anne's, the clank of iron doors shutting had seemed the perfect antidote to the din of church bells, a thrill that never quite wore off. She had found her true calling as counsel to the condemned. Though impervious to charm and manipulation, she was on the inmates' side, a position they could sense.

Excluding the brief interlude of marriage, her life at Ste. Anne's spanned nearly forty years. Her retirement gift from the administration was a watch. The inmates gave her an olive tree, dedicated to a thousand years of life. The watch soon stopped but the olive tree prospered, and retirement didn't last. Every Wednesday afternoon, she made her way along the familiar winding route to the prison library where she volunteered as assistant to the head librarian, Hervé Brunet.

A scrupulous bachelor with thinning hair, he spent his days muttering against the tide of forms and letters that floated down from Paris, leaving the matter of books to Nelly, who took great interest in the chatter of readers. Her latest task was dealing with several dozen boxes of books that had come to Ste. Anne's following the death of an eminent Sorbonne professor. The bequest sparked an irate letter in *Le Monde* from a circle of intellectuals. Why a remote provincial prison had been chosen to receive such a valuable collection was a mystery bordering on outrage. Brunet had studied the cache, as if the books themselves might provide a clue. A minor scholar with a thin publishing record, the late professor's sinecure had rested on a brief though highly acclaimed study of Genêt, often referenced by subsequent studies but out of print for decades. Dipping into a stack on his desk, Brunet had examined one volume after another.

"I suppose," he mused, "one must consider that Genêt was …" He drifted off, seemingly lost in contemplation.

Nelly prompted, "Genêt was an inmate?"

He looked up, straight at her, suddenly paying attention. "Yes. He was that too, wasn't he?" A sly smile exposed tiny kernels of teeth. "These books will have to be vetted before we let them into circulation, if indeed we ever do. Madame Reboul, I hope I can count on your help. You may prefer to read these *particular* volumes at your leisure, in which case you have my permission to take them *home*. In fact, I would strongly advise you to do so. We mustn't rush the matter. That wouldn't do at all. Would it?"

She had taken the books he'd set aside, wondering why he was looking at her so intently. Was she expected to refuse?

"Thank you," she said, without understanding at all.

He nodded, and clutching two titles to his chest, retreated into his office and closed the door. I will take them home, she'd resolved. No need to have him peering over my shoulder while I read.

By the time Nelly turned onto rue des Griffons it was almost dark, the air still damp from an unexpected downpour. Her canvas bag was heavy. Her arms ached. Rounding the corner, she set the load down and glanced ahead. A shaggy figure stood huddled in the doorway. Snatching up the bag again, she quickened her pace and shot past the door. From behind, a hand grabbed her arm. A voice called out, "Aunt Nelly!"

It was Magali, her hair gone wavy from the rain.

"I forgot my keys," she said. "Don't worry, Auntie. They aren't lost. Come on, let me help you with that load."

Still shaking as they entered the house, Nelly blurted out a warning against the dangers of wet clothing, turning brisk to hide her confusion, ordering the girl to change into dry clothes and then come straight to the kitchen for a hot drink.

"But I like the rain," she protested, following her down the hallway.

The electrical switch spluttered. Fed by ancient wiring, the kitchen light assumed a will of its own. Nelly knew the trick, how to wiggle the button until the current connected. It was early in the season to be lighting the stove, but the sight of Magali's wet hair made her fear a chill. She doused the oil burner with starter, tossed in a lit match. A ring of flame shot up sending out pungent fumes. Magali watched, absorbed by the ritual. She's never seen such old-fashioned ways, Nelly thought. Brought up in a sprawling split-level in the suburbs of Orange, she pushes buttons, microwaves.

In four weeks under the same roof, they hadn't

seen much of each other. A reluctant riser, Magali rushed out the door each morning and stayed in her room all evening. On weekends she was out late, sneaking upstairs like a mouse in wooden shoes and lying in bed till noon. In the absence of sightings, her presence could be verified by a trail of lights left on, doors ajar, taps dripping, clothing dropped, half cups of tea on the kitchen table. Entrenched disorder was one thing, but Nelly hated carelessness, so she took to leaving notes. Progress had been made but a talk about the rules was overdue. Filling a saucepan with milk, she resolved to speak her mind.

Rain pounded hard against the kitchen window. Gusts of wind penetrated the creaky frames and made the curtains sway. Magali sat perched on a stool while Nelly rummaged through the pantry, searching for a tin of cocoa, filling the void with chatter about the dangers of a chill. The lights flickered. Nelly emerged from the pantry in time to catch a swirl of wet shirt landing on the table and a flash of Magali's bare shoulders, a pale camisole on skin like butter, before they were immersed in darkness.

"I have a flashlight upstairs," Magali volunteered.

"No, stay put. The whole house will be out." She'll say we're living in a barn, Nelly thought. Won't certain members of the family enjoy hearing about this!

Groping through the drawers, she found a stub of candle and lit a match. The flame caught a glimmer of Magali's mischievous smile and died as the candle took hold. The room opened up with light.

When the milk was warm, Nelly stirred it into the cocoa and sugar, filled two cups to the brim, and handed one to Magali, who whispered thanks. They sat in awkward silence, Magali rocking back and forth on the kitchen stool. An unnecessary movement sure to loosen the joints, it made Nelly anxious.

"Stop!" she snapped.

Magali stood up to leave but before she could get away, the telephone rang. An urgent peal in the distance, it startled them both.

When Nelly had disappeared into the dining room, Magali moved closer to the stove. She was cold and hungry, but knew her room would be even colder. On the hunt for a loaf of bread, she peeked into Nelly's bag, found nothing, only old books. A title caught her eye: *Le Livre d'Amour de l'Orient*. Before she could open it, she heard a dulcet voice from the hallway.

"Magali, *chérie*. Telephone call for you." An unfamiliar singsong voice. For an instant she thought there must be someone else in the house. There was no time to put the book back. She slipped it into her satchel, and sat up straight on the stool.

The kitchen door swung open. Nelly's face was rigid, chin pointed upwards, lips bowed into a tight smile. A strangely formal melody: "Your grandfather wishes to speak with you."

With Magali out of sight, Nelly retrieved the wet sweater and draped it over a rack by the stove, muttering to herself about the dangers of staining the wooden table. Inhaling the pungent mixture of lamb's wool and cigarettes, she changed her mind, added a few lavender grains to a basin of water and set the sweater to soak.

Through the half-open door she could hear Magali's voice, and moved closer to catch the drift. An animated description of university life: her courses, English, accounting and law, the core subjects of a business degree. Léonce must be proud, she thought. Money always meant so much to him. Under his care, Brigitte's stony heritage in the Haut-Vaucluse had been thoroughly transformed. He'd added land in Gigondas and Vacqueyras, uprooted the orchards to plant prize-winning vineyards until Les Hirondelles was worth a fortune.

Hearing Magali's laughter, she closed the door and put a jar of *pistou* to heat on the stove. Still a charmer, she thought, a man who lives to please women. And so many of them! Poor Brigitte had had to endure the talk. Nelly lit a second candle and placed it on the counter, then a third for the table. The soup began to bubble, filling the air with savoury warmth until the dank room resembled a real country kitchen.

The door swung open. Magali entered, breathless. "Grandpa says hello!" she announced. Her cheeks were flushed. "He sends his love, and guess what? I'm invited for Christmas, just Grandpa and me. No parents, maybe Marc and Estelle if they can get away. He's coming to pick me up December twenty-first. What day is that? I think it's a Thursday." She stood still, as if expecting a response.

Nelly turned away, slid the pot off the gas burner and reached for a ladle. Hands shaking, her sleeve brushed too close to the candle. A handkerchief, tucked inside the cuff caught fire. Magali lunged at the flame intending to blow it out, instead knocked the candle over. Hot wax burned her hand. She shrieked and burst into tears.

Clumsy girl, Nelly sputtered to herself. So impulsive. But she said nothing. Moving quickly, she rubbed the singed sleeve, examined the burn which was superficial and not nearly as serious as the girl's reaction had suggested. Taking out her medicine kit, she applied a thin layer of salve. The skin was cool to the touch, her fingers icy. Standing close, she caught the mixture of cigarettes and soap, hair still damp with rain, and underneath the common smells, a bone-deep aroma, faintly animal. The sensation of being so close to a familiar body, she hadn't felt in years. Her head spun. She steadied herself against the table and sank into the chair.

"Are you all right, Auntie?"

Nelly struggled, groping for an answer, but no words came. The look of bewilderment on the girl's face, she suspected, must mirror her own.

"Sit down, I've heated soup." She hadn't intended to be sharp, and attempted to cover the mistake by an offer of escape. "You can take it to your room, if you like." Without waiting for a reply, she turned her back and headed for the dining room, as though a pressing chore needed attention.

When Magali had finished the bowl of *pistou*, she stretched out on the mattress and covered up with the duvet, a gift from her grandfather. She was grateful for his phone call. The news about Christmas gave her hope. Only a few more weeks to go. The sound of his voice always lifted her spirits. He never judged, never pried into what she was doing. He was not among the relatives who said she was spoiled; he was one of the spoilers. She decided to get a cookbook and surprise him by making something her Gran always prepared for the *réveillon*. Or maybe they'd go to a restaurant, she knew she could count on him to have a plan.

From a corner of the rose room, a gas radiator groaned as though making heat was a terrible effort. Everything in this house is old, she thought. The mattress was her raft, surrounded by books and clothes, empty water bottles and half-eaten packages of butter biscuits bobbing on the sea.

Reaching for the satchel, she dragged it under the cover and searched inside for the prize she'd pinched. So easy, maybe too easy. Nothing like the first time, a thrill, an impulse, in Paris. Wandering around the Galeries Lafayette waiting for the rain to stop, she'd seen a salesclerk cast a mean look in her direction, and decided on the spot to lift a lipstick. She picked out a colour and looked away, keeping an eye on the surroundings, watching who was paying attention, then slid the tube up her sleeve and left the store at a casual pace. Once out on the street, she'd been sure everyone was looking.

Next she tried a silk scarf, then a book, one she didn't even want, but the people in the bookstore were smug. She took it out of spite. A week later she slipped a wheel of Camembert into her shoulderbag. A pudgy grocery clerk noticed and came running after her but she lost him easily in the winding streets of St. Germain des Près.

As for the lipstick, she had ducked into a nearby café to try it out, a horrible texture and colour, she tossed the tube into the washroom trash. But the thrill lingered, proof it doesn't matter what you steal. The rush comes from taking the risk and getting away with it, having power over strangers. Stealing displaces numbness, for a few hours at least.

Those first experiments in petty crime had followed hard on the morning at the Paris clinic when she'd undergone a lecture from a nurse, after a demeaning procedure by which she got her life back. Destiny brought under control by medical science, blood flowing out through a plastic tube, down the drain and into the Seine. In former times, a girl in her position might have jumped into the river. A swirl of thoughts and moods gave that crazy time the disjointed rhythm of a high. Afterwards she was prone to sudden bursts of anger, a lingering sense of violation. Of something stolen, something nameless.

A few weeks later her parents caught her smoking dope, which led to an awful row. She'd made promises. So had they. Afterwards, she knew the minute she walked into her bedroom whether they'd been in there searching for evidence. It was easy to tell if something private had been seen or touched. They made her angry, and then depressed. She figured the feeling would wear off just as everything wears off, the buzz of shoplifting, the swoon of good dope, even the pleasure of knowing somebody really great likes you.

Books were the easiest, because the clerks in bookstores were always distracted, far more interested in talking to each other than keeping an eye on customers. Poking around the house on her own, she discovered Nelly had dozens of books, dusty and thick. They all looked boring. She hoped the volume she'd taken was different, but it looked old. Definitely used. A soft tan cover with red lettering: *Le Livre d'Amour de l'Orient,* and in smaller black type: *Le Bréviaire de la Courtisane. The Courtesan's Prayer Book.* So, old ladies like to read porn, she thought. Of course, this one would be considered literature. The first page bore a bookplate and an important-looking signature but the second was blank, as were the rest. Creamy vellum paper, as thick as cloth, empty pages, some kind of diary with a false cover. Private. Suddenly, taking it didn't seem so easy.

Wrapping the notebook inside a bulky sweater, she decided to make a quick trip back to the kitchen before Nelly noticed. On her way downstairs, she met Piers coming up. He nodded and stopped, mumbled good evening and extended his hand. The gesture surprised her. As she reached out, the book

slipped and landed on the step in front of them.
Piers bent down to pick it up, and reading the title
as he handed it over, flashed a wobbly grin.

"So, you're interested in the Orient?"

She nodded.

"Have you been there?"

"No," she stuttered. "I've only visited Italy and
Spain. Well, London once."

"London! Ah, yes." He sighed, as if there was
much he could say on the subject, but instead, began
to walk backwards up the stairs. As she turned to
go, she heard him stumble. Hurrying on down the
stairs, she felt his eyes following her.

Nelly observed the exchange on the staircase through
a crack in the sitting-room door, and watched
Magali's furtive dash into the kitchen. She'd noticed
the missing book immediately. A thief in the house?
No surprise, she thought. After all, the girl is
Brigitte's progeny.

FOUR

LIKE FLOCKS OF migrating birds, giant rusty leaves
swirled around the university's ancient stone facade,
settling on manicured grounds connecting the old
building with a sleek new library made of glass and
green girders. Piers walked through the gates in late
afternoon. It was warm for the end of October.
Spying a stone bench half hidden behind a clump of
laurel bushes, he settled down to survey the courtyard, a grazing ground for students, some stretched
out on the grass, others huddled in friendly circles
and amorous pairs, killing time, making time and
smoking.

He had set himself the task of recording their
day, jostling, sparring, the body talk of exquisite
girls and cocky boys. Like lawn ornaments or extras
in a movie, half were dressed for comfort, the other
half for show. Their clothes looked new, their faces
fresh and crafty. He was amazed by the self-assur-
ance of youth, at least on the surface. Slobs talked

confidently to peacocks and no one sat alone. Must be a new code, he thought. Nothing like the old.

A burst of laughter erupted from the nearby circle where a tall beauty held forth to a circle of admirers. Teetering on platform shoes, she was poured into skinny slacks that flared mid-calf, a brief t-shirt outlining her ribs. Piers opened his notebook and scribbled: rich, lean, bold = youth. Not how he remembered education, but then wasn't that the point of research? It was the only way to keep the personal from creeping into fiction.

As he opened a newspaper and pretended to read, his thoughts flowed back to his own school days. A series of boarding schools, followed by several lunges at higher education, Ivy League on the east coast, and a stint in draughty Edinburgh. Never the same place for long, yet always another to take him in. No expense spared. Nothing but opportunity thrown his way by a father he rarely saw.

The accidental parents, he had named them as an adolescent, turning them into a jocular legend, part of his carefully constructed private-school persona. A famous (married) writer and an actress half his age — their brief encounter during an Adriatic cruise and a series of stormy rendezvous in the years that followed had rekindled the aging author's stalled career and ruined a beauty's life, or so she claimed. Craving warmth and devotion, the child-mother leaned on her son for everything. She died gracefully in a hotel room smelling of orchids. He marked her passing with a Pacific voyage and vowed not to follow in the old man's footsteps. The first of many broken vows.

He had never heard the other side of his mother's story, couldn't summon the nerve to ask. His meetings with his father had been formal and faintly shameful for them both. After the funeral the old man softened, sent for his secret son and graciously offered the use of his famous name. His son declined politely, while raging inside. After that, no name felt like his own, though he tried on several.

From half a lifetime spent in the chains of formal learning, he counted only one friend, E.B., a self-diagnosed genius who studied all night by flashlight so that he could lounge by day, giving the appearance of natural brilliance. The last news of E.B. had come years ago, a cryptic postcard from a mutual acquaintance reporting that the lamplight genius had entered an institution full of like-minded men. No hint as to whether it was Bedlam or Harvard. The main point was in the postscript: E.B. still considers you odd. A madman's second-hand comment was the only hard evidence of himself he possessed from those years.

What if I could go back? he wondered.

Surrounded now by so much youth and beauty, the idea of formal study seemed luxurious. Following a course, taking home assignments. Preparing for exams. Receiving a grade! What joy, to be sure that all answers to all questions lay right over there in the green-glass library. He was tired of improvization, ready for cunning girls, sure he could stride over, introduce himself, borrow a cigarette and shuffle off to class. Balance irony with levity and emerge at the end of term with an album of colourful memories and an address book full of life-long friends.

Soaked in reverie, he began to sweat without noticing. Beads formed on his crown. Leaving the house early, he had mistaken a grey dawn for the day's weather and worn his raincoat. A rumpled reminder of London, it had spent the summer under a pile of books. Whenever he relied on instinct, Piers expected rain. Extremes always caught him off guard. Provence, for example: from photos and brief childhood trips, he'd pictured a paradise of sun and scent. Instead it was a violent, moody place, prone to sudden storms and heat waves. Much like his mother.

The hard bench made his muscles ache. He got up to stretch, tucked the newspaper into his briefcase and began to walk, cutting a wide circle around

the courtyard and heading toward the main building, an elegant eighteenth-century facade built on a
curved stone arc dating from the Middle Ages. The
modern glass doors were open. Clutches of students
and professors, casual weather-beaten men and styl-
ish women spilled out into the promenade, chatting
gravely, making plans.

It was cool and dark inside. His eyes adjusted to
the cavernous foyer. Wide marble staircases on both
sides leading up to a gallery on the second floor. The
grand scale struck him as better suited to justice than
undergraduate education. Glancing at his watch, he
headed up, hoping the rhythm of his stride signalled
purpose and destination. At the top a cheerful aqua
corridor with open doors revealing banks of com-
puters, classrooms, offices. On the other side,
windows looking onto an interior courtyard filled
with rows of lavender. Recently renovated, the building had a long history as Avignon's main hospital;
he knew it from Nelly's stories of her early days at
Ste. Marthe's, her first posting as a young nurse in
the mid-fifties.

All physical evidence of that world had disappeared. The morgue was now a café, the surgery
refitted as a lecture hall. Former sickrooms had become classrooms, the whole edifice washed in
bright antiseptic modernism. Yet the deeper he

wandered, the more the building's historic purpose seemed to seep through. He would not have been surprised to meet a limping soldier or a white-robed nun dashing, head-down, bearing an urgent vial of morphine. Nelly's stories followed him, the ghosts of feverish patients mingling with the exuberance of youth. He thought he heard her voice, the crackling lilt of verbal calligraphy.

A door in his path swung open. Two young men emerged, laughing. Piers slid past into the WC and the door swung shut, leaving him in darkness. He groped for the switch, found none. Suddenly the automatic light flashed on, illuminating a mirror. The sight of his face was a shock. Blotches of red, stringy hair matted with sweat and a strange, startled expression. Guilt.

He felt foolish, caught in the wrong place for the wrong reasons. Research exposed as a vague pretext. Nelly's rambling tales of long-deceased strangers, an idle reverie, yet there *was* a reason for this visit. He was looking for someone. Hoping for a chance encounter. Counting on it.

The automatic light went out. He bolted for the hallway, made his way quickly back through the maze of offices and classrooms, sure that every professor was looking at him strangely and all of the students grinning, whispering. As if they knew.

Magali entered the gated square alone, half expecting to see Mouloud, who often tracked her down. He claimed he'd found a job but wouldn't reveal more, implying intrigue of some sort. A lie, she suspected, calculated to get her attention. Instead, she was surprised to find Piers sitting on a bench, legs spread apart, elbows resting on his knees like a clumsy spy. Her first thought was, he's waiting for me.

Standing close, she said *bonjour*. It startled him. He slid his sunglasses onto the top of his head and answered back.

"What are you doing here?" she asked, just friendly enough to mask bluntness.

"Research."

"Really. Research into ...?"

"My book."

"Ah, yes."

He stood up, and pulling himself to his full height, glanced at his watch.

"What kind of book are you writing?" she asked, taking a step back.

"I'm looking into the life of Petrarch."

"Ah! Well, I doubt there's much on him here," she said, waving at the library. "Very few books in there at all."

She took out a cigarette, offered him one. He declined, but pulled out a lighter to light hers. She took a long drag, exhaled in his direction and tossed it away. Keeping his eyes fixed on hers, he slid the toe of his boot over the butt and flattened it into the gravel.

"Well, I should be going," she said, tilting her head to one side.

He nodded, murmured yes, then he turned and walked away. The pivot took him straight out through the iron gates and into a narrow street. He could feel her eyes on his back, cool, interested, he was sure. A fresh picture of Magali lightened his steps, the way her dark eyes danced as she quizzed him. He was a good foot taller but she had pulled him down with her gaze.

He stepped off the curb. A small car came hurtling around the corner and swerved to avoid him. Deaf to the driver's shouts, he caught the crash of bumper against stone as a distant rumble. He kept on walking, did not hear two police officers approaching from behind, calling out for him to halt. Intending to circle the block and head back to the library, he quickened his stride. The police bolted ahead and blocked his path.

"*Vos papiers, monsieur!*" the officer barked.

Piers fumbled through his briefcase and produced his carte de séjour. The inquisitors exchanged knowing glances. He was not a French citizen, that explained everything. He knew from experience that trouble in France begins and ends with paperwork. Innocent until proven guilty being a vague concept in the Republic, a foreigner could not expect to be given the benefit of the doubt. In his experience — and certainly in his books — police were stiff and hostile, these two no exception. One was tall and arrogant, obviously in charge. The other, reserved but mean, brandished a pen and notebook.

What was he doing on university premises?

Not an idle query, Piers suspected. Someone must have spotted him wandering through the halls or sitting in the courtyard, and made a phone call. He shot a glance above their heads. Magali was watching from the open gate, along with a gaggle of other students.

It seemed to take them ages to verify his existence. While the tall one shouted into a cell phone, his partner delivered a dissertation on the French state's generosity toward foreigners, clarifying that these privileges, however, did not include the right to loiter in university courtyards. Public property — research — writer — novels — London: none of his objections tempted them into conversation.

Three girls in tight jeans walked by, giggling. Piers looked in their direction. The officers noticed. The short one wrote it down. Finally, after a warning that his name was on record, he was free to go.

The sun had dropped, the streets were in shade. He was exhausted, angry, thirsty. On the way through Place de la Pignotte, he caught his reflection in the window of a dress shop and saw what the police had seen. His shirt was soaked with sweat. He needed a haircut, a shave, or maybe a beard. The coat was a pitiful ghost of its former glory. Shapeless shoulders, torn pockets, a gash of lining hanging loose from the hem. The French word fit: *affreuse*, to the exile's ear a combination of frazzled and frightening. He ripped the coat off and stuffed it into a garbage bin, enjoying an instant surge of relief. All he needed now was a beer.

As he made his way along the narrow streets, the day took on a chill. Gloom crept into his thoughts. All he could think of was the missing coat. An old friend, they'd been through a lot. Why had he abandoned that raincoat? He considered going back to rescue it from the trashcan, but before the interior argument could be settled, found himself standing in front of O'Leary's, an ersatz Irish pub the likes of which were springing up all over France. Walls covered with shamrocks, kilts, red rugby shirts, top-o-the-morn' joke plaques. Once he'd even spotted a beefeater mannequin. The careless juxtaposition of symbols made him boil. In many other cities of the world, a mistake like that could lead to a fight. He slid onto a barstool and ordered a Guinness, grateful for a familiar scent, even if it wasn't quite real.

The last Friday in October, Nelly placed a tray of black olives and pistachio nuts on the stone table beside a pitcher of water, two glasses and a bottle of *pastis*. The season's final Friday aperitif in the garden, an unspoken ritual begun shortly after Piers arrived; from April until October, a rendezvous in the garden; in winter, nut wine beside her sitting-room fire. Old themes stretched over weeks, stories of her nursing years at Ste. Marthe's, the dramas of her true vocation as a prison counsellor. An enthusiastic student of Avignon history, Piers was interested in it all, stories of the war, medieval themes too; the popes and cardinals of Avignon were his special fascination. He'd read everything that touched on their history. She'd tried to be interested, but as a long-time agnostic who spurned religious institutions, had a hard time hiding her contempt.

When she'd declared herself an atheist, Piers had laughed, then gone silent. Assuming she had insulted his beliefs, she had muttered a change of subject. He laughed again, a peculiar nervous chuckle. She'd been afraid he would say something religious, try to save her soul, and the whole image of a worldly writer would come crashing down. She had imagined the cause of literature was his true belief, so closely did the rhythm of his work resemble a monastic regime. As a deadline drew near, he lost all sense of time and often stayed awake for days, typing, pacing, hardly stopping to exchange pleasantries. Only when the bundle had been dispatched to London would he emerge from his state of rabid concentration and seek out company.

Taking up gardening shears and gloves, she busied herself trimming recalcitrant climbers. He was late, but she had confidence in his ways. The explanation would be simple; he must have forgotten the day.

Gathering up the last of the vines, she piled them in a corner of the garden and glanced up at Magali's window. Her room was still in darkness, curtains drawn. The night air was turning cool. It was too late now for an aperitif in the garden.

As she started for the house with a tray of un-used glasses, the garden gate swung open. Piers entered, bearing a large bouquet of flowers. She set the tray down and stared at him, a tall, thin man in a summer shirt, smiling warmly, walking toward her with his arms outstretched. She closed her eyes, reached up to receive his kisses and felt his arms around her, lifting her almost off the ground, a snug embrace pulling her against his chest. He smelled of beer and running. She caught her breath. Her greeting seemed to gush out involuntarily, a nervous trill, full of relief.

Ahhh, magnifique! Vous me gâtez toujours, Monsieur Le Gris. Quelle beauté! Vous êtes toujours si charmant.

Too much Guinness made his head spin. The sudden clasp of her body, lean and nervous, surprised him. He felt his touch race through her into the ground. He could have held on longer.

Drawing their chairs close, they sat under the olive tree, sipping a warm *pastis*. He had tried to think of a suitable excuse for being late, but she seemed to have taken no notice. Perched on the edge of a wicker chair, small and familiar, hands fluttering, she chattered about the day's events: a weather report predicting rain, a phone call from Madame Noiret complaining about the climbers shadowing her garden over the wall. Their regular gardener was still down with a bad back and the young replacement hadn't worked out at all. Noiret's nephew had recommended another name, but Nelly was reluctant to give the task to a stranger. Inept pruning could be ruinous!

The sound of her voice pulled him out of despair, into a mellow mood. He could happily have fallen

asleep, no offence at all, a delicious safe stupor re-
placing the trials of the day. Struggling to keep his
eyes open, he shifted in the chair and sat up straight.
Images of the day flickered through his thoughts, a
wasted afternoon of delusion while the only woman
who mattered had been here in her lovely walled
garden, waiting for him. His mother had wasted her
life waiting for a man she hardly knew. Thinking
about her always sapped his energy. So much
wasted time. She deserved more, so did Nelly. The
day hung heavily on his spirit. And yet there she sat,
oblivious to his thoughts, chattering on about the
garden, holding him with vigorous conversation as
she had held him so many times before. The evening
light was fading quickly, a stone-lit glow descending
around them.

Above her head, a light went on in an upstairs
window. Magali's room.

Nelly saw his eyes dart upwards. She knew the
cause immediately. He shifted in his chair, eyes
glancing away from the window, then back, as if he
could not turn away. She was sure the girl was smiling down at him.

"It's late," she said. "We should go inside."

She stood up and began stacking dishes on the
tray, though they'd hardly touched the *pastis*.

"I could make a fire," Piers offered. But it was

too late. She was already headed into the house, holding the tray unsteadily, heels crunching along the gravel pathway.

It all happened so quickly. She was alone before she realized what he'd said. *I could make a fire.*

Had she listened, nodded, walked more slowly, they would be sitting by the warmth now, caught up in Friday conversation. But she hadn't heard or at least had not digested the offer until it was too late. Now he was gone.

"You must be part bird," Adèle had said. "While other people are still wondering what to do, you've gone somewhere, into the clouds, nothing left but footprints and dust." The echo of a dear friend filled her head. Adèle was right. The too-quick dance was disastrous. A familiar, hectoring voice, if only I had taken more time, listened to what he was saying instead of leaping up. A vital friendship, sabotaged. Possibly, the last new friend I will make. Life is finite, time running out. One remembers a first kiss, first love, first anniversary, but who ever dares to pronounced the words *last kiss, last love*?

The word sounded odd, and yet it was true. She did love Piers Le Gris. He might not return her love, but surely he took it in. Unconsciously or not, he lived on her love, wrote his books by her love's warmth. The ridiculous difference in their ages — she expected nothing. And yet, being forced to watch his attention drift up to a lit window was painful beyond endurance. Suddenly she was standing in the middle of the room, swept up in a rage of memory, shouting at the top of her lungs. Then, as quickly as the rage had come on it lifted, and she realized she hadn't been shouting at all. The voice was inside her head, though her body was shaking as if it had all been real. Tears streaming down her face, she collapsed into the reading chair, stayed rigid until the outburst passed, took a deep breath and leaned back, exhausted, relieved.

Turning to a stack of books beside the chair, she looked through the titles. The Marquis de Sade. *The Kama Sutra*. A thick novel by an Englishman, D.H. Lawrence, in translation. A smaller book with a soft tan cover, the one Magali had taken away, and then changed her mind and brought back. The title was embossed in red:

Le Livre d'Amour de l'Orient.
Quatrième Partie : Le Bréviaire de la Courtisane

Blank pages, waiting for words. Such an odd choice. Why would Hervé Brunet pass her an empty book? How disappointing for a thief. She held it in her lap, turning one white page after another. It occurred to her that she could fill the pages easily and then some with the endless conversation waged incessantly in her head. Or, she could put down what she knew, stories that would make Hervé's cheeks burn.

The first word cannot be I. And yet the subject is. She spoke the words inside her head, picked up a pen and began to write.

The following pages concern certain events that occurred during and immediately after the Second World War, as subsequent generations have named it. At the time we spoke of the war, or usually, the occupation, Paris and area being controlled by the Nazis. The southern part of France, named for its capital at Vichy, was under the governance of Marshall Pétain, whose collaboration with the Nazis some residents of these parts chose to defy (although definitely not as many as is claimed today). This writer's purpose is to record certain experiences of youth, specifically between the ages of 15 and 19. The circumstances include defiance and betrayal. No harm is meant to persons living or deceased, these events having occurred in the past. No ill will is borne towards anyone. Nevertheless, it is intended that the following will be a complete and truthful disclosure of events that have never been part of any discussion or record, either in written or verbal form.

May 22, 1943
Sometime in the night, my father woke me from a
sound sleep, saying nothing except that I should
wear dark clothing. It was well after curfew and
sometimes the Milice patrolled on foot so we stayed
off the main road, instead taking a path through the
orchard that led away from the village of Ste. C—
and into the woods. He walked quickly. It was all I
could do to keep up. Rose branches scraped my
bare legs.

After walking for hours (or so it seemed) we
came into a meadow. He pointed at a clump of trees
in the distance, indicating I should stay there, and
gave me a torch with instructions to wave it towards
the sky when he flashed the signal. He was nervous.
I could tell he wanted a cigarette. He kept turning
the package over and over in his hand, but he de-
nied himself the luxury as we waited. Even the
flame of a match could give us away!

Finally, we heard the sound of a motor overhead.
He pointed me toward my duty, and ran off to a far
corner of the field. The night was cloudy, lit by a
hazy slice of moon. I heard the drone without ever
seeing an aircraft. I tried to keep my eyes on the
dark form of my father, so as not to miss his signal.
When the motor faded, he flashed his light. I swung
the torch in the air, back and forth, like waving a
towel to call field workers for dinner.

Four corners of the meadow lit up with bobbing torches. I caught sight of movement in the night sky, a big, black balloon floating downwards, dangling a body like a toy. I waved. The parachute veered, and landed a few feet from where I stood.

As the figure hit the ground, the jolt knocked him down. He lay on his back, still at first. I ran over, thinking he was hurt, but he rolled onto his hands and knees and stood up. He was tall and dressed in black, wearing a hat with flaps and a leather pilot's jacket. He was surprised to be greeted by a girl, though at that age I made a concerted attempt to look older. Removing his hat, he shook my hand. He was still trembling from the fall. He kept holding my hand for what seemed like a long time as if he might never let go. Finally, two other torch-bearers and my father reached the landing spot, where they introduced themselves by their code names. The visitor told us his name was 'Roland.' Under the circumstances, I was to remain nameless. Later I would become 'Murielle.'

FIVE

A TACITURN SPINSTER with tea-stained teeth, Isabel
Tweed was senior wordsmith at Putterly Publishing,
her first and only job since coming down from
Oxford (medieval studies, a thesis on the Venerable
Bede). She managed her far-flung order of scribes
with care and respect, as long as they obeyed the
rules of genre and met their deadlines. Tweed had
little tolerance for the clever turn of phrase, even
less for the stench of irony. Action verbs ruled.
Nouns assisted. Adjectives and adverbs might bloat
a first draft, but must be gone when the glue was
dry. Putterly paid by the word.

Characters were less important than plot, though
Tweed kept an eye on gender balance which she referred to as "the sizzle." She once ventured that all
of Piers' female characters were the same woman. He
hotly begged to differ, pointing out that each had a
unique name, face, body shape and perfume. He insisted the feminine protagonists in his nine published

novels were discrete individuals drawn from live sources, hard research. When it came to writing women, the Putterly style did not encourage cribbing from other scribes or populating books with shadows from the author's past. The genre favoured concrete reality. Piers went hunting in the streets of Avignon and put the tab on expenses.

By trial and error he had perfected the art of unobtrusive observation. He spent hours, sometimes days, in carefully selected cafés and bars, lingering over an expensive meal if the plot required a sophisticate, haunting dives if it did not. Never was a man more attentive to a woman's choice of dress, her natural beauty and comportment, potential, the mixture of strength and vulnerability revealed by her aura than was Piers Le Gris at work.

He scribbled adjectives in the margins of a folded newspaper, details of how she held her shoulders, the breadth and duration of a smile, the angle and length of the neck, each fold and curve abetting speculation on the shape and density of her breasts, the dusky geography below. Surreptitious observation led inevitably to acts of mental striptease, a small indulgence he permitted as a break from taking notes. And why not? It was hardly an imposition. The subject continued to eat and chat with friends, unaware, though sometimes he detected a faint blush, a quick knowing glance his way. And from these hints, a theory arose: attractive women are instinctively attuned to appreciation, even when it is launched from a distance by a man bent over a newspaper.

Only once had he veered from his dedication to strict anonymity, a deviation from policy dictated by circumstance. It began with a stack of blank pages, *The Faithful Husband* (titled ironically), his first foray into domestic felony. According to the plotline, a man storms into a married woman's life and several chapters later drives her to violence. He had no trouble picturing the man, but the woman was vague.

One day, sifting through a pile of mail on the dining-room table, he had stumbled upon a marketplace flyer and paused to peruse the classifieds, his eyes lighting on the offer of a large oak bookcase, Louis XIV–style. As he savoured the order this treasure might bring to his overstuffed office-cum-bedroom, his eyes drifted downwards toward the personals column: badly married woman seeks affection, discreet liaison. The dialectical leap from order to its antithesis being instinctive, he picked up the phone and punched in her number.

In the weeks before they met, he dreamed of her every night. So fully did *la femme mal mariée* enter his imagination that he broke another rule and began to create her on the page from thin air. She was small and soft with red hair, lavish lips, striding through his plot with a confident swagger, delectable and eager. Meanwhile, practical problems plagued the real-life encounter — her dentist, a visiting aunt, Easter.

When the day finally came, he paced the parking lot outside the Porte St. Michel and walked straight past the tallish woman in a raincoat who was leaning against a silver Peugeot. She came striding over and shook his hand.

"*Bonjour*, Chanelle."

A woman seeking sex names herself after perfume? He liked the choice of pseudonym, was tempted to steal it. Smiling, she held up the car keys. He hadn't driven a car in years. He rarely ventured outside the medieval walls of Avignon except to cross the Boulevard St. Roch en route to the train station.

"Oh no," he said. "You drive. It's your car."

She shrugged and turned away.

Their destination was an unknown suburb called, somewhat ominously, Les Angles. Angles worried Piers. He would have preferred angels. He had hoped for a quaint Provençal village full of cheerful children and crusty gents in berets playing *boules*, an exotic location for a thriller-in-progress.

As he folded his lanky frame into the bucket seat, inadvertently squashing a loaf of bread, his thoughts hung onto the official purpose of this mission. In a few moments he would face the task of removing this substantial woman's clothes.

As they glided over the Pont de l'Europe, he observed her from the corner of his eye, noting a lean, efficient face, carefully made up, faintly enthusiastic. She was not the woman he had imagined. Burying his hands in his pockets, he gave his notebook a squeeze and wondered where to start.

The house was a newly built split-level bungalow surrounded by high brick walls, with a yard and a swimming pool. Chanelle locked the iron gate, picked up a bag of groceries, and led him inside a cool, orderly sprawl of bright rooms furnished in sleek, self-assembled pieces. Photos of family celebrations decorated the walls; men's and boys' shoes cluttered the hallway. A warren of domestic routine soaked in the fruity smell of family life, the house made him aware of how thoroughly accustomed he had become to the gloom of rue des Griffons. He sat uneasily on the lemon sofa, sipping Scotch while Chanelle chattered from another room.

A few moments later she returned, dressed in lace lingerie, a yellow that complemented the interior decor. Her tanned legs dominated. If his panic was

obvious, she seemed not to notice. A take-charge
personality, she put little store in conversation, for
which he was grateful.

Afterwards, Piers accepted a glass of water and
offered to take a bus home, but Chanelle said she
had to stop by the dry cleaners anyway, and could
just as easily run him back across the bridge. Her
tone was neutral, her mind already on dinner.

In a subsequent thriller published under the
Putterly imprint, the man whose advances led a
badly married woman into a life of murder and
clandestine activity took her savagely that day, beginning in the drawing room, a rough embrace
conducted with her back against an oak bookcase,
a priceless heirloom, circa Louis XIV. While they
tore madly at each other's hungry bodies, a crystal
vase hit the marble floor and splintered into a thousand pieces, first casualty of a passion charged with
the fury of too many delays. She was lithe and light
and easily hoisted. He was tough and sure, more
adept with hooks and snaps than any man has a
right to be. When it was over — and it was over
quickly — he gathered her into his arms, carried her
across the debris of broken glass and into the bedroom, a dark, masculine chamber with a hard
mattress and barren walls where they lay together
in a careless angle across the marriage bed, oblivi-

ous to the creak of antique boards and groans of pleasure until every moment of the dangerous delay had been exhausted, and nothing remained of their lust but the knowledge that it could never be cured, only calmed by frequent surrender.

By the time he transformed his first afternoon with Chanelle into nighttime prose, there was no trace of the first awkward fumble on her cheery home-office sofa. By the time the book was finished, she had begun to find excuses. Their Tuesday afternoons stretched from once a week to once a month, and finally not at all.

Chanelle Lambert had been vacationing in New Orleans when she came upon *The Faithful Husband* in the living room of her bed and breakfast. A ragged paperback left on a stack of newspapers, the salacious cover drew her attention. When she caught the author's name, her first thought was, there must be another Piers Le Gris. Could there be two? The photo on the back cover left doubt intact — a shadowy profile of a man's face all but hidden under a black fedora, pulled low over a beguiling half-smile.

Armed with a dictionary, she tackled the first chapter. The scene of the murder was the inside of her home. Once the truth hit, she stopped pausing over unfamiliar words and raced ahead. The yellow walls could have been anyone's walls, but the moles on her breasts, her thighs, her noises — page after page of dead-accurate detail bent to the services of cheap crime and punishment. It was thrilling. She returned to France with a shopping bag full of Putterlys written by a man she thought she knew, determined to find him and pry out the truth.

It was three in the afternoon when the phone rang. Piers was asleep. Mistaking the unfamiliar clang for a caller, he ambled sleepily towards the door but there was no one there. The muffled noise persisted. By the time he located his cell phone under a pile of clothes, Chanelle was on the verge of hanging up.

"It's me," she said. "… Remember?"

"Of course," he stammered. Charlotte? Chantal? Her voice sprang from the pages of *The Faithful Husband*, though he could not remember her name.

"I've been travelling in America," she said, somewhat breathlessly. "How have you been?"

"Chanelle!" he said, hitting the mark.

Her laughter evoked the scent of cigarettes, lipstick, a powerful perfume. He pictured her hand on the stickshift, the pert no-fooling profile as she fixed her attention on the task of driving him home. Standing with his ear pressed against a familiar voice, he knew he wanted, nay, desperately needed to be driven outside the medieval walls, past suburban sprawl, through locked gates and taken into a warm home-office hide-a-bed by a mature, available woman who had already known him naked. No dreams, no novelty, certainly no research. Where the lemon-flavoured nest had once filled him with impatient longing for the bachelor comfort of his avocado sanctuary, the prospect of flight from the same now filled him with joy.

Circling the Porte St. Michel parking lot for the tenth time, he leaned against the wall, attention focused on the search for her car. He checked the time. He'd waited half an hour. Maybe she'd had an accident. Maybe her watch had stopped. His mind festered with excuses.

Taking out his cell phone, he retrieved her call and pressed redial. A male voice answered on the second ring. He hung up, waited a few moments, and tried again. When the same man answered, he felt obliged to speak.

"Sorry … I'm looking for … Chanelle."

"*Ah, oui.* Chanelle." A mocking tone. "May I tell her who is calling?"

Piers said nothing. The man let the phone drop. She picked it up immediately, her voice a rainbow of signals including affection and unease.

"Where are you?" he shouted in a hoarse whisper.

"At home, of course. Where you called."

He stumbled. "I meant, why aren't you here?"

"Where?"

"The parking lot. Porte St. Michel."

"I was there yesterday," she said tartly.

"Oh dear. Isn't today Tuesday?"

"It is not."

"I'm sorry. I wanted to see you. I, ah ... Could you come into town? For a drink?"

She hesitated. He pictured the husband looming in the background, wondered what she would say to explain his call. Recalling *The Faithful Husband's* gory end, he shivered, then reminded himself: this is life – a bleak genre featuring many unfinished sentences and dial tones, relatively few murders.

He had never met Chanelle outside the trajectory of parking lot and pull-out sofa. As he made his way along rue de la République toward a rendezvous he hoped would launch a new chapter in their affair, he conjured up an image of her pillaresque legs, the thighs especially. Magnificent, impeccably taut, they seemed to run all the way to her waist; she favoured a style of panties that accentuated their length. He tried to recall her smile but the face he saw was the face from his book, a figment that had starred in his dreams for months.

The Bar Américain was almost empty. He took a window table. Surveying the wine list, he paused momentarily at the high end, wondering if the rendezvous might not be classified as research and therefore a Putterly expense, then rejected the idea as guaranteed to doom the rendezvous, and ordered an unpretentious bottle of Côtes du Rhône with two glasses.

In a department store across the street, the house detective kept his eyes fixed on a young Arab who had slipped from ladies' lingerie into kitchenware without the slightest hint he belonged in either. A former discothèque bouncer ill at ease in a suit, the detective knew he looked out of place amid the rows of pastel sweaters and beauty products, but he carried a clipboard and hoped to pass for management.

When the kid ducked behind a display of candles, the detective slid over for a better look. Just then a young woman came up and asked him something about a certain brand of shampoo. She had dark wavy hair and carried a backpack. She was cute and stood awfully close and in the few seconds it took him to respond, the kid got away. In the end, she didn't buy the shampoo.

Mouloud caught up with Magali outside the store. She was standing on the corner, staring straight ahead, as though she didn't know him. He whipped a foolish teddy bear out from under his jacket and offered it to her, a prize to prove he could play her game. She rolled her eyes and walked away.

"See, we make a great team," he said.

"You'll get caught," she warned as they dodged traffic to cross the street. "Your father will send you back to Morocco. You'll be banished forever."

"No way! Nobody tells me what to do."

"Ha! We'll see about that. You'll get caught. You'll get caught. You'll be gone," she sang, snatching the teddy bear away and throwing it up in the air. He was sure that if she kept on with this spectacle he'd soon feel the hand of a cop on his shoulder. Outside the Bar Américain she tossed the bear so high it landed on the sidewalk. Mouloud scooped it up and stuffed it into his bag. As she leaned against the window of the café, scowling, he wondered what he could do or say to make her listen.

Then she turned and waved to someone inside. A man waved back.

"See, I do know people. I'm not alone in the big city," she said, throwing her arms around him. "I don't need protection." Her joking tone was unusual, the embrace too. He was sure she did it for the man inside.

"Who is he?"

"Piers Le Gris, a writer. He lives at Auntie's."

Mouloud peered through the window. For a moment he had both faces in view: his own reflection and the dim outline of an adversary. He recognized the man inside as the same one he'd met on the stairs the first time he'd visited Magali's room in Avignon. He remembered the glowering look. Like the house on rue des Griffons, it gave him the creeps. How could she bear to go back there every night? Someone had died in that house, he was sure. The walls reeked of death. The so-called writer was dripping in it. Even the aunt was weird. He'd seen her on the street one day and followed her home. She dressed like a blind princess or a spirit from another century.

Magali was smiling into the window, watching herself reflected in the glass. She knows what's on his mind, Mouloud thought. French girls have a special pose for panting men. She's teasing. As if she'd read his mind and decided to torture him, she said, "Do you want to go in? Look, Piers is inviting us."

"No," Mouloud said, turning away. "You go if you like."

"Never mind." Wrapping her arm around his, she steered them away. That made twice she'd touched him in one day. He wanted to believe the embrace was real, that it was meant for him and not just a taunt for another man. But he knew better: she was using him to get Le Gris' attention.

Turning around, he saw Piers standing on the sidewalk, watching them walk away. No pride at all, he thought. Tongue hanging out in broad daylight. So, why not take advantage? He slipped his arm around Magali's waist. Of course she didn't protest. With French girls it's all a game, he reminded himself. She would have to learn another way of love. He tightened his grip and vowed to teach her.

Nothing went as Piers had imagined. The moment Chanelle sat down, he knew everything had changed. There would be no more Tuesday afternoons at Les Angles, no more delicious time free from conversation and consequence. Conversation was what Chanelle had come into town to get. She began by describing her husband's heart attack, a dramatic brush with mortality that had acquainted him with hospitals and inspired a re-evaluation of priorities. He'd emerged with a permanent scar and a renewed interest in life.

Piers was tempted to laugh. Instead he emptied his glass while Chanelle rambled on. They'd had a calm talk about their marriage and decided that as long as no one was harmed, there was no need to resort to the tired dictates of melodrama. (Piers translated: no need to resort to telling the entire truth which will lead inevitably to shouts and tears.) Nevertheless, she said she had more or less decided against affairs (the plural caught his attention) at least for the time being. He wondered if he was expected to protest. Since it seemed unlikely anything he said could save Tuesdays, he nodded gravely and muttered, "Of course, I understand."

"What about you?" she said, folding her arms. "How are you? More to the point, *who* are you?"

His laugh came out as a hiccup. "What do you mean?"

Her eyes brimmed with mischief. The question was a test.

He pinched his cheek. "If you cut me, I bleed."

Ignoring evasion, she pressed on. "I know you're a writer but that's about all I know."

"Then you know everything worth knowing about Piers Le Gris. Besides, I thought you wanted it that way. You've told me almost nothing about yourself."

"Untrue. You've been in my home. This is me," she beamed, stretching out her arms.

"Chanelle?" he said, defensively. "I don't even know your real name."

"What are you saying?"

"Isn't Chanelle your Tuesday name?"

She reached into her handbag and, taking out a

wallet, opened it to a photo ID showing a shiny face above the name Chanelle Lambert.

"Why would I lie? More to the point, why would you? Surely you can tell me who you are? Why did you come to Avignon? I would like to read all of your books. That's why I'm here. I would like to know you, Piers Le Gris. If that is your real name.... Is it?"

He winced.

"So you want to remain mysterious. Then answer one question."

He shrugged. There was no stopping the barrage.

"Have you ever killed anyone?" She was staring straight at him, nothing flirtatious about the question. When he didn't answer, she said, "You know an awful lot about killing. It always happens from behind, doesn't it? I mean, your killers sneak up on their victims."

In a year of Tuesday afternoons he had never noticed the ring of blue inside the grey centres of her eyes. She had a solid, sculpted face that just missed great beauty, yet from a certain angle could suddenly disarm. Lost in discovery, he forgot to think about the question. His mind emptied. His hands were resting idly on the table. She reached out and touched his fingers lightly.

"I'm waiting."

"Have I ever killed anyone?" he repeated, vaguely.

"That's what I was asking. You can be honest. I won't tell anybody."

He laughed, a nervous ripple guaranteed to telegraph guilt and lead to further questions. By the excitement in her eyes, he knew she wanted more. He was tempted to say, imagination is a thief. It steals from reality. The more you steal, the more you long to confess. But at that precise moment, when he felt himself strung out on a wire, unable to improvise escape and sorely tempted to blurt out the truth, Magali Martel appeared before his eyes. She was standing outside the café window, smiling. His face lit up from inside. Chanelle followed his gaze.

"Well, well," she said, when Magali waved at him. "This explains everything."

Before he could respond, Mouloud turned up and tossed her the teddy bear. They began to dance, Magali throwing it up in the air, Mouloud struggling to get it back, looking over his shoulder. The dance was playful, posed and somehow, Piers thought, cruel. When Mouloud saw him watching, he stopped. Piers waved but they'd turned away and were talking. He looked back at Chanelle.

"Why don't you invite her in?" she said.

He shrugged.

"Go on, do it."

Piers leaped up and ran out into the street, but

Magali and Mouloud were walking away. He called her name. Mouloud looked back, and tightening his arm around Magali's waist, scowled and hurried her off.

Chanelle was on the phone by the time he returned, making plans for dinner. He'd intended to ask her to spend the evening but now it was too late.

"I won't ask any more questions," she sighed coolly, as he sat down. Getting up to leave, she kissed him on the forehead, a gesture he had come to recognize as the blessing of goodbye. He reached for her hand.

"May I call you?"

She shrugged. "Sure. But not about Tuesday."

When he returned home that night, a light was on in the dining room, but there was none of the usual cacophony of television to cover his footsteps. He stopped at the bottom of the staircase, wondering what Nelly could be doing up so late. Careful not to startle her, he pushed the dining-room door open a few centimetres. She was sitting at the end of the table, writing, oblivious to his presence. He let the door shut softly and made his way upstairs.

The sight of an unmade bed was so much more inviting than a computer screen. He stretched out, drifting, and called up the night's work in his mind's eye, trying to picture the pages yet to be written. In the distance he heard voices. Struggling out of half-sleep, he forced himself to sit up, and checked his watch. An hour had slipped by.

Magali and Mouloud entered the rose room on tip-toe. He'd promised to be quiet, drink a glass of water and leave. The new Mouloud, a friend for life. No more demands. Or so he'd said.

She handed him a bottle of mineral water and a wet cloth. He wiped his face and pulled up a chair. As she lifted his coat off the floor he started to speak, but she put a finger to her lips and nodded in the direction of Piers' room. He'd hardly settled in when she was standing beside the open door with his coat over her arm, a signal meaning he had to leave.

There was nothing more to say, yet he desperately wanted to stay even if it meant going over the same bitter territory one more time, anything to forestall the moment when he had to go downstairs and into the street alone, without her. So little time left, everything was on the line now. His chance to study in Toulouse was gone. The Arab community of Avignon was tight and well connected. Someone was sure to have passed along the news that Ahmed Mourabed's brilliant son was working at the market, mooning over a piece of French tail. Any day now, his father would find out and come after him and he'd never see her again. He loved her so much his body ached. Love made him weak. He was terrified of the awful debilitating power of his love. Sometimes he thought he might die of love.

"Magali," he whispered. He tried to move but his body was a dead weight in the chair. He needed to tell her one more time how it could be. The way she was looking at him made words impossible. His face felt frozen.

"You've got to go now," she said in a low murmur. She opened the door a little wider.

He pulled himself up so quickly the chair fell backwards. Suddenly full of rage, he wrenched the coat from her grasp. "You're a murderer. You killed our child." Then he began to sob.

She closed the door, shook her head with the familiar bored expression he hated so much. "It wasn't a child," she moaned. "It was a mistake. I've told you a hundred times, but you refuse to accept the truth."

She grabbed his arm and began to pull. He slapped her face hard leaving a red blotch on her cheek. Tears welled up in her eyes. She glared at him but did not move. He could have hit her again. He could tell she expected it but she held her ground.

"You see?" she snarled. "Can't you see how wrong this is?"

From the other side of the insubstantial partition, Magali's voice was sharp and pleading. At first Piers thought she was on the phone. The conversation seemed to be one-sided. Finally he made out the low register of a male voice punctuating her monologue. Then silence. He leaned against the wall trying to hear what they were saying. Muffled words soon gave way to sobs and dry lamentations stuck in the mourner's throat.

He shot out of his room and down the hall, banged a fist on Magali's door. No answer. He knocked again, this time calm and firm as though he deserved to be let in. She opened the door a crack.

"What do you want?" Her eyes were cold. She held a hand up, covering her cheek.

"I thought I heard someone," he said.

Beneath the wash of hostility, her face was flushed, eyes wide. She was breathing heavily. She's on some kind of drug, he thought.

"Are you all right?"

"Fine," she said. She was hanging on to the door. He glanced over her head and caught a glimpse of the Arab boy, who was kneeling on a mattress in the middle of the floor. Catching Piers' gaze, he sank into the bedclothes and turned away.

Piers tried to step forward but Magali closed the door on his foot.

"If you don't mind—"

"Is there anything I can do?" he interrupted.

"Go back to your room."

She laid one foot down on top of his. He wondered if the gesture was a sign, some communication of danger she didn't dare express in words.

"Magali," he whispered. She shook her head. She was standing close to him, glassy-eyed, half-smiling, giving him a look that made him feel naked and foolish. She enjoys the power, he thought. A middle-aged man in a bathrobe and a bawling boy, both pleading for her attention. She loves it.

He pulled his foot back and said, "Goodnight then."

Walking away, he was sure he could feel her eyes sweep his body with contempt.

As quickly as anger had taken Mouloud out of himself and into an alien realm of hatred, it passed, leaving him limp with remorse.

"I'm sorry," he moaned. His eyes stung.

She wasn't crying. She was kneeling beside him on the mattress, whispering lethal words into his ear.

"You see what I mean? I am so, so right, Mouloud. Your love is full of hatred and control and selfishness. It makes me puke." She spat out the word *love*, kept after him, twisting his words. "You say you love me but you can't even get it through your head that I don't want what you want, at least not right now, and it isn't some kind of temporary sickness I'll get over, it's me, how I am. Anyway, your putrid little promises wouldn't last past the first time it rained."

He reached out to touch her hair, but she pushed him away, eyes radiant with triumph.

"I would never break a promise to you, Magali."

She sighed. "I don't want your promises."

"Well, I'm going to make one anyway, and then you aren't going to see me again, ever."

"Shhh. Keep your voice down, the whole damn house is listening, can't you understand. He's listening." She pointed at Piers' room.

She was close to him now, so close he could feel the heat from her cheek. No matter what he did to her, he could tell she didn't care. She didn't love him, didn't even hate him. Even if he drew blood, she would swallow it and stand there telling him to leave. Nothing could touch the cold in her. Even in the middle of sex, she hadn't really been there. She didn't lose herself. But then neither did he, he held back and watched them watching each other.

Taking up his coat, he stepped outside the door so she would know that this time he meant to go.

"I promise—" He stopped, waiting to be sure she was listening.

"What do you promise?" she said, glaring at him.

In a normal voice, he said, "The next guy you fuck will die."

"Don't be silly!" she laughed, but her voice trembled.

He turned and headed downstairs.

"Mouloud! I'll see you around."

"No you won't," he said, without looking back.

She closed her door and turned the key.

From a crack in his door, Piers watched Mouloud disappear down the stairs. He waited a few seconds before following to make sure the chain lock on the front door was in place. When he passed Magali's door on the way back, her light was out. Careful not to signal a presence, he slipped off his shoes and carried them into his room.

SIX

....

ALPHONSE REBOUL had elaborate plans for the house by the time he inherited 9 rue des Griffons in 1961. He had explored every crevice and corner as a child. Poring over picture books on Sunday afternoons, he pretended not to listen while his mother and uncle Clément talked in hushed tones, knowing their conversation would soon turn to his absent father, a doctor who led a series of vague medical missions in the Polynesian Islands. Ruinous adventures, according to his mother. She consoled herself by reminding Alphonse that her brother's house would someday be his. Steeped in her longing, he never quite began to live; he was waiting for the house.

By the time Clément died, in his ninety-fifth year, Alphonse was 50. Hardly had the door closed on mourners when he set about realizing a long-nurtured list of improvements. A cellar-to-roof renovation would fulfil his late mother's dreams and transform a dank mausoleum into an elegant townhouse, fitted out with conveniences, tasteful and contemporary yet respectful of the architect's intentions. Modern plumbing, white walls, lightness and air wherever possible: the new owner proceeded with fervour, certain fresh paint and glass could banish the shadows of a miserable childhood. In the seventh year of renovation, he met Nelly St. Cyr.

There was still much work to be done. The skeleton ceiling of rafters reminded her of a barn. The stark white walls seemed crude, the overall effect more like a convent or museum than a home. She did not share the memories her husband was desperate to erase. But before they had time to confront the decor, Alphonse fell ill and entered a slow decline. His dying words: "Don't ever abandon this house."

His last wish hung heavily on Nelly. In the weeks after his death, she'd been desperate to leave. Instead, she embarked on a thorough cleaning of the house which led to change. In the third floor attic, she found a trove of magnificent old furniture and moved it all downstairs: Clément's heavy oak armoires, various dark pine dressers, plant stands, wicker chairs, a horsehair recliner and travel trunks full of china, paintings and sundry *objets d'art*. Telling herself the monastic white plaster walls would surely crack and let in dangerous drafts, she covered the downstairs rooms with wallpaper, elegant brocades and stripes. Soon the house was back to where Alphonse had started. Taking in boarders seemed like a sensible plan. The two main bedrooms were emptied of personal belongings and transformed by warm colours: green like the underside of olive leaves for one and a cheerful antique pink in the other. She moved into the tiny alcove at the end of the hall and covered the cracks with lavender wallpaper. A single bed sufficed.

All of this happened in a single year of mourning, a time in which she had kept to herself. When the work was done, the only remaining evidence of her late husband was a photograph of General de Gaulle pinning a medal on his chest — in Nelly's opinion, the highlight of Alphonse's life. He had enlisted at the first sign of action and risen to the rank of Captain in time to meet the invading Germans in the Ardennes, but was wounded on the second day of fighting and spent the rest of the war in convalescence. He would not be quizzed on the details, though she persisted. When he finally produced the medal, she whisked it away for cleaning and kept it hidden in a cedar box with her nurse's graduation pin and a few pearl buttons.

If only Alphonse had talked about the battle, told stories of the front, even hinted at memories too terrible for words. Instead, his silence stood between them like a lost child. She kept the photograph hanging above her bed. De Gaulle's hot eyes followed her around the room, while Alphonse remained frozen, his profile almost hidden.

The month of November brought an invasion of dreams, sharp images without stories: Alphonse standing at the top of the staircase, looming over her. At first she'd written quickly, every night, feverishly filling loose pages, re-reading, revising, rewriting, before finally copying the polished phrases into *The Courtesan's Prayer Book*. But since the dreams began, the words had stopped. She could feel his quizzical expression; it said, you're a fool. I am, she thought, without remorse. But this story is not for you. Still, his gaze burned. Who is your reader, then? Alphonse had a way of jumping straight to the point. He would have made a good soldier, had fate given him a chance.

On her way up to bed, Nelly paused outside Piers' door. At first she thought it was a radio. Then she recognized the low drone of his voice, punctuated by Magali's laughter. The sound made her weak. A girl young enough to be his child! Suddenly, it came to her, the answer to the question posed by a dead man's ghostly presence: she was writing for

Magali. Brigitte's nosey progeny deserved the truth. From now on, she decided, nothing could be held back. She turned and hurried downstairs, into the kitchen.

The General was curled up under the table. A burst of light entered his sleep as a bad omen, but the warmth of her stockinged feet slipping under his belly was reassuring. He fell back into a dream where every chase led to conquest and all smells were friendly.

From the moment Roland came into our lives, I began to take an interest in the war. Until then it had been a nuisance, like rain or a sore throat. He came from the north. He had been sent to us by de Gaulle himself, they were still in touch. He spoke to me like an adult, so my father could hardly object.

Once a week, we met in the basement of a café in Ste. Cécile to catch the General's broadcasts on a short-wave radio. De Gaulle's voice rolled over us like ocean waves, as if he were speaking to millions, though it seemed he also spoke directly at Roland, who sat with his eyes turned away from the radio. From the BBC, I learned to hate Pétain, the traitor who settled with the Nazis and yoked us to their cause. And a Frenchman, a hero of Verdun! Like my father, who had lost his health in the first war.

*Of what did this fight for freedom consist?
Bundles of newspapers smuggled from Marseille
bringing the latest news from Paris and London. We
slid copies under certain doors at night, or slipped
them into baskets of eggs. I delivered some from my
schoolbag in broad daylight. Gathering information
on the Germans, to be sent to Paris. All with the ut-
most secrecy. In the beginning, I had only a vague idea
of what the Maquisards were up to, their obsession
with train times, secret meetings, breathless excur-
sions into the wilderness. Had the Germans
questioned me, I'd have been hard pressed to tell them
much. I might have been embarrassed.*

*Still, one truth did not go over my head: it was
clear that for those who threw in their lot with the
fight for freedom, the ordinary rules of smalltown
life no longer applied. Once you were known to be
active, you could come and go as you pleased. No
one raised an eyebrow when Roland and I linked
arms in broad daylight. The common assumption
was that we did it as a disguise, a bit of theatre to
throw off the enemy and confirm Roland's place in
the community. The Germans liked to see evidence
of normal life in their midst. Love convinced them
the French had accepted the Reich.*

*Only one person was not disposed to accept our
excuse: my mother. She disliked Roland on first sight.*

Her only clandestine activity consisted of watching us, broadcasting her disapproval with a sharp word or a grimace. But she knew better than to defy my father by objecting to a man who had parachuted into his meadow.

One night, Roland came with a truck to deliver supplies to a cell in the mountains, somewhere in the Drome; he assumed I would go. I slipped a note of coded explanation into the sugar bowl, but apparently no one drank coffee the next morning. My return the following night brought down the wrath of mother. She grabbed my arms and shook me, shouting. I thought she'd gone mad.

"Do-you-know-what-you-are-doing!? Fool! Harlot! Consequences! Such behaviour!" She wouldn't let go.

I answered back, "What have I done?"

She kept calling me a fool. Fool! Fool! I could see her hand coming but made no effort to move. She slapped me hard on the ear. Her violence was frightening. I hid in my room, determined to tell my father everything. But the next morning she was careful not to leave us alone, so I said nothing.

My arms stayed bruised for days. I thought, that was not something a good mother would do. I decided she must be jealous. Roland had my father's full attention and I had captured his. In effect, I had them both. I resolved to keep out of her way. From *then on we continued as if nothing had happened, though when she looked at me from the corner of her eye, I caught the rage. Oui, Maman, I know the facts of life, how easy it is to lose your reputation, slip into misery, ruination, etc., etc., etc. I had no intention of making the common mistake, if that was her fear. The ferocity of her attack hinted at worse, as though my behaviour carried the threat of destruction to us both.*

Only after the war, months, years later, did we realize the real horror, such terrible suffering. The camps, decimation of Jews, gypsies, communists. And so many millions of young men slaughtered on all sides. Those desperate Japanese people caught and burned at midday. Our little sufferings seemed insignificant. And now, I sit here writing, warm and safe. What personal malady cannot be quickly diminished by remembering how much other people have endured? The temptation lingers, one's own small woes must be resisted.

For a few years after the war, thoughts of humanity suffering so much weighed on me. I wanted to escape to Africa or the Far East, where people were hungry and sick and without relief, but for many reasons, my mother, etc., I stayed back. We all had to put things out of our minds, in order to get on with life. The French, Germans, Japanese

*too, even the Jews, so I've heard, we put it all be-
hind us. Took pains to forget.*

*If memories are to endure, they must be seen to
on a regular basis, like plants and dogs. Otherwise
they disappear. Some experiences are good to forget.
It is late, I feel old.... Written down, the past seems
small. Looking at the page I see this one is ruined
by rambling. Writing directly without revision is a
mistake. Stop now, begin again tomorrow ...*

Head resting on her arms, she slept for a while.
Waking, she saw that it was still dark outside, and
turning to a fresh page, started in again.

*As the wind turned against the Germans, they put
pressure on Vichy France, declaring all able-bodied
men would be sent to work in German factories, on
the war effort. Of course, there were few volunteers,
so as an incentive they offered an exchange: one
French prisoner of war would be returned for every
four working men who agreed to go. Needless to
say, the pressure from desperate mothers and wives
was great. My brother Didier was among the prisoners, so we all hoped and prayed. My prayers
included a secret postscript: take anyone but
Roland. A selfish prayer, but it was answered: the
Resistance leadership decided that to give up their*

best men was unthinkable when the real battle for liberation must be near.

The fall of 1943. Roland was one of a dozen essential members of the movement sent into hiding. We weren't told where. Christmas passed without a sign of life. My father, who had survived Verdun, was not hopeful about the direction the war was taking. His gloom was contagious; our life became an ordeal of waiting. I began to hate Ste. Cécile, its empty streets whipped by wind. I was stuck in the middle of nowhere. I woke up every morning wishing the day were over.

Soon enough, news came that made me long for an hour of innocent waiting. On the night of March 2nd, one of the twelve, Mallet, passed through Orange on his way south to Marseille, and he spoke to someone in Ste. Cécile. I heard the news later that week, third-hand, from my father whose duty it was to tell the families. His indifference to my feelings came as a shock. But that's a selfish thought. Wives lost husbands, mothers, their sons. What was Roland to me? Only I knew the answer to that.

According to the man who met Mallet, the twelve had made it to a camp in La Roque du Buis, an abandoned village west of the Mont Ventoux. They were living in a chapel, existing on sparse provisions provided by locals, staying out of sight during daylight for months on end. But they were found out anyway. Someone tipped off the Germans. Two were hanged immediately in the town square, as a warning to local sympathizers. The others were forced to walk to the next village, pulling heavy carts filled with the guns, ammunition and equipment they'd amassed in preparation for the final battle.

The youngest, Renard, tried to escape. He was shot. Thomas and Roland took turns carrying him. This encouraged the men to think they might be taken prisoner. Why else bother to save a wounded man? But it was a false hope. Nazi trucks were waiting to take the equipment. As soon as they were loaded, the commanding officer appointed a firing squad, and headed for the local café.

As the commander turned, Mallet seized his moment and bolted, tearing through an orchard along a route he'd worked out carefully from the day they'd left La Roque du Buis. The plot had been discussed as far back as the chapel. Four men followed suit, thinking it was better to be shot in the back than face a firing squad.

The man who passed this information to my father had no idea how many men escaped, or which of the others had made it out. Mallet heard shots as he ran. He could not look back.

The next day, a party was organized to go after the bodies. To my mother's chagrin, I begged to go along, and was allowed. The journey took all night. By the time we arrived, a half-centimetre of snow had fallen on the village, a cold, white shroud covering a heap of familiar forms. Roland's body was not among them.

All my strength went into making a brave face. I had to hide my relief. A few minutes later, a woman came over to where we were standing and in front of everyone, including my father, asked if they knew of a woman named Murielle. My secret name! The men looked at me. I nodded, and she handed me a crumpled piece of paper. It was a letter found under a stone in the chapel, ripped into tiny pieces. She'd glued them together.

The first word I saw was a bold signature across the bottom of the page: Roland. I started shaking. I could feel my father's eyes on me, a fever of shame rising in my face. The man standing next to me took the note, read it to himself, and sighed. "Nothing of importance," he said, handing it back. Then he nodded to the others, and they started loading bodies into the truck.

Standing there in the snow, I read the crooked lines slowly, then once more, certain they were a dead man's last words. All that he had never said to me in person was on the page — a complete and absolute declaration of love, in the spiritual and physical sense. He regretted that we had been too careful and now might never know each other intimately. He asked for my prayers.

I could see the men glancing my way. They'd already been informed of the letter's intimate contents. Even my father! I folded the page and tucked it out of sight, trying desperately to keep in mind the fate of those poor wives and mothers for whom the loss was tragic, and beyond all doubt.

SEVEN

MAGALI CLOSED A TEXTBOOK and began her nightly routine, counting deep-knee bends under her breath. At a hundred and one she tossed the sweaty t-shirt aside and crawled onto the mattress. The house was draughty. Nelly kept the nighttime temperature low but insisted on installing a mobile petrol heater in Magali's room "because young girls are prone to chills." It was so hot she could still sleep naked in November.

After a swig of water from the bottle next to her mattress, she turned off the light and started counting back from a hundred, relying on numbers to empty her mind. But on the verge of sleep, her bladder muscles flinched. Relief was a long, cold walk to the end of the hall. Plucking a flannel nightshirt from the floor, she peeked out the door to be sure the way was clear.

In the darkness, the small piece of paper pinned to the WC door was illegible, but she could easily imagine the message, the familiar nervous handwriting, formal French reminding Dear Occupants not to flush intrusive objects down the toilet or leave the tap dripping or running and upon departure from the water closet please turn out the light. Notes from Nelly appeared mysteriously and frequently, reminders of how things worked and how they did not; generous notes too, offering yoghurt on the verge of expiration and ripe plums that must be eaten.

She had expected dutiful conversation and long boring dinners, but after the first few days she was quite alone. Piers slept all day and Nelly was either rushing off, watching television, talking on the phone, or shut away in the sitting room with her books. There was always food in the kitchen, yet apart from breakfast no one seemed to eat a proper meal. Nelly's notes were the strongest evidence of her presence, impersonal signs that someone was watching, and no doubt judging.

So I've left the light on again, she thought, crumpling the note. She flung the bathroom door open. Piers Le Gris was standing under the glare of a naked light bulb, his hand on a chain dangling from the ceiling.

"*Pardon!*" he said, and gave the chain a nervous jerk, leaving them standing in the dark. Light from a tiny window to the street formed a halo, his face in shadow.

Magali had been carrying her nightshirt, and raised it to cover her breasts, a graceful, listless motion Piers would later recall as perfectly beautiful. Keeping her eyes fixed on his, she stood motionless for an instant, then brushed past, murmuring, *bonne nuit,* as though there was nothing at all unusual in their meeting.

He bolted down the hall, veered toward the stairs. There was a light on in the dining room, but the door was closed. Reaching the entrance foyer, he found the front door locked. He had no key. Then he realized he was wearing slippers and his bathrobe. He'd been working, had no plans to dash out of the house on a chilly night. As he slipped into the darkness of his room and closed the door, still dazed by the potent afterglow of naked shoulders, bare arms and breasts, his heart was pounding. I need a whiskey, he thought.

Someone was turning the handle from the other side. He stepped away. The door opened. Magali walked in, and tossing him a puzzled look, said, "May I ask what you're doing in my room?"

She was wearing a nightshirt that stopped above her knees and clunky shoes that made her seem ridiculously tall, as though walking on stilts. Her hair was damp. Only when he had fully taken in this new version of the girl who made the room dance did he catch what she'd said and verify with his own eyes that, yes, this was *her room* and he was in it.

"My mistake," he shot back, hoping it sounded ironic.

"That's all right." She picked up a package of cigarettes. "Do you smoke?"

"No! Well, I did but I've given it up."

"Shit. I'm out of matches."

"I have matches!"

She tilted her head to one side and smiled. "Would you mind?"

Relieved to be charged with a simple task, he headed back to his room. She followed.

While he rifled through drawers, she surveyed the room with the detached curiosity of a museum-goer, one arm wrapped around her waist, the other waving an unlit cigarette. Yesterday's shorts and socks lay in a heap on the floor. He kicked them out of sight.

"So this is where you write your books," she nodded appreciatively. "How can you stand these fungus green walls?"

"I didn't choose the colour."

"You could have taken my room. It's bigger."

"I need this magnificent table."

He ransacked the dresser and a nightstand by the bed, but no matches were to be found. As he started to go through various jacket pockets, she said, "Never mind. It's not important. I'm not addicted or anything."

"Could I offer you something to drink?"

She brightened. "Sure."

As he poured two shots of whiskey, hoping she wouldn't ask for mix or ice, he watched her from the corner of his eye, a perfect contraposto, one knee slightly bent, shoulders back, chin thrust forward. He was beginning to appreciate the clunky shoes, how easily she transcended their awkward shape. Handing her the glass, he imagined an urn balanced on her head, held gracefully with one lithe arm. She will be a beautiful woman, he thought. She knows this already.

"Cheers," she said, in English, raising the glass.

"*Saluté*," he replied.

She took a sip and winced. Suddenly it struck him that she was far too young for hard liquor, definitely under the drinking age in every place that had one.

"You don't have to drink it," he said.

"I love it, really! What is this?"

"Glenfiddich."

She tried to say the word. Her accent made him think of Campari, soda, fresh strawberries.

He wheeled the swivel chair around in her direction. Clearing old newspapers and sweaters from a wicker armchair, he sat down carefully, hoping it would support his weight.

"Is there something wrong with that chair?" she asked, pointing at the horsehair recliner.

"It's for napping. Certain chairs have their function. I don't violate functions."

"So what's the function of the chair I'm sitting in right now?"

"That's my writing chair."

"Ah! You're not writing."

"No."

"Am I keeping you from writing?"

"Not at all."

"What would you be doing right now, if I were not here?"

She crossed her legs, which were long and smooth and covered with fine golden hairs. They've never been shaved, he thought. A shade between pink and brown, like the colour of her room, the word was flesh, not naked or even nude. By the light of the reading lamp, they were simply bare, a wholesome natural state that left him feeling strangely calm, because she was calm. The shock of naked beauty almost in his arms had worn off and he was deeply relieved to have her here, sitting in a familiar chair.

"You sure have a lot of books," she said, taking in the wall of shelves.

He nodded. "This is a fraction of the collection."

"Really? Where are the rest?"

"In storage."

"Where?"

"Various places."

"Such as?"

"London. Montreal, mainly."

"Do you have furniture too?"

"A few pieces."

"How long are you planning to be away?"

"Away?"

"From your stuff."

"Oh. I don't know," he shrugged, his voice trailing off.

"… So you're English?"

"No, Canadian. But I've been away for years."

"But you are planning to go back someday?"

"Yes, definitely. I will return to my books at some point."

"What are you waiting for?"

When he didn't answer, she pulled her knees up under her chin, wrapped her arms around them. Noticing goosebumps had formed on her legs, he reached for a wool blanket from the bed and handed it to her.

"Thanks," she said, tucking the blanket around her shoulders so that it formed a tent. Her toenails poked out under the edge. They were painted purple with silver sparkles.

"Your aunt said you're studying business," he ventured.

"Yes, and languages, so I can get a good job and make lots of money. I had a talk with my father. It seemed to be the best choice. Actually, the only choice. He's paying."

"What would you rather study?"

"That's the problem, I don't know. I've always been good at math, though you don't need that for business. They have machines."

"So what do you need for business?"

"A nice smile, nice ass. Lots of clothes. I'm not really interested, but we'll see." She sighed, and took another sip of whiskey, a big one this time.

"Not too fast. That's powerful stuff."

Ignoring him, she leapt up, and wearing the blanket around her shoulders like a cape, went over to the bookcase and surveyed the contents.

"I'd like to read one of your books. I'm studying English, you know." Then she added in carefully articulated English, "I am told I speak the language rather well."

He laughed. The arch construction, its combination of French pronunciation on a plumy British base, surprised him. He hadn't meant to insult her, but she blushed. Just as well, he thought. As long as the conversation remained in French, a wall existed between them, but if she dipped into broken English, the urge to help would be irresistible, and once he held out a hand, there was no telling what would happen next. But she didn't; a boast about her high marks in the subject seemed to settle the matter.

"Why do you have so many books on ancient history?" she said, taking a volume off the shelf. He leapt up, went over to check on what she might have found.

"Not ancient," he said. "Medieval."

She was leafing through a picture book of the Papal Palace. "The Popes in Avignon, right. I've studied the period. What are you reading now?"

"Now?" He was standing beside her, so close he was sure he could feel the heat from her breath. "The Book of Daniel."

"A novel?"

"No, the Bible," he blurted out, realizing he must have sounded sarcastic. "Re-reading it, that is. Strange story. Gabriel the Archangel tries to help Daniel interpret his dreams and ends up confusing them both. Totally mysterious, like there's a message encoded in the text that we can't yet understand. Or else, the winged vixen is losing his grip, and that hardly seems likely. You know Gabriel has had quite a hectic career: wrestling with Jacob, the voice from the burning bush that saved Isaac's son, Joseph's guide on his flight from slavery, helping Noah load up the ark." He knew he was babbling but couldn't seem to stop. "And that was only the old testament, the Jewish part. The same Gabriel told Mary she was preggers with the messiah." Magali laughed. "Didn't mention the boy's fate, did he? And Mohammed: do you realize it was the same Gabriel who tapped an illiterate desert merchant on the shoulder and told him to write down the Qur'an? Well, I'm not sure he wrote it down right away. I think they memorized it for a few decades and then somebody else took notes, but don't quote me. Anyway, it was the same Gabriel. So why are these religions at each other's throats?"

She shrugged. "Don't tell me you're religious?"

"I was an altar boy for years," he said.

She laughed. "You *are* religious! Sorry, I don't mean to offend. I've never met anyone who believed in all that, except maybe Auntie, and she's ancient. Not to mention a little strange. But never mind.... Do you have any children?"

The question jolted, broke her spell. He was glad of it. He turned away and in a voice that was little more than a whisper, answered, "Yes."

"How many?"

"One."

"Girl or boy?"

"Girl."

"How old is she?"

"She's ..."

"You don't know?"

"Thirteen."

"You hesitated. Why?"

"I wanted to be sure."

She picked up her glass and, reaching for the bottle sitting on the floor, poured a generous shot. He didn't approve, but stayed immobile, as if suddenly he'd lost the right to interfere.

"So I take it you don't see your daughter very often?"

"No."

"Why not?"

She was talking to the floor, avoiding his eyes. The whole conversation had suddenly turned heavy. He didn't want to answer. He was leaning against the bookcase, propping himself up as though at any moment he might fall. All the strength seemed to drain from his body.

"Are you all right?"

He nodded. She splashed an ounce of Scotch into his empty glass and handed it to him.

"I'm sorry," she said, "but I didn't expect, I mean, you don't seem like the type to be someone's ... father. Well you could be, of course. Anybody could. But I thought ..."

She sat down in the wicker chair, crossed her legs

and, cradling the glass in both hands, said, "I wouldn't mind having a father like you, someone who writes books. That would be all right."

The thought seemed to slip out, sounding more like truth than anything she'd said all night. The tension disappeared. He stretched out in the recliner which had until now been kept for creative meditation, and closed his eyes.

"Where do they live, this mother and child?" she said softly.

"Montreal."

"Ah! Now that's a city I would like to visit. Especially in the winter! I've seen pictures of a hotel built completely out of ice. Is there really such a place?"

"Yes," he murmured.

I wouldn't mind having a father like you, someone who writes books. That would be all right. Her words hung in the air. His chest tightened. She wanted to know more. What more was there to know? He could tell her everything, the story ran like a loop, a recurring dream buried under a firm decision to forget. But once begun, the words were unstoppable.

It isn't the ice that matters, it's the snow.

Her eyes were green.

Her hair was fair. An actress! Fresh out of theatre school and on the proverbial trip to Europe we all took in those days, before real life began.

I was reading Meister Ekhardt in the original German, open to the power of suggestion, ill-equipped to draw distinctions. Every creak in the floorboards seemed to mean something. I was a raw bundle of faith and concentration. For the first time in my life, I had plans. I was sure of who I was and what I was put on this earth to do. A life of contem-plation. But we kept running into each other, first in Paris, then Amsterdam.

She was on her own and seemed (though I was wrong) completely lost. I suggested we might travel together for a while, but she wouldn't hear of it.

"I've come over here to learn to be alone," she said.

Ah! Imagine thinking you must learn to be alone. I'd always been alone.

I was not equipped to tangle with her logic, so I followed discreetly. Rotterdam, Antwerp, Ghent, Bruges. Standing by a stinking canal, she turned around and said, You're following me.

I denied it, of course. The idea of coincidence had lost credibility. Some of the back roads of Britain are absolutely desolate. You can walk for days and still be alone.

So we headed north, hunted down desolation in

the wilds of Scotland and Wales. I think she began to see the merit of travelling together. I'd wander off for hours every day. Spent time reading, kept up a diary, all of it to give her space. I said I was on a mission and would soon have to leave, which seemed to put her at ease. It was true ... a spiritual mission. Weeks went by.

Finally, she said she had to meet up with a friend in Spain. She'd be back in Paris in a couple of months. We agreed to meet, and said goodbye.

A few months later, I saw her again. She was wearing one of my shirts. She looked good. I had to have the facts of life pointed out to me by a waitress who asked about the date: she was pregnant.

I'd already taken my first vows. I had plans. So did she. Everything happened so quickly. She said the decision was hers, she'd take care of it. She's a fearsome person, doesn't like being followed or told what to do. I offered what I had to offer, and we parted. On good terms, or so I thought. The minute I was on the train to Rome, a horrible sense of desolation descended. I was sure I'd taken the wrong decision. It gnawed at me. The emptiness.

Months went by. I wrote the occasional letter, always received a cordial reply. I was about to take the final vows that would make such letters impossible or at least unwise. I wanted to tell her in person, so I booked a ticket to Montreal. It was early January, the streets were a mess of slush and salt. Believe me, worse than the legendary cold. I phoned her from the airport, said I was passing through on my way to a conference in Boston. She sounded surprised. We agreed to meet the next day at a deli on Metcalfe Street. I cased the place first, arrived early to secure a window seat. When she walked through the door my first thought was, she's carrying a birdcage under her coat.

I babbled on about my travels, world events, the books I was planning to write, did my best to present a credible life plan. She knew about my vocation. She said she had learned to be alone, a talent I'd cultivated for years, so the conversation went smoothly. We agreed to have dinner the following Friday. It was an outstanding night, as if we'd picked up an old conversation without losing a beat. When it was time to say goodnight I hung back, waiting for her to make a move, and it worked. She said her uncle had a cabin up north. Maybe we could go there for a couple of days, enjoy the snow.

I rented a car and the following weekend we set out for the cabin. It was farther than she expected, her map was not to scale. By late afternoon, after doubling back on a barely passable road, we found the landmark red mailbox and a few minutes later had a roaring fire going in the stove. The sun went down, the moon came up.

In the meantime, I had read up on the changes a woman's body undergoes preceding birth, but nothing had prepared me for the spectacle of how far a lithe form can expand to accommodate life within. As she lay back naked before the fire I thought, there is nothing in all of art to compare with this astonishing feat of nature.

At dusk it started to snow. Huge flakes, no wind. Snow fell all night and on into the next day. Her uncle kept the cabin well stocked; we could have stayed till spring, and I secretly hoped this might come to pass. Sunday morning, as we sat by the fire, reading, I heard a clunk and looked up. Her book had fallen on the floor ...

'I think it's time to go,' she said, standing up. The chair and her skirt were wet.

I ran out into the yard and started the car. I tried to back up. I grabbed a shovel and shoveled for two hours, hoping to clear enough for a run at the road, but it was no use. The way was blocked. Inside the house things had become less calm. All I could remember was a single passage from the *Penguin Book of Childbirth*: the majority of human beings currently walking around on the planet were born without the assistance of medical personnel. So was my daughter, Celia.

While Piers confessed, Magali listened, Nelly wrote and slept. No one heard screams on the front doorstep. Piers came upon the bloody mess when he opened the door to retrieve the newspaper. He found Nelly in the kitchen, asleep with her head on the kitchen table, and rested a hand on her shoulder so as not to startle her. She looked up, thought she was dreaming.

"I'm sorry to wake you," he whispered. "Could you tell me where I might find a mop and a pail for water? There's a problem in the front entrance."

The General caught his mood and growled.

"What kind of problem?" She leapt up but he caught her by the arm. "No, please, I'll take care of it."

Still in the mist of the story she had written, where every mention of trouble was serious, announced or followed by gunfire, Nelly could feel the blood drain from her face, and leaned on the table for support.

"Don't worry," Piers said. "It's just a stray cat. I opened the door and she got in somehow. Bit of a mess."

The mention of an animal, there was no holding her back. She headed down the hallway, the dog and Piers in tow. Magali was kneeling over what looked like a lump of bloody rags on the floor. Badly mauled, its ears bloody, the cat had crawled into the entranceway, and died. Looking closer, Nelly noticed movement beside the cat's belly, a tiny ball of fur.

"Look, kittens!" Magali cried. "She must have given birth just before she died. They're all dead, except this one. He's still bloody from the womb. His mother didn't have time to lick him off. Oh, dear kitty. I hope you don't die. Do you think he will?"

Nelly picked up the barely moving body in one hand and with the other began breathing gently into the spaces between her fingers. Taking it into the kitchen, she instructed Piers to light the oven, lined a wicker bread basket with cloth napkins and, placing the kitten in the centre, set it on the open oven door along with a pan of water laced with camphor. In a few minutes, the air was heavy with a sweet, damp odour. Using an eyedropper she placed a few drops of warm milk on the kitten's mouth. It squirmed at first and kept its eyes firmly closed. Before long, a tiny pink tongue slipped out and licked the first drop. Its eyelids twitched. It took another lick. The next few drops went down quickly then the pink tongue disappeared. The kitten curled up and fell asleep.

EIGHT

....

A PASTILLE-SCENTED incantation steeped in tobacco, Isabel Tweed's voice on the answering machine sent discomfort through Piers' body. In the hierarchy of threats, a phone call from London fell somewhere between an inquisitive email and the dreadful reality of a sealed letter. As usual, she opened on a casual note, as if her attention were somewhere else.

"Hello Piers. Tweed here."

Pause.

He pictured her tight smile dissolving around the remnants of a cigarette, and waited for the cough.

"Where is the manuscript? Haven't noticed anything in the papers about a postal strike in La Belle France."

A second pause, wherein she expected him to laugh.

Tweed's telephone style avoided personal pronouns, as though I were too intimate and you too specific. Her approach to the instrument was visceral, invasive.

Leaving a voicemail, she proceeded on the assumption that Piers was sitting by the phone, mute but attentive. Punctuated with thought-filled pauses and background noises, her rambling memoranda sometimes stretched over two or three calls before she was through. Even when replayed hours, days, weeks later, Tweed's messages retained their terrifying immediacy. This one was short and ended abruptly. One final puff before she dropped the receiver into its cradle, a reminder of how hard a writer might fall, should Putterly decide to let go.

He erased the message. Turning on the computer, he called up the previous night's file and began to read, slowly at first, from the beginning of Chapter Seven, then more quickly as the words lost their strangeness.

From behind the wall, footsteps and the whish of running water. His eyes followed the sound but he forced them back, sliding over one page and onto the next, but not reading at all, his mind cold to the blur of words. An aversion to *The Lethal Guitar* had been building up for weeks, surrounding his desk like a magnetic field, the moment of sitting down made painful by a fiery ring of doubt. Now Tweed's eyes on the back of his neck clarified the problem: *The Lethal Guitar* was …

He groped for a word. He came up with Bad.

Searching further, he found Very, Very Bad. Finally, Awful.

Spinning away from the screen, he looked up at the plot chart pinned to the wall, a maze of coloured arrows pointing from one scene to the next, the stepping stones to a perfectly saleable Putterly thriller. Had he followed the plan, the book would exist. But something had gone wrong. The answer was in front of him. The slide began in Chapter Seven with the introduction of a junior detective, female. Intended as a catalyst, she had taken over *The Lethal Guitar*.

Who was she? Young, yes. Wise. Beautiful and gawky. Savvy, silly, an innocent-savant whose first action was to raise a cup of coffee to her lips, enough to send the seasoned police chief into reverie.

In a thriller?

A line, a paragraph perhaps, but no book released by Putterly Inc. would devote an entire chapter to *reverie*.

As for Jenkins, the weather-beaten gumshoe, a clear-eyed loner known to readers of the series as a man able to crack the most convoluted crime, Jenkins had ceded his drive to a misty female whose cheerful insights were responsible for every single advance of plot since her first appearance on page sixty-four.

Turning back to the screen, Piers skimmed pages

at random, picking out snatches of words, until finally
he began to grasp the meaning of bad. Fragments.
Metaphors. Far too many boldly inventive, sensually
assaulting, palpitating, noisy, thirst-inducing adjectives. The whole thing was hopelessly tainted by
poetry, long passages spent on lyrical descriptions of
a junior detective whose name he did not know. He'd
changed her name a dozen times and still none
seemed to suit. As a temporary measure he'd begun
typing XXX, planning to slot in the name as soon
as he was sure, but now he knew the name was the
least of it. For all the hundreds of words spent,
XXX was still a bundle of contradictions: delicate,
dark, wispy, imposing, statuesque, fair, sallow, pale,
nimble, awkward, guileless, shrewd, poised. In
truth, he had no clear picture of the junior detective,
yet she had overtaken his story. He was lost.

He regretted erasing Tweed's message. A blast
from London would be welcome now. He thought
of picking up the phone, but it was 3 a.m. She'd
have gone home long ago, wherever that might be.
He could not imagine Ms Tweed at home. She did
have an answering machine though. The sound of
her recorded message might suffice. Punching in the
fourteen digits, he waited for the crackle of connec-
tion. London's distinctive efficient buzz always
made him sit up straight. The phone rang once, then
stopped. A familiar voice barked: "Tweed here."

He froze. A Tweedlike pause followed, dented only by the sound of chalk-red lips sucking on a menthol light. In the exhalation, a severely rhetorical question, "Is that you, Piers?"

How could she know?

"Yes," he whispered meekly.

The words had hardly left his lips when she laughed, a sound like crumpling newspaper: *The Observer*, book review section.

"Glad to know you're on the job. What can I do for you?"

He cleared his throat. "Has the manuscript arrived yet?"

"It has not." She took a sip of liquid.

Her confidence inspired him with the strength to lie. "Well. That is quite … inexplicable," he said, pinching his buttocks tight.

"Is it," she said. No trace of a question.

Tweed's quest for truth required few words. A master of silence, she knew the power of a pause. He admired the method. He had even tried to use it on the page, building interrogation scenes around the brittle discourse between a huntress and her prey. But inevitably he broke down, identified with the underdog, slipped him a deft comeback or two and watched the whole thing collapse into repartee.

His hand was slippery with sweat, his throat as dry as a blank page.

Clock ticking, London time, Tweed turned brisk: "Are you working?"

He was, yes, oh yes, the computer was on.

"Of course," he said, straightening his shoulders. "Just thought I'd ring and let you know ... it's coming."

"Fine then, I won't keep you," she said, and dropped the receiver.

Still holding the live end of conversation, Piers took a deep breath, another. He set the phone down gently, returned to the keyboard, and raised both hands.

In a few seconds, twenty-five chapters had been selected, blackened, sent into oblivion. The machine paused, incredulous. Are you sure?

Yes! He answered, DELETE.

Every word written since the beginning of October, in one push of a key, the manuscript was shorter by seventy-three percent. All reference to XXX gone. In her place, a new junior detective entered wearing a day's growth on his strong, manly face. He thrust his hand at the chief, offering an unambiguous grip and introduced himself as Max. After a few words of exposition and a knowing nod to account for Jenkins, who would be back on the job in a page or two, Max walked out the door, bound for Marseille with a clear sense of purpose, a mission to accomplish. Not a whiff of poetry.

That the agent of his plot now wore man-sized Adidas and carried a gun filled Piers with resolve. *The Lethal Guitar* proceeded at a steady pace, according to a revised timetable both realistic and capable of staving off a showdown with London. For the first time in weeks, he resumed his morning dash around the ramparts. The effort left him agreeably exhausted, ready for a day of dreamless sleep. Heartened by the old rhythm, he began sorting through a summer's worth of loose papers. He had his hair cut by a musk-scented woman on rue de la Carreterie. He took his winter coat to the dry cleaners, and stopped at a flower stall behind Les Halles to purchase a potted plant.

Nelly met him in the hallway. Chrysanthemums made her think of death. After All Soul's Day the graveyards were full of them, ragged pots leaning up against headstones or planted hopelessly in the hard soil. Hardy winter flowers, tinsel gold and rust, they looked dry and already dead at the peak of bloom. But she could not blame a foreigner, who had acted with good intentions. She complimented his haircut and suggested a cup of tea.

"Madame Reboul," Piers began, followed by a pause calculated to build anticipation. "Would you be free for dinner Friday night? It's so long since we've visited the Oliveraie."

"You've finished your novel!"

"No, but it's going well. And the fall menu is up. May I make a reservation for Friday?"

"Well! Of course," she beamed. Once the pressure of a deadline was over, they usually celebrated with a meal at the brightly lit family restaurant a short walk outside the walls. The owners knew them by name and always enjoyed chatting.

He followed her into the kitchen. The kitten lay curled up in his basket. Hearing their voices, he stretched, green eyes sparkling at the prospect of food and attention. Christened Caesar, after the Roman hero's untimely birth, he'd quickly grown into his name. Piers watched him lapping warm milk from a bowl as if he hadn't eaten in weeks. He wondered whether the animal's existence wasn't somehow a message. Was Mouloud behind the gory birth? He wanted to think otherwise. He couldn't bring himself to raise the subject with the only other person who might know.

Magali's cheery hello rang out from the hallway. She came bounding into the kitchen, tossing her bookbag on the table, and after a hasty greeting, headed straight for Caesar's basket to stroke his belly. At the sound of scratching on the kitchen door, she leapt up to let in The General, who'd been banished to the windy courtyard. She fed him crackers from her satchel. He licked her hand and wagged his tail. She knew just where to scratch under his chin. Thankful for the affection, he barked approval.

In the presence of Magali's girlish enthusiasm, Nelly felt her own damp spirits give way. Piers was perched on the kitchen stool, arms folded, his face lit up. There was an easy banter to their conversation. Surely they were friends, she thought, nothing more. Anyway, what did it matter? His concern was genuine, and Magali's presence lit up the room. The spell of youth was working on them both.

Declining a cup of tea, Magali excused herself, saying she had a term paper to write and needed to work all evening. Piers made no move to go, so Nelly refilled his cup and told him about an invitation she'd received to a reception Friday night at the Petit Palais. She wondered if they might drop in on their way to dinner at their old haunt, the Oliveraie?

A fine idea, he agreed. As they sat discussing plans, Nelly relaxed into anticipation. He was telling her about a museum he'd visited in Rome when Magali burst through the kitchen door, announcing she'd forgotten her bookbag, which was sitting on the counter. Piers leapt up and handed it to her.

As she turned to go, he said, "Your aunt and I are planning to eat in a restaurant Friday night. Would you care to join us?"

Magali glanced at Nelly, then at Piers. Her aunt's face was unreadable, her posture rigid, but Piers' half-smile seemed to suggest it was all right.

"I would," she said. "I'll have finished my paper by then. Thank you!"

When Magali had gone, Piers sensed the chill and wanted to say something — I hope you don't mind. But it was obvious Nelly did mind. When he tried to re-open a conversation about the Petit Palais, she answered politely and, turning her back, began rinsing out the cups.

Later he had second thoughts and reserved at table at the Grande Café. It was not part of the old routine, and more Magali's style.

NINE

....

GOOD FRIDAY, April the 6th, 1327.

So, all my misfortunes began in midst of
*   universal woe.*
Love found me all disarmed and found the way
was clear to reach my heart down to through
*   the eyes*
which have become the halls and doors of
*   tears.*
It seems to me it did love little honour
to wound me with his arrow in my state
and to you, forearmed, not show his bow at all.

From Petrarch's third *Canzoniere*, a bitter lamenta-
tion marking the moment he first set eyes on Laura
in the chapel of Ste. Claire, a stone's throw from rue
des Griffons. The day he was touched by the blessing and curse of unattainable, unrequited love.

Rain turned the cobblestones as sleek as snails.
Mouloud was late for work and had no good excuse.

He'd slept through the whining alarm clock and stayed in bed, rising only at the last minute before there was no hope. As he made his way toward the Sunday-morning market inside the walls at Porte de la République, he shoved a hand into his empty jacket pocket, anxieties focused on the present. He needed the job. The pay was a pittance but there were other compensations. He'd made important contacts.

By the time he got to Abdelkarim's fruit and vegetable stand, the tables were already set up. The old man was nowhere to be seen. A subordinate barked at him. He started unloading crates of fruit from the back of the van. It reminded him of the grape harvest at Les Hirondelles, which had come and gone without him. Hard work, though it always felt like a holiday. Distinctions disappeared and everybody was friendly regardless of age or where they were from. All that counted was hefting grapes and getting the wagons down to the co-op before they began to ferment. He loved the rhythm of the days, rising early to pick from dawn to noon, taking lunch under the trees or, if it was too hot, in a stone *cabanon* at the side of the field. They ate well and slept till it was time to begin again. He thought of a hand on his shoulder, his mother shaking him awake. She wasn't there this year either. She wouldn't be, ever again, so just as well he'd missed this year's *vendange*.

His mind far away, he didn't see a juicy scorpion
climb out of a box of figs and land on his ankle. He
shook it off and slammed it hard with his heel, reducing the carcass to a grey smear. Even in a useless
insect, the moment of death was fascinating. Now
alive, now dead. He thought of Fatiha caught in the
headlights of a car, thrown onto the rocks. She died
instantly, or so they said. The driver was drunk and
didn't even stop. He heard something but thought
it was a stone. There was blood on his fender, her
blood. Someone else came along and saw her purse
lying in the middle of the road. The details made
Mouloud sick, but he'd insisted on knowing. Now
her death played through his mind on a loop. Over
and over he saw the headlights approach, his
mother close her eyes and fall forward into darkness. He was sure she had closed her eyes before the
hit. Why was she walking in the dark? She'd gone
to visit a neighbour, she could have phoned for a
lift. Why didn't she call? If only she'd called. A
thousand ifs beat against his brain but he could turn
them off at will, close his eyes and drift into the
glare of headlights, waiting for the thud. He was not
afraid to die. He knew she was waiting on the other
side. Thinking of death made him strong.

"Mourabed!"

Behind his back, a shout. Then a hard-toed boot

slammed against his ass. As he shot forward, knocking over a crate of oranges, he heard roars of laughter, the boss and his cronies slapping their knees in delight, and Abdelkarim's growl, "Get back to work. Clean up the mess." More laughter.

He picked himself up from the pile of scattered oranges. His forehead throbbed. In a flash he saw a piece of the splintered crate fly through the air in a graceful arc and sink deep into Abdelkarim's white bulging eye, and suddenly the blue day was splattered red, like blood on a windshield. Then the flash was gone.

He ducked behind the tent flap that separated one seller from the next, and spat into a puddle of rain. An ugly bruise was rising over his eye, where he'd hit the crate. It throbbed. He felt a hand on his shoulder and turned around. It was Selim, one of the old man's gang, but he had his fingers in many pies. He knew where to find quick money, good dope and pretty well whatever else a stranger might need. Most importantly, he was independent, not part of the knot of old Arabs that led straight to Ahmed Mourabed.

"I found what you're looking for," he said.

Still dazed by the fall, Mouloud stood staring at the gold chain around Selim's neck. He was tall and muscular, with hard brown eyes and confidence to spare. Everything about Selim was exactly the way it should be. He reached down, took hold of Mouloud's hand and drew it toward his chest, to a spot near the heart. A weird sensation. He wanted to pull away, until he felt the hard barrel and curve of the handle. Touching the gun through Selim's jean jacket was thrilling. He swore softly.

Selim's eyes glowed. "Who are you going to do with this?"

"Nobody, I just need it. You know, in case."

Selim shrugged. He wasn't one to press for information.

As they stood in the Sunday-morning drizzle, Mouloud was uneasy about the next move. This was a major favour, and it hardly made sense, it was all so easy.

"Come on," he said. "I'll get you the cash."

They set off down a crooked street toward the bank machine at St. Didier Square. The transaction could tip off the old man, he thought, if he had the brains to call the bank. As each day passed and he wasn't in Toulouse, the chances of being found out grew. So did the inevitable cost. Someday soon, there would be no point in going home. Abdelkarim's boot was nothing compared to the beating his father would deliver when all his reasons for rage joined hands.

He handed over the money and was about to go

when Selim slipped a piece of paper into his shirt
pocket.

"Hey, my good friend, I want you to pick up
something and deliver it to my place tomorrow
night, after midnight."

Mouloud looked at the paper. The address was
on the outskirts of the city. "I don't have a car," he
said.

"You don't need a car. It's very, very small. Take
a rucksack."

Back in his room, he lay on the bed wearing
headphones, playing tapes of his mother's music
until the too-familiar sounds made his heart slow
down. Sweet rhythms of al-ala, the rich Andalusian
tunes he'd heard forever. The malhoun, a wild over-
ture and then the eerie sound of his mother's voice
singing ancient poems, immortalized on celluloid.
He closed his eyes, sank into the pool of sound and
floated over the landscape they had known together.
Desert and vines, but always the scorching sun gave
way to chilly dusk and with darkness came the glare
of the headlights, a light so real it kept him awake
at night. Nothing settled him down for long anymore; the drug of music was no escape. Fatiha's
wails reached a crescendo. He slid his hand under
the pillow, looking for the gun, which was wrapped
in a cloth. Fumbling through the folds, he found the

steel barrel and held on tight. For the first time in months, he was safe.

Spiteful Madonnas made Piers queasy. Following Nelly's pilgrimage through the Petit Palais' permanent collection of Gothic art, the weight of holy eyes bore down on him from the walls. The accusing gaze of Mary, mother of God, holding the infant to her breast; little Jesus, looking wise and wizened, like a midget cardinal, two fingers united in a beneficent blessing; their matching halos tilted inward, two pairs of eyes fixed on the spectator. He wondered who they saw, staring out from the canvas. Generations of the faithless? Or the artist? Were they scowling on behalf of some wronged deity? Or blaming the painter for some personal slight? He pitied the painters, hired hands compelled to draw inspiration from a ready pool of furious wives, neglected children and grieving mothers in their life. Judged by the icons of religious art, women bore the fruits of divine intervention grudgingly: abandoned Madonna, betrayed Madonna, clairvoyant Madonna mourning the pain to come. So it was not enough to be impregnated by the Holy Ghost, rewarded with sainthood and a lifetime of fidelity from the cuckolded carpenter? The female presence in pious art was a spider crawling up his spine.

Nelly's pace was steady, respectful but nothing more. He kept up a few steps behind, slowing only when she stopped to point out a detail. Though she claimed to dread museums with their artificial lighting and resemblance to cemeteries, she took an avid interest in receptions. Ste. Anne's chief librarian made sure she was on the official guest list. This one celebrated the museum's acquisition of a tapestry dating from the time of Giuliano Della Rovere. As the Vatican's representative in Avignon after the papal court had reverted to Rome, legate Rovere spurned the draughty Papal Palace for apartments in a proto-Renaissance cardinal's palace, which he decorated with a flourish foreshadowing his future as Pope Julius II. A benefactor of Raphael, it was Rovere as pope who set Michelangelo to work on the Sistine Chapel.

Having paid the walls their due, they arrived at a crowded reception room dominated by a finely laid table and buzzing with talk. Nelly disappeared. Piers plucked a glass of wine from a passing tray and turned his attention to the crowd. Of the fifty or so guests, three-quarters were female; he estimated well over half deserved scrutiny. In keeping with the exhibition, he restricted his musings to the field of aesthetics, specifically the ironic contrast between divine and secular art. He had given the matter serious consideration and developed a theory: religious art encourages atheism, whereas nudes arouse piety. He could stand for ages before Ingres' *Odalisque*, soothed by the mystery of a curved torso, all material cares and licentious fantasies quelled by an unclothed lady in a turban. Womankind rendered in her divine state of undress revealed a higher power, a master craftsperson at work in the world. Female beauty in art made him want to weep and sing, conflicting urges that could only be reconciled in the act of prayer. While meditating on Botticelli's *Venus* he'd been overwhelmed by an urge to join the priesthood, whereas touring the *The Last Supper* had aroused a fierce need to curse. The Muslims have it right, he thought. Earthly depictions of the Unknowable are sacrilegious. He envied Nelly's casual French attitude to religion, her painless agnosticism, neither hostile nor enthusiastic, part of her European heritage. She seemed indifferent to the sour Madonnas. They were simply art, beyond reaction.

Looking around, he saw Nelly had wandered to the other side of the room and was standing beside an elfin man whose head bobbed gratefully as she talked. She was wearing a deep blue Chanel suit, impeccably cut, with a double strand of pearls, her hair swept up in an elegant swirl with a few strands allowed to stray. Even in a crowd containing a few real beauties, she drew attention, exuded the magnetism of celebrity. Closer to royalty than fame, he mused. An air of patient dignity leavened by madness.

Watching Nelly from a distance dissolved the gloom brought on by sacred art, and he began to think as he sometimes did when they were together in a crowd: if only she were younger. The thought embarrassed him, the cruelty of judgement based on age. He acknowledged she was an attractive woman, yet his imagination stopped against the hard taboo of time. Or maybe she did it herself, spun a halo of dignity to keep him away. Who was this little man beside her? What did he see when he looked at Nelly Reboul? Fortified by a second glass of wine, he wandered over to inspect the stranger at close range.

Hervé Brunet's handshake was limp and damp. Nelly introduced him as the prison librarian and presented Piers as The Author. Brunet claimed he knew the name.

"What are your books about?" he asked.

Rocking back on his heels, Piers delivered his stock answer, "My books are studies of man's elemental flaws, his highest worldly aspirations and his inevitable failure. I'm afraid most of my characters end up in prison, or dead."

Nelly's eyes narrowed, as if this description did not fit the impression she held of the leather-bound

tomes sitting on her mantle. Brunet nodded enthusi-
astically and promised to order copies for the library
the moment they appeared in French. "Have you by
chance read or heard of *The Perfumed Garden*?"

"I have, though only in translation," Piers replied.
"I'm afraid my classical Arabic is weak."

Obviously impressed, Brunet's eyes widened.
"Which translation?"

"Sir Richard Burton."

The librarian's knobbish head bobbed deliriously.
"A sixteenth-century masterpiece penned by Sheikh
Mohammed Nefzaoui. Do you know the story?"(He
did, but thought it best to feign surprise.) "Well,"
the little man began, rubbing his hands together.
"You see, the Bey of Tunis was determined to em-
ploy Sheikh Nefzaoui in some tedious administrative
post. A great honour but a terrible labour just the
same. Being someone who cherished freedom more
than honour, the Sheikh devised a masterful escape:
he said he would accept the post as soon as his work-
in-progress was complete. The Bey agreed. So he
wrote *The Perfumed Garden*, a roaring success —
the first known manual of sexual practice! Naturally,
the infamous author's credibility as a servant of the
state was ruined. He effectively disqualified himself
for the post. The Bey had to rescind his invitation.
And Nefzaoui remained free!"

He burst into laughter, a Rabelaisian torrent that

drew stares all around. Then he leaned in close, and murmured, "The original translation appeared in 1850, by a certain Baron R—, a Capitaine d'État-Major in the foreign army. Your man Burton worked from the French."

Piers nodded gravely, as if agreeing to take the blame.

"I've given Madame Reboul a collector's edition, yet she finds so little time to read."

Nelly sighed. "Such a lovely title. I'm saving it for last."

"Madame, is it too soon to ask what you think of the bequest, in general? A provisional judgement?"

After a hasty explanation of the bequest to Piers, she added, "I see little reason for censorship. Surely the mind cannot be imprisoned."

Brunet's face lit up. "Excellent! I'll start on my letter to Paris. In the case of Anaïs Nin—"

"I'm afraid we'll have to leave you, Hervé," Nelly said, catching Piers' eye. "It's nearly eight o'clock and we've another engagement."

He nodded and taking a quick breath, kissed her delicately on both cheeks. "We must order your books immediately, Monsieur Le Gris. Even if they're only in English. As an exercise! Some of our men may be interested in foreign languages. Why not? After all, they don't have much to do."

Piers followed Nelly to the door. When they were alone and heading across the wide plaza, she said, "By the way, Magali's grandfather phoned earlier today. I invited him to join us. Léonce Martel, I'm sure you'll find him interesting."

Her tone was matter-of-fact, as if delivering an insignificant bit of information. Piers murmured polite approval, though it was a lie. He did mind. He'd been looking forward to an evening alone with Magali and Nelly as his guests in a great restaurant. The three of them chatting over a bottle of wine, the most innocent and natural scene he could imagine. In the presence of a stranger, conversation would have to be made.

TEN

....

AHMED MOURABED was locking his rifle away in the toolshed when Léonce pointed the electric starter at his Mercedes. The instant roar of the motor startled Ahmed; he dropped the clutch of keys and stooped to retrieve them, a painful gesture. A short, thick man of sixty, his bones ached from a life of farm labour.

"Any luck?" Léonce called out, as he sauntered down the tree-lined lane connecting his house with an L-shaped row of outbuildings.

Grim-faced, Ahmed shook his head. "Don't count on wild boar for the holidays."

"Ah! You give up too quickly," Léonce chided, tossing his jacket into the back seat. "It isn't Christmas yet."

The Qur'an forbade pork and the smell of it cooking revolted Ahmed, but he loved the chase. He hunted alone and would have rejected the noisy joviality of a hunting party, had he been asked to join. On the cusp of sunrise, he liked to take a quick two-kilometre walk along less-travelled paths. Most mornings he was sure to surprise a drowsy herd that had foraged all night.

Léonce had no interest in guns, though he savoured the taste of fresh game and prided himself on knowing how to create a succulent sauce and which wines went best with wild boar. A ritual stretching back some thirty years, it served them well. Léonce hailed from the north, and even after half a century was still considered an outsider by the clannish society of Ste. Cécile les Vignes. A native Moroccan, Ahmed had worked in France long enough to earn a state pension, but his soul belonged to the other place where family life went on without him. The only permanent residents left at Domaine des Hirondelles, Léonce and Ahmed lived according to entrenched routines, an unspoken pact of duty and respect.

Ahmed emerged from his quarters next to the machine shed, wearing a suit jacket over his flannel shirt. He held the iron gate open as the Mercedes rolled through and locked up behind.

"It's warm," Léonce said as he pushed the car-door open. Dutifully, Ahmed removed his jacket, laid it on the back seat, and climbed in beside him.

Part of the Gigondas appellation, Les Hirondelles was a spectacular 100-acre estate, an enterprise built up through decades of hard work and foresight. Prize-winning vineyards, productive olive groves, orchards and woodlots were managed from a central hub of house and barns set back from the highway, surrounded by stone walls and trees. Léonce took pride in his latest coup: convincing an ambitious young neighbour to manage the time- and labour-intensive duties so that he could play Lord of the Manor, enjoy his golden years, giving up nothing but the slog. Five years on, the arrangement was working well. It pleased him to know it made tongues wag.

Solitary by nature, he enjoyed the quiet life. Tall and trim, he was still fit into his seventies. Since Brigitte's death, he'd become a popular dinner party guest, though he saw no need for pointless socializing when silence would do. At first he enjoyed the quiet, but lately he'd fallen into a slump. Idleness, once a luxury, had begun to grate. He was restless. On the slightest excuse, he got into the car and headed out the lane.

By force of habit, he slipped a CD into the player. The clover-honey voice of Lynda Lemay roared from the back-seat speakers, *Je voudrais te prendre dans mes bras*. Lemay, a young Québécoise, was his latest discovery. The woman could fill a stadium, and the hollow space in a man's life. Her voice assailed his sombre state and always won.

He glanced at Ahmed whose face was tight with worry. Suddenly aware the love song might be an intrusion on his passenger's thoughts, he turned it off. The silence was awkward.

"Do you have any idea where he is?" Léonce ventured.

Ahmed shook his head.

"But you know people who've seen him?"

"He's working at a market."

Ahmed had resisted the truth of Mouloud's life on the lam. Only when he'd received a pointed call from Fatiha's sister did he admit to himself the boy was not just too busy to call or write. He was not at university in Toulouse, never had been. He'd run away, chasing the girl. Then a letter came from the university declaring Mouloud absent. He'd skimmed the page and tossed it aside.

His other children had grown up in the midst of an extended family in a village near Tangiers, on wages Ahmed sent back from France. He visited every year, attended their graduations and weddings. Ahmed had missed family life, but exile made his family rich. Everything changed when Fatiha finally moved to France. Mouloud was born that year. He was younger than their first grandchild. The only one of seven they raised together, he was a mystery.

Ahmed blamed himself for the kid's rebellious

ways; he'd grown soft with age. Fatiha blamed France. The day Mouloud started school she said, we'll lose him now. She begged Ahmed to send them both home to Tangiers but he resisted. After she died, Mouloud seemed to spin out of reach. He was sullen, refused to speak Arabic and started drinking, money slipping away like sand. After Magali came on the scene, his joy returned, at least until she ran off to Paris. Mouloud followed. He came back alone, his mood sullen. It was a relief to see them both leave for university, but the peace was short-lived. A phone call from Fatiha's sister in Montfavet meant he had to take action. Mouloud had been seen in Avignon. He was in with a rough crowd. Ahmed had hesitated before bothering Léonce, but the alternative had seemed worse. Now he wished he'd swallowed his pride and asked an Arab neighbour to drive him into the city. Chances were they all knew more than he did anyway.

Lost in anxiety, he failed to notice the urban clutter of malls and warehouses. The traffic picked up. Ahmed blurted out, "Turn here, Montfavet!"

Léonce braked just in time to make the turn and followed Ahmed's directions past the sprawl of used-car lots, warehouses and apartments until they reached a block of four battered apartment buildings in the Arab quarter. Barely had he stopped the car when Ahmed leapt out, thanked him and said goodbye. Léonce had assumed they would look for Mouloud together, at least for a few hours.

"What time should I pick you up?"

Ahmed shrugged.

Taking a card from his pocket, Léonce scribbled his cell phone number and handed it over. "Call me when you're ready," he said. "Take as much time as you need. I've got things to do."

Ahmed's face remained impassive as he tucked the number into his pocket. All right, Léonce thought, you want to handle this alone, it's understandable.

"Look, Ahmed," he said. "I went through something like this with my son, Paul. He had to get out on his own, take a few bruises. He shaped up, at his own pace. Mouloud's a good boy. He's smart. Give him a few years and he'll be running Les Hirondelles. You and I'll be sitting in the shade, drooling old men."

Ahmed's eyes flickered with a smile. He didn't need to say anything, his gratitude was obvious. For a moment Léonce thought Ahmed might reconsider and let him help with the search. But the smile passed and he disappeared inside a nondescript apartment building.

A glorious November day, sunny and warm, the kind that lulls travellers into believing Provence has no winter, Léonce was happy to walk and observe, browsing in bookshops and stopping to read *Le Monde*, first in one café, then another. The energy of strangers brought his solitary life into relief, reminding him of an idea that had broken through his ennui since Brigitte's death: he might return to Paris, where he'd lived as a young man, take a flat in the quiet residential quarter of St. Germain-en-Laye. The landmarks would be familiar, though whenever he visited Paris now the roar was exhausting, the prices outrageous. By midafternoon he'd heard nothing from Ahmed. On an impulse, he called rue des Griffons hoping Magali would be home.

Nelly's brisk hello caught him unaware. If Magali was there, she normally handed the phone over quickly. But this time her tone was cheerful, friendly. How are you? Her question so warm he was tempted to say, I'm not well at all. But he caught himself. Surely it was only a formality, she didn't actually expect the truth. In the pause that followed his innocuous reply, she mentioned they were eating in a restaurant that evening. Would he care to join them?

He said yes immediately. Hanging up the phone, he wondered if he might have misunderstood.

Softly lit and alive with diners, the Grand Café's cavernous interior countered the medieval weight of Avignon with a touch of Left Bank chic. A classic French bistro with high ceilings, its battered charm was calculated to the last detail, the walls stripped down unevenly to a ravaged look and decorated with gilt-framed mirrors and Art Deco lamps. Lean young waiters buzzed around dark oak tables lit by candles floating in brass bowls.

The maître d' led Léonce through the crowd of smartly dressed patrons to a table at the far end of room, where Nelly and a man were sitting elbow to elbow, in deep conversation. Seeing him, she flashed a broad smile and introduced her companion as the writer, Piers Le Gris. Up close, he looked younger than he'd seemed from a distance, dressed entirely in black, his long salt-and-pepper hair slicked back off his face, sharp grey eyes too intense for comfort.

Le Gris was drinking Scotch. Léonce ordered the same and they fell into conversation about the building, an artillery warehouse during the war, when the Papal Palace had served as a military compound and prison. He was surprised to find a foreigner so knowledgeable about French history, especially the papal presence, how it had come to a sudden, bloody end in 1791. The Palace had been declared French territory, and used as a prison for enemies of the Revolution. Le Gris became quite churned up about Commandant Jourdan, "the head cutter" who was responsible for the Glacier massacres — 60 suspects thrown to their death from the Latrine tower. "Miraculously," he said, "the Palace escaped a post-revolution demolition order, and for better or worse was assigned to the army."

For better or worse? Awfully generous with your opinions for a foreigner, Léonce thought. He was about to ask what else they might have done with it when Nelly said, "I wonder what happened to Magali?"

Léonce handed her his cell phone. "Why not give her a call?" She did, but there was no answer.

ELEVEN

AS SHE OPENED the front door on rue des Griffons, Magali's first thought was of Caesar. His hungry cries reached her midway down the hall. On the kitchen table was a note from Nelly saying she and Piers had gone to the reception and would meet her at the restaurant. A postscript mentioned her grandfather would join them, a pleasant surprise, though puzzling. He'd phoned on Sunday and said nothing about a visit. She boiled the kettle and added hot water to a bowl of milk, set it in front of the kitten and turned her attention to The General, who was waiting impatiently, always faintly hungry.

Nelly's note confirmed the house was empty yet she couldn't shake off the sense of eyes watching as she tiptoed into the dining room. The table had been cleared and covered with a linen cloth, fresh flowers placed at the centre. Scanning the bookshelf, she took a quick look through the stack of books by the fireplace. The small brown volume she was looking for wasn't there.

She had not set out to read Nelly's private diary, but the familiar cover had caught her eye one day by accident, and she hadn't been able to resist a peek. Nelly's handwriting — the first few lines read like an official historical account or a newspaper article about the war. But as soon as Roland appeared, it got interesting. Afterwards, she began to notice Nelly spent most evenings in the dining room with the door closed, and looked for the book again, but without success. Weeks went by. Finally she found it one afternoon, sitting on the dining-room table in plain sight, and raced through the new pages. The story stopped suddenly, just as the Germans took Roland away. She was sure it hadn't ended there.

Some families like telling their stories, but not the St. Cyrs, she told herself, as she approached the bookcase. They behave as if nothing at all had ever happened and the reigning generation of parents somehow appeared fully formed at family gatherings. Knowing Nelly was safely ensconced at the Grand Café, she decided to make a thorough search for the missing diary. She rifled through a stack of newspapers in the corner of the living room and searched the bookshelf. No luck.

Racing up the stairs, she hesitated outside Nelly's room. There was always a chance she might come back. The consequences of getting caught would be dire; family might forgive, but they never forget. Pushing the door open, she saw the clock on the dressing table said 19:05. Surely they would go straight from the museum to the Grand Café.

"Aunt Nelly?" she called out. Then closing the door, just to be sure, she began searching through the dresser drawers and the bedside stand. She was about to give up when she noticed a corner of the brown cover under a silk scarf on the dressing table chair. Careful not to disturb the folds, she slid the notebook out and sat on the bed. It opened easily at two pages separated by a bookmark, a black-and-white photograph of a girl in a print dress standing beside the town fountain. She had dark hair and wore it pulled back off her face, a roll pinned up over her forehead. Only half smiling, yet she looked happy. The expression was lively, almost defiant.

Magali's first thought was, it's me. The resemblance was startling. She held the photo up to the dressing table mirror. It was a much younger Nelly. Flipping past the familiar pages, she came to the new chapter.

If not for the letter he had left behind, I might have been able to forget Roland, dismiss him as a girlish fantasy, or mourn his death, so total was the silence that followed his departure. He simply ceased to

*exist — no letters, no communication at all, not even
to the Maquisard. Others took his place in the movement. My father remained his gentle, silent self.
Mother was content to imagine him lost. A few times
I found an occasion to mention his name in front of
someone who might have information. The response
was a shrug. If you weren't born in Ste.Cécile, you
simply did not count. (As far as I know that hasn't
changed.) I was too young, too troubled by fierce
emotions to ask the right questions and demand answers. I could not lift the veil that fell over that
summer. The war was over and France liberated.
Naturally, it was an occasion to celebrate, though I
have no recollection of celebration.*

*Only one person knew of my love for Roland,
his qualities, his whispered promises, the immeasurable force of feelings he aroused, how terribly I
suffered from his absence. The misery of waiting
made me weak. I was naïve and maybe desperate,
or surely I would never have confided my feelings.
The confidant was my cousin B, daughter of my
mother's oldest sister. She was nineteen and had
more experience. Her own tragic story drew us together. Her fiancé and first lover had been killed in
'42, so she had no one to wait for. In the many
hours we spent together commiserating over fate,
my stories of Roland moved us both to tears. I was*

foolish. I took pride in the pathos of details, squeezing every memory for the last drop of Roland. I retold stories of those moonlight moments so often it seemed they belonged to both of us. We cried together, finally decided he was dead, and cried for our loss.

In the fall of 1946, I was accepted into nurses' training in Carpentras. B enrolled as well. We were eager to start our lives and resolved to leave the tight horizons of Ste. Cécile together. But at the last moment she changed her mind, saying her family needed her on the farm. They owned a great deal of land, and her brother had been killed in action. I did not envy her. The day I left she cried, "You're the lucky one. You won't end up a dry old maid like me."

Leaving that village was a relief. I enjoyed being on my own with the chance to meet new people and be known by strangers. Convinced Roland was dead, I resolved to mourn him properly and then forget. Mourning took the form of prayer. I talked to him night and day, telling him my troubles, asking for his help in the trials of study. He was dead and yet he lived and was loved.

A few months later, Ste. Cécile welcomed the last of the missing men who were destined to return. Midwinter, he travelled down from Paris under his own name which none of us had ever heard: Léonce

Martel. He visited my father's house. He was seen at mass in Ste. Cécile. He met B's father who needed a man to replace his son. He met B. He asked after me, this much I am sure. My father admitted later he did try to contact me.

Magali stared at the page. Roland was Léonce. B was her grandmother, Brigitte. Her face burned. Suddenly it seemed there were eyes everywhere, a smiling but stern General de Gaulle watching from a photo on the wall above the bed. Nelly looking up at her from a snapshot. As if she'd been caught! Still, she couldn't leave the room without knowing how the story ended.

Did he really try to find me? To this day, I don't know. By that time, my ever-curious friend Adèle was engaged to be married. She wrote me a strangely vague letter by which I knew he'd come back, yet something was wrong. She said he'd changed. Then she said, maybe it was only a rumour. What rumour? I re-read the letter several times, finally decided to find out for myself. So I came home at Easter.

My mother knew immediately what I wanted, and lost no time saying to no one in particular (though in front of my father) that the mysterious hero had returned and he'd been courting B. I was too proud to show I cared. The next day, I called on B, but her sister said she was out. Days passed. She knew I was home but did not come calling so I figured the rumour was true. Did I dream the truth, or hunt it down on purpose?

B's family owned the farm next to ours. The two properties were separated by a barn we shared during the war. I needed an excuse to go there at night so I picked up the egg basket. Why would anybody be collecting eggs after midnight? My alibi didn't go that far.

I was lucky, no dogs barked, no roosters crowed. But as I stepped into the stable, one of the milking cows started bawling. I rubbed her swollen udder until she began to chew calmly. When it was safe, I went through the door that led into the haystack.

I did not want to know about what would happen on the other side, yet I had to know. I dreaded knowing. Dread, and its most unsettling opposite — I was pulled through the door by a fierce desire as strong as any sensation aroused by a man. Roland! I knew he was on the other side, and yet he was not. He had returned, and not returned.

I took my place behind a stack of wooden crates, which offered a protected view of a certain place where the hay was flat. I did not have to wait long.

They came in through the outside door, whispering. B's familiar throaty laugh filled the darkness. He must have hushed her. She turned quiet and started kissing him, a picturesque embrace straight from the movies. He didn't kiss back for long. He reached for her blouse and pulled it off. Her hair was loose. She was wearing a full skirt and gathered it up around the waist. She was naked underneath. She laughed and began to do a little dance in the hay, lifting one foot at a time, her fleshy thighs and big milky breasts swaying, like a stout gypsy. Who could have imagined? From an open window, moonlight fell on her bleached skin. She kept her eyes on him, excited by her power.

Suddenly he stepped back, leaned against a pillar. He was looking straight at the crates, staring. For a moment I thought he'd seen me. Then he turned away as if he would walk out the door. I held my breath, hoping he'd recognize his mistake and run. I sent my wishes like invisible spears but she came up behind him, pressed herself against his back, reached her arms around and undid his trousers. He gave in, and pulled her down onto a bed of straw.

He was on top of her. His shoulders heaved. Such urgency, a kind of panic! I wanted to shrink into a tiny ball and disappear into despair but my whole being defied good sense and entered into the force of his desire. B moaned. I thought it must be me. I put a hand over my mouth to stop myself from crying out. I was weak with fear and shrinking deeper into the corner until it was no longer possible to see them. I didn't want to see them. Hurried whispers, sounds of dressing, they ran off almost immediately. When I was alone I couldn't move. The image of him standing naked from the waist would not leave my mind. How many times I'd felt him next to me, but never inside, he would never let himself go or even let me look at him. Every time we were together, he was half ashamed, as if he was afraid. No, no, we have to wait, he'd say. Wait until all of this is over and it's safe. He said he couldn't leave me in trouble with a war to finish. So this was what I'd missed? Aroused and naked, he looked so greedy, as though a strange force had taken hold of him and he had no choice but to fall on his knees and submit. From the angle of a girl hidden behind the crates, the act of copulation seemed less like pleasure than hard work in the service of an animal urge. His foolish bobbing sex. The experience left me confused and drowsy. I cried, I fell asleep.

They married. Six months later, a son was born. They named him Paul.

A life was stolen. The thief paid no price. On the contrary, she lived long and well and died at a respectable old age, surrounded by family without suffering much, or so they said. The man who came home had changed. Let Brigitte have her way. He was someone else.

I made up my mind to forget about Roland. I decided he had died in a German prison.

TWELVE

AS SHE HURRIED towards the Grand Café, Magali tried to think of an excuse for being late. She settled on a story about being held up at the university, but facing the three of them staring at her, it was all she could do to mumble, "I'm sorry." Sliding into the seat opposite Nelly, she kept her hands under the table so no one could see they were shaking.

As the waiter handed her a menu, conversation resumed, something about a castle in Scotland and the labour of restoration. The table was small, their elbows almost touched. Nelly's attention seemed to float between Léonce and Piers. Magali tried to catch her eye but it was impossible, almost as if she was making an effort to avoid contact. The velvet bouquet of Nelly's perfume, irises with a hint of musk, seemed nothing like the scent of a girl who had forged ahead into life and emerged years later with so many secrets. How many more must there must be, she wondered.

Nelly had dressed up for the occasion in a serious suit and pearls, her hair swept up in a roll held tight by pins. An expert at good behaviour, yet so unpredictable, unlike Grandma Brigitte who'd been stout and laughed a lot, a simple person. She remembered her brother's comment: Nelly's a strange bird. Marc watched other people's lives closely, especially men with women, checking up on the quality of their love. He said some people were meant to be together, and you had to watch them, get the sense of how love works. How much did he know about Nelly and Léonce? She tried to picture her grandfather as Roland but could not at all imagine him the hero who'd landed in a moonlit meadow.

When the waiter came to take her order she was tempted to ask for Scotch but lost her courage and settled on Perrier. The entrées arrived, *tarte aux olives* for Piers, salmon marinated in dill for Nelly, rabbit *pâté* with sweet onions for Léonce. Unable to decide, she'd ordered the same and, ravenous, ate three pieces of bread while Nelly picked at thin slices of salmon. Piers Le Gris looked strangely out of place, as though he didn't quite know what was happening. The St. Cyrs are like that, she could have told him. A sociable situation might be excruciating or completely phoney and yet everyone will laugh and talk as though it's all quite normal.

The subject moved from Scottish castles to

Britain. Piers was telling them about the Druids, pagan priests before the Romans came north. The Celts' main festivals revolved around the solstices. She accepted a glass of red wine with her lamb and apricots and tried to relax. On her way to the restaurant, she'd imagined making some clever, subtle remark that would tempt Nelly and Léonce to talk about their past, bringing on an eruption of reconciliation, joy, relief. But now she saw the idea was ludicrous. The evening would disappear in a blur, not a word worth remembering.

And then, without warning, the conversation seemed to enter a lull. Fearing the opportunity would get away, she took a deep breath and to no one in particular said, "I've decided to change my program of study next year. I hope you won't be disappointed, Grandpa."

"Why would I be?" he said. "You're not leaving university, are you?"

"Oh no."

"Well then, do tell us more."

"It's just that I don't much like business. I mean, I— That was all pretty much Daddy's idea, because I didn't know what I wanted to study. Now I do. At least I've been thinking it over."

She had hoped to disguise the impulse as a well-considered change of plans. For the first time since she sat down, all three were listening to her. "I'm going to study history. Modern history. World War Two."

Léonce kept his eyes on the glass of wine, apparently lost in the colour red, as deep and rich as the taste. Nelly remained still as stone. As if she had slipped into a well of silence, they let her fall.

Finally Piers came to the rescue. "Well, it's a fascinating period. I did a bit of work on the Resistance while I was at university. Jean-Pierre Azéma came over to give a lecture. He's at the Sorbonne, or at least he was then. He might be dead. I can recommend his books, though."

Léonce frowned. "History?"

Magali nodded.

"Where are you planning to study? Here?"

"Well," she hesitated, "I don't know. Maybe Paris. I'm not sure they offer modern history in Avignon."

"Of course they do!" Nelly sputtered.

"I'll have to look into the details. It's, it's just something I would like to know more about. History, in general. But especially the Second World War in France."

"I must say," Léonce said, picking up the bottle to replenish their glasses, "I have difficulty thinking of the war as history. Of course it is, but when you've lived through a time and hear it called history

— well, it certainly makes you feel old. Don't you agree?" His question was directed at Nelly.

She replied with a bemused smile. "Of course we *are* old. How we feel is another question." Turning to Magali for the first time all evening, she said, "A great deal more information is available about the period today than any of us could have known at the time. Yes, I think this would be the perfect moment to study that particular history. You have the benefit of distance, yet there are still people living who remember. Might I ask what prompted your decision?"

Magali felt the colour rise in her cheeks. Clearly, her sudden interest in history had been a clumsy ruse. Her aunt knew she'd read the diary. It occurred to her that she'd known all along. The first time she'd peeked, the diary had been sitting on the dining-room table; after that, on top of a pile of books, and finally on a chair in the lavender room. Left out on purpose! With a picture of the writer as a young girl tucked between the pages, meant for discovery. Still, she doubted her own judgement. She glanced at Nelly, who seemed to be smiling. Her thoughts raced forward to the possibility that if she said anything more, Nelly might explode and accuse her of stealing secrets. Yet if the conversation slipped away onto some ordinary subject, the moment would be lost forever. She might never know more than one person's side of the story.

Hoping they didn't notice her voice shaking, she pressed on, "You did live through exciting times, Grandpa. And yet I've never heard. Well, no one ever …"

Léonce was twirling a dessert spoon in his fingers, as if transfixed by the gesture.

Nelly finished the sentence. "No one talks about the past?"

"Not in this family," Magali blurted out. "At least, not to me."

Nelly looked away, at a point in the room above their heads. The silence was uncomfortable, as though the subject of secrets must itself be kept secret. Piers seemed to notice too. He shifted position slightly in his chair, brushing his knee against hers. Magali caught his eye and knew he'd done it on purpose. The gesture gave her confidence.

"Grandpa, were you part of the war?"

In a flat voice, as though it was a simple fact that everyone surely must know, he said, "Yes. I spent time in a German prison camp." Then he leaned ahead on his elbows and sighed. "You might be better to ask Nelly. She was around too, you know. I'm sure she has a few stories to tell."

"Only at the beginning," Nelly said, as though answering an accusation. "I lost touch."

"Yes. Everything happened so quickly in those days," he replied. "It's hard to imagine now, how it all happened so fast, it was a blur. Though at the time, we didn't live it that way. Each day was … an adventure."

The air around them crackled. Piers' leg was now resting firmly against hers. The silence seemed to paralyze them. She knew nothing more would be said, at least for now, yet a great deal had been revealed. She wondered if Piers knew the details. Had Nelly told him the story of Roland and Murielle, their secret names? How they were in love but Roland ruined it all. A mistake, meaning her father should have been Nelly's child, Nelly her grandmother. Her thoughts whirled and she thought of Brigitte, a big, cheerful, utterly loveable woman. She had great memories of sitting on her grandmother's soft lap in the rocking chair. But what an awful thing to do! How could she steal Nelly's love?

She could feel tears rising and bit her lip, but just then the cell phone rang, startling them all. It was sitting on the table beside Nelly. Léonce took the call. Murmuring a few words, he jotted down an address on a table napkin and stood up.

"I'm terribly sorry," he said. "There's someone I have to meet. I'm afraid it's quite important. I hope you will excuse me."

"Oh, Grandpa, please!" Magali pleaded. "We haven't finished our meal."

Léonce apologized but remained firm. He insisted on paying the bill, promising Piers an opportunity to return the gesture.

With Léonce gone, Magali and Nelly began to relax. Piers signalled for the dessert menu and the women embraced the decision with enthusiasm. Nelly weighed the choices and settled on a rich pastry which, as always, she would nibble and abandon. Magali ordered a chocolate mousse and savoured it to the last morsel.

"So, history," Piers began, hoping the subject could be revisited with greater insight now that a mysteriously tense mood had lifted. But Magali said she'd have to give the idea more thought, and Nelly started on about the exhibition at the Petit Palais, telling Magali she should pay a visit. Don't you agree, Monsieur Le Gris?

As they walked back to rue des Griffons, it occurred to Piers this night would surely be revisited in his mind's eye. At moments during the meal, he'd felt like a stranger lost in the spaces between words. Despite their pretence at conversation, on the walk back, both women seemed deep in private thoughts and had no intention of letting him in. He said goodnight at the door, claiming he needed a walk.

THIRTEEN

....

ALMOST MIDNIGHT, the streets were empty, shutters closed, shop blinds pulled down and locked. A battered instrument case slung over his shoulder, Mouloud followed the side streets, dodging bright lights, keeping in the shadows. He was sure his old man must be gone by now, back to his vines and grief. A friend had tipped him off to his father's unannounced visit. He'd stayed out of sight all afternoon and spent the evening in the basement of an abandoned building on rue Roi René, playing music with a chaabi band.

Entering Place de la Principale at a fast clip, he was thinking about Selim and how lucky he was to be in on the action. It was all so simple when somebody showed you the ropes. Selim knew the music scene in Marseille and had offered to give him connections. There would, of course, be favours to return, but for the first time in ages a road stretched ahead. Avignon was a hole. Once he got to Marseille, everything would change.

Lost in thought, he didn't hear the clop-clop of hard-soled boots approaching from behind. A hand grabbed his arm and twisted, yanked him into an unlit alley, shoved his face against the wall. The instrument case clanked and fell to the ground. He caught a glimpse of the thick-necked stranger with a switchblade in one hand, gripping the back of his neck with the other.

"You've got something for the boss," he growled, jamming Mouloud's head against the stone. "Hand it over."

"I did!"

"All of it."

"Marco— Marco took everything," Mouloud gasped. "I didn't—"

"Shut up, liar," the thug hissed. "You're stupid, kid. You thought Selim wouldn't notice? Well he did, and he wants his shit back, all of it." He tightened his grip and slammed him again, as if he were barely holding back from crushing him like a flea. A stab of pain, blood gushed from his forehead into his eyes. From somewhere behind, shouts in a language he didn't understand and the thug released his grip. Mouloud slid down the wall, wiped the blood from his eyes in time to see the attacker backing away. His face was scarred, eyes wild with hateful glee. He had deeply bowed legs and massive shoulders. From a distance, somebody shouted at him to follow.

"You'll hear from us," he snarled at Mouloud, and took off.

Mouloud staggered over to pick up his case and started walking. He could hardly see for blood. Leaning on the side of the building, he bent over, gripped by a wave of nausea.

A voice from the shadows called his name. He looked up. It was Piers Le Gris.

"You all right?"

Mouloud turned away, but Piers blocked his path. The pool of water at his feet was red. The sight of his own blood made him dizzy. His head throbbed. He began to sway, felt a hand on his elbow. As if his feet no longer touched the ground, he was floating down the narrow rue du Chapeau Rouge. The storefronts were blurry.

Finally the strange dance stopped outside an open door. Peering into the gloom, he saw the place was crowded, some kind of bar with music in the background. Piers gave him a shove and they lurched ahead, through the crowd, toward the back of the room. A woman with masses of stiff blonde hair and big earrings was on her way out. She shrank along the wall when she saw them, as if the mess might rub off. Piers dragged him into the toilet, turned on the tap and pulled down a handful of towels. It hurt like hell, but a few minutes later Mouloud's face was presentable.

They took a booth at the end of the room, Piers sliding in with his back to the wall. The last of the jazz spots to close, Bazou Bar had a murky warmth, candles in jars on each of a dozen thick wooden tables and spots focused on a makeshift stage along the side wall. A rag-tag band was playing a sloppy kind of improv to a handful of fans, most of them crowded around one large table next to the stage. The centre of the action was a buxom woman stuffed into a shiny white tube dress, enthralled by the delusion she could sing like Billie Holiday.

"What's your position on drink?" Piers said. Unsure of what he meant, Mouloud said nothing.

Piers caught the waiter's eye, held up two fingers, and a few minutes later, two glasses of Stella Artois arrived at their table. He took a sip and sat back, closed his eyes, lost in the music. Mouloud didn't much like the taste of beer but he was thirsty. Glancing at the door, he considered leaving but hesitated, wondering if the thugs would be waiting. The encounter had left him dizzy, confusion far worse than the gash on his head. What did the lout mean: Selim wants his shit back? He'd delivered the parcel, as agreed. Marco had tipped him. Maybe

he'd lied, kept it himself and thrown the blame
back. Fear of Selim's anger made his stomach
tighten. He was counting on Selim. Everything de-
pended on their deal and Selim's help.

Finally the tubular diva brought her song to a
close, drank in the applause and joined her table of
fans. An innocuous background CD came over the
sound system, played low. Piers woke up, drained
his glass and signalled to the waiter. Pointing at the
case propped up against a chair, he said, "So you're
a musician?"

Mouloud nodded.

"What do you play?"

"The oud," he said, figuring that would stop the
interview in its tracks.

Piers' face lit up. "Magnificent instrument.
Ancient. Is it a bass? So you're from Morocco? Or
Algeria?"

Stupid questions got on Mouloud's nerves. He
looked at the door. "Ste. Cécile les Vignes."

"Point taken. Okay. What's your style? Rock?
Hip hop?"

"Rai," he said, thinking that would shut him up,
but quite the opposite. It only got him interested. He
started showing off, going on about chaabi, dropping names — Cheb Mimoun, Hanino — saying he
collected their CDs and had been to a concert in

Marrakesh. It all sounded spurious, like he was just trying to make conversation, but still Mouloud was curious to see how far an American could go without running out of patter. Then, of course, the questions.

"Do you write your own stuff?"

Questions were annoying. He could go on all night if he let go. If he started talking about music he'd start feeling bad about Marseille, the time he could be having if he'd gone straight to Marseille, skipped this crazy detour, running after pain. He took a long slug of beer, stared at the glass and decided he couldn't let this conversation go any further, even if Selim's thugs were waiting for him outside. This was not the time to sit in the dark talking music with a man who deserved to be dead. He needed to figure out why Selim's hoods were tracking him. What to do. More questions. Short, nasty answers didn't seem to matter. Piers began to babble on about places and people he'd known. Mouloud resolved to resist the bait and eventually it worked, the monologue trailed off.

They sat in silence until a commotion at the singer's table commanded attention. A guy with a camera started taking pictures. Buoyed by raucous laughter, the fans clustered around the singer and flashed their cheesy smiles. He was shooting fast from different angles, dancing. Suddenly he aimed the lens at them, dove in close and snapped Piers, then Mouloud, stepped back to catch them both. Mouloud swung his arm over his face. The man tossed his business card on the table. "Call me if you're interested in prints," he said. As if.

Piers pocketed the card, and start up again, his monologue about the Crusades. How the knights in shining armour had been dazzled by Islam. Inspired by the discovery of pure love, female beauty hidden behind the veil, they had dreamed up their own version, called courtly love. The world of the Harem, women beyond the reach of men's lust, had inspired great verse. Poets killed themselves for courtly love. Chastity, fidelity, denial drove them mad. But what a death! Imagine the poor Christian sods, he said, going home to wives they'd acquired through business deals cooked up by their parents.

As he rambled on, he leaned in close until the scent of his body mingled with the words. Beneath sweat and beer, Mouloud detected a sweet, stale smell, like burning spices. It made his nose tingle. Piers went on and on about the Troubadours who raised love out of the depths of animal desire until it hovered close to heaven. A religious experience, he said, beyond the reach of poor dirty mortals, and anyway, wasn't hopeless love the only love worth having? Petrarch's the man, he said. The bard of hopeless love. The low drone of his voice bored through Mouloud's head, words blurring with the strange scent, making him dizzy. He knew enough about Petrarch, could have said a thing or two but he was too spun out, couldn't listen anymore.

Finally, the diva jumped up on stage to start into her second set. A blast of music put a stop to the deluge. Piers leaned back against the wall and stared into the crowd.

As if a tight grip had loosened, Mouloud seemed to wake up. His head cleared. He took a sip of beer and resolved to get a plan, face facts: the future with Selim was washed up.

Two girls slipped into a table next to theirs. One of them had long black hair and fine features. She laughed and for a moment he thought it was Magali.

He glanced at Piers. He was looking at them too, thinking the same thought. Of course it wasn't her. But the way the hair fell over her shoulders ... As if on cue, Piers leaned in close and said, "Look, man. Keep away from Magali, okay?"

The sound of her name in this place was a violation. It made him want to puke.

"Fuck yourself!" he murmured.

"That's an option," Piers snorted, reeling back. "Probably good advice." He raised his glass and drained it. "Hey, take it easy. Don't worry about me. I'm old enough to be her father. Yours too, for that matter."

The candle on the table had burned down to a translucent pool of liquid wax in the bottom of a jar. Mouloud looked across at the grim stubble on his jaw. Lit from below it looked like the face of an animal. All he had to do was let his mind conjure that mouth pressed against her breasts and his chest filled with rage. She was trapped in Piers Le Gris' mind, stripped bare. He tried conjuring Marseille, the horseshoe port full of boats, a gypsy band, the open sea, but all he could see was her with him.

The path to the door was cluttered with drinkers. He got up slowly, picked up his case and edged through the crowd, out the door.

It was a relief to escape the bar's oppressive atmosphere. He hurried toward the other side of town, cutting through Place du Carem and turning down the narrow rue de la Palapharnerie toward a seedy stretch of crumbling walls covered with graffiti. The battered metal door leading up a stairway to his room was ajar. He stopped, wondering if his father might somehow have doubled back and be waiting. A tiny window in his room looked out on the back of the building. He decided to circle around and see if there was a light on before going up.

When he stepped into the alley, a fist shot out

from the dark and grabbed his hair, hauling him into the light. The thug had been waiting. He recognized the snarling face, an ex-con, Remy. He'd seen him hanging around the market. Selim claimed he couldn't be trusted. He was backed up by a massive fair-haired bruiser who held a length of pipe in both hands.

Mouloud stepped away and started to explain, but the accomplice thrust the pipe at his case and sent it flying into the street. It bounced to the ground, cracking open with a discordant twang. He reached inside his jacket for the gun but a second crack with the pipe caught his hand. The gun exploded with a deafening crack and fell on the pavement. His head swelled with pain.

From a second-storey window across the street, a woman swung open rusty shutters and shouted at them to move on. As Remy snatched up the gun, his accomplice thrust a calloused hand around Mouloud's throat, lifted him off the pavement and slammed his face against the wall. All he could see was the thick bare arm and massive chest pinning him against cold stone. He heard shouts, then a thud followed by a sickening crunch. His attacker's grip went limp. Mouloud turned around in time to see him teeter and groan. His eyes bulged. The look of shock stayed frozen on his face as he slid onto the pavement like a scorpion smeared under a flick of the heel. The instant happened in slow motion. Mouloud stood transfixed, watching life ooze out of him like a weightless fog, drifting up and away.

From the distance, a shout, "Hey, chaabi."

He looked up. Piers Le Gris was standing beside the crumpled body. He reached down, scooped up a fist-sized cobblestone smeared with blood and fired it over a high wall into a clump of laurel bushes. A siren wailed in the distance. He picked up the gun.

"Give me that, it's mine," Mouloud said.

"You want to go to prison? Okay, stick around. Otherwise, run."

The siren grew nearer. Mouloud looked at Piers, then at the delicate pear-shaped instrument lying in the gutter, strings ripped by the fall. His mother's most prized possession. She'd taught him how to play. Slowly, as if he had all the time in the world, he put the rosewood antique back in the case. The sirens were closing in as he walked away. Three sharp gunshots rang out behind, ugly blasts that burned his ears and made his skin crawl, but he kept walking at a steady pace, transfixed by an image of his attacker crumpled on the pavement, blood trickling from his mouth.

Of course he'd be blamed. Even if it was a demented writer who picked up the stone, the finger would be pointed at him. Turning the corner, he broke into a run.

Piers stood watching until Mouloud was out of sight. From behind came a thud. The police siren died. Everything went black.

FOURTEEN

A SICK SENSATION of falling, flailing, nothing to hang onto. And then it stopped. His first thought was, I'm blind. He rubbed his eyes but the darkness refused to take shape. Silence, broken by episodic growls, the rhythm of breathing and pounding in the distance. Thump-thump-thump. A rusty metallic odour, faint at first then overpowering. It occurred to him the sounds were his own heartbeat, his breathing. The smell was blood, his blood. He was inside his own body, there was no other room. A terrifying claustrophobia. I'm trapped in a coffin, he thought. He was fighting for air, chest heaving. His hands, helpful reliable appendages, reached out and grabbed the side of the bed—

The sensation produced a word, *bed*, the word rescued him. He could feel the edge, meaning he was lying down. Digging his elbows into a hard surface, he hoisted himself up, and in one quick movement swung his legs around till they dangled over the

edge. The air was thinner, as though a higher alti-
tude than it had been when he was lying down.
Everything is amplified, he thought. The sound of
breathing, thumping, like an old dog, struggling.

*So I am not dead. No, whatever death is, this is
not death.*

His panic began to subside, like flood water
seeping away.

I'm alive though possibly dying. The sensation
of falling crept back but he stopped himself from
thinking about it and the sensation went away.
Wilfully breathing deeper, taking in more air, he became conscious finally of an inside and an out. He
reached one hand in front of him, into the black. It
moved slowly in an arc, as if equipped with radar,
and stopped at a solid presence. Warm, damp
breath on his fingers. The breathing disappeared,
now he heard only the sound of someone waiting,
thinking. A void bursting with expectation.

"Is that you?" he ventured. The words came out
dry, like crumpled newsprint.

No answer. And yet the answer hung in the air.

Finally, a whisper with the weight of thunder, "It
is I."

He was overcome by an urge to cry, couldn't
stop. Deep childish sobs rose up from the bottom of
his heart, spilling out into the darkness occupied by

a whisper. He felt foolish. He felt good, let himself go for a few seconds, then quit. Blew his nose into the crook of his arm and gripped the side of the bed, steady, steady. A gulp of air. Whatever would come next would come anyway. He was empty, ready.

Minutes ticked by. The rhythm of their breathing fell into time, synchronized. The longer he listened, the more ridiculous it seemed, like dancing. They were doing it unconsciously, the rasping presence and his noisy lungs. He started thinking they could not continue like that, the overlapping breaths were taking his freedom away. Worse than falling, out of control. "Stop," he snapped. "Please, stop it."

"Petras."

The word gripped him like an accusation. A hypodermic. The liquid form of the word entered his bloodstream and he felt warm, a good feeling, but at the same time a dangerous one. To be resisted at all costs. *Haven't heard my name spoken out loud in so long.*

"It's all right, all right, Petras. Don't worry. It's all right. Allllll right. Alllll—"

"Stop saying that!"

"Petras?"

"I didn't mean—"

He broke off. Waited, fearful and sure the next words would be another *it's all right*. The way his mother used to rub his forehead in a fever, her hand sliding across his brow, over and over and over until he wanted to scream. She meant well. He missed it now, the rubbing, the well-meaning. He missed everything about her and yet he did not wish her alive again. Nor the old man, no, he was better off dead. If there was one thing he was certain of, it was that we are not all together in death. We are all eternally apart. Otherwise, death means nothing. And that cannot be true. Death is the one certainty against which all other probabilities are measured. He'd had this conversation many times. He knew the dance, what was permitted and what was forbidden. He knew who had raised the questions in his mind. Who had access to his thoughts. One person only lived on the edge between here and the other place.

"Is that you, Père? Have you come for me? The rendezvous? Listen, I was there on time. I was in the right café, I'm sure. According to the letter …"

The answer, a deep sigh. He didn't need to be told, he could sense recrimination coming. I'm sorry, he was about to say, but stopped.

"Petras, it is not important. Everything is … all right."

A distinct iciness in the voice. Consolation was worse than accusation.

Silence.

A dry cough. Followed by another. The same annoying cough that had once made silence hell. The presence beside him shifted, swallowed. Any attempt to stifle the cough was worse than the cough itself, reducing the atmosphere to irritation. Then, from nowhere, a statement delivered with a hint of accusation:

"You told that young girl everything."

"I didn't! Did I? Maybe, but she hardly believed … Was she listening?"

"It's all right, Petras. Good. Good. You should speak about the living more often. Speaking their name keeps them alive and fresh. Otherwise, they fester."

I know, I know. It bothered him to be told what he already knew, and yet being taken by surprise left him weak. He shivered. A draught, as if a door had opened somewhere letting in a pale light, the room began to take shape. It was a small cell with a hard bed, a wooden door, a book-sized window with bars. His lips were cracked, caked with some kind of disgusting mixture of blood and pus. His back hurt, the pain spread until every muscle ached.

I'm going to lie down now, he thought. Get some sleep. But he didn't. A sudden flood of nausea sent him reeling into the darkness and the sensation of falling came rushing back, except that this time the feeling was not unpleasant. It was real.

FIFTEEN

....

AFTER THREE DAYS when Piers did not appear at
breakfast, Nelly called her old friend Olivier Fare who
had been the chief of police when they knew each
other years ago. He still had contacts in the department and promised to make enquiries. True to his
word, Fare called back later in the afternoon to report
that no one by that name was on file, nor could the
hospitals offer a clue. He'd gone as far as to contact
Marseille. Before hanging up, he took the opportunity
to ask how she was.

Fine, she said.

Was Monsieur Le Gris a relative, he wanted to
know.

No, an author.

He tried to prolong the conversation, asked if
they might have dinner sometime. She was too dis-
traught to indulge his chatter. Hanging up the phone,
she wondered how hard he'd tried, whether he'd
thought to ask the Gendarmerie, or simply restricted

his investigation to a few old cronies in Avignon. By evening, she was beside herself with worry.

A firm believer in discretion, Nelly made a point never to enter the lodgers' rooms. In the beginning, the agency had sent a young man over to inspect the premises. She could tell he wondered what her story was, did she really need the money, or was she just another lonely widow in search of company? His mute curiosity was irritating; she'd vowed to leave meddling to a cleaning lady who came in once a week. But the sudden disappearance of Piers Le Gris was unsettling. She needed tangible evidence of his existence.

His room gave off an eerie impression of flight, as if he'd left on impulse. The door to the armoire was ajar, the bed unmade. He'd left the cap off his fountain pen and books open on the table, a fat volume of philosophy by Meister Ekhardt beside an illustrated paperback, *Capital Punishment Through the Ages*. She took a quick look at drawings of guillotines, hanging scaffolds and electric chairs, and put it down.

The furniture had been rearranged, the table moved to the centre of the room, covered with computer equipment, a maze of electrical wires, piles of files and open books. A stack of typed pages in English were marked with indecipherable comments in a flamboyant script. The bookshelves were over-flowing, paperbacks and newspapers everywhere. The room seemed darker and smaller than she remembered. When Alphonse was alive it had been the master bedroom, dominated by a high double bed facing the window. She thought of the hours she'd spent bathing his burning skin with cool cloths, keeping an eye on the morphine drip. For a full year, his dying had usurped all else, though the effort had not been a chore. He was boundlessly grateful and never complained.

Sliding open the drawer in the table, she found a navy blue passport containing a picture of Piers' unsmiling face. A relief. At least he hadn't left France. But next to the photo was a strange name. Her first thought, it doesn't suit him at all, surely a mistake. She studied the details: nationality, Canadian; birthplace, Montreal, 1955. Visa stamps from China, Japan, Thailand, Italy and France. Wedged between the middle pages was a snapshot of a young girl with light brown hair cut in a straight fringe, a sweet lop-sided smile, an unmistakeable resemblance to Piers.

She shut the drawer quickly. So, he had a child. The idea seemed implausible. Of course he would have a life elsewhere, but an unknown family and another name? His sudden absence was all the more unsettling. She hurried out, closed the door quietly and turned around to face Magali who was standing at the top of the stairs.

"Is there any news?"

Embarrassed to be caught coming out of Piers' room, Nelly managed a feeble no.

"Where could he be? I wonder if something has happened to him?"

"Oh, I should think not," she said, hoping to escape conversation. "In any case, I don't suppose there's anything we can do."

"Maybe the police know something," Magali insisted.

"No. I've telephoned. I'm sure it's about the novel. He needs to get away sometimes when he's close to a deadline. Frankly, this house has been a circus lately. I don't know how a writer can manage to work at all. You've had guests, haven't you? At night?"

"No, Auntie. Well, a friend of mine came around a few times. Mouloud — but that was ages ago. I stopped him."

"Yes, well, Monsieur Le Gris spoke to me about the noise."

"I'm sorry. It won't happen again."

The girl's contrite stammer made her realize she'd been harsh. "I don't mind if you have friends in," she added hastily. "It's normal. But during the daytime, all right? At a reasonable hour."

Magali nodded but didn't move, as if she had more to say.

She didn't much care whether Piers Le Gris came home at dawn or never. What she wanted more than anything was to talk to Nelly about the diary, get answers to the deluge of questions it inspired. Do you have any pictures of Roland? What was he really like in those days? And why did you run off and leave him to—

When she looked from a certain angle, sometimes caught a gesture or a way of thinking, Nelly had recognized uncanny resemblances between this sometimes gawky, often quite beautiful girl and her own younger self, especially in moments like this when she stood tongue-tied, incapable of saying what she was thinking or feeling, yet unable to hide it either. Magali should have been contrite; she'd just been spoken to for having a stranger in her room. Instead, her curious half-smile was ripe with questions.

So you've read the story, Nelly wanted to say, but years of reticence closed off the possibility of a direct approach. She'd left the notebook in plain view, peeking out from under a scarf on her dressing-table chair, a hairpin hidden in the folds. Sure enough, the hairpin was on the floor when she returned, the scarf folded carefully. I needn't have bothered, she thought.

Magali's outburst at the restaurant made her clandestine reading quite evident. Now they were both
caught, sharing awkward corners of a secret. For the
moment, she enjoyed knowing she had Magali's full
attention. No pressing need to give up the power.

As she started down the stairs, Magali interrupted. "Auntie, wait. I was thinking, Piers has a
cell phone. Maybe we should call him."

Telephone him?

"Do you have the number?"

"No," she said weakly, wondering why she
would take the phone number of someone who
lived under her own roof.

"He might have written it down. We could check
in his desk," Magali said brightly, and headed for
his room as though she had every right to be there.

Whereas the first venture had felt like a transgres-
sion, this one seemed like a practical necessity. While
Magali chattered on about possible explanations for
his absence, Nelly took charge of the search. She slid
the passport under a pile of envelopes, leafed
through his address book and, turning to the Ls,
found Le Gris, Piers, 9 rue des Griffons and a number. How odd, a man who lists himself in his
phonebook! She was tempted to look up the name
on the passport for a possible clue to his other life,
but Magali was watching. She scribbled the number
on a scrap of paper and headed for the hall phone.

Two rings, the sound of his voice, a deep author-
itative *bonjour* unleashed a flood of relief, until she
realized it was only a recorded message. Tucking the
number away, she resolved to keep calling, if only
to hear his voice.

An empty evening stretched ahead. There was
nothing to be gained by worry, she knew, yet could
not resist thinking steps should be taken. But what
steps? Hoping for distraction, she turned to the pile
of books, Hervé Brunet's request, which led her
straight back to Piers Le Gris and the reception, how
strangely he had responded to the Petit Palais' collection of Madonnas. When she'd tried to interest
Magali in paying a visit, he exploded and said they
were all terrible, vindictive women. Probably mod-
elled on the artists' unhappy wives, he thundered.
She'd had to change the subject, or risk ruining
dessert. Now the outburst made sense. He'd been
thinking of his past. She preferred the old image of
a solitary writer with no other life. Taking a leather-
bound volume off the shelf, she thought, what a
shame they're only in English. Opening at random,
she came upon pages of short phrases liberally sprin-
kled with quotation marks. Who were these people?
What were they talking about, she wondered? Was
there a voice among them as deep and impressive as
his? But it was no use, the words lacked meaning.

She collapsed into the reading chair, forced herself to take a book from the top of the pile. On the cover was a shadowy silhouette of a young woman under the title, *Vénus Erotica* by Anaïs Nin. She tried to read, but the words resisted. The next was *Justine*, a weighty tome by the Marquis de Sade, tiny print, hundreds of pages. The hours it must have taken him to fill those pages — exhausting! She could hardly hold Sade's tome on her lap. She wondered what it must have been like to spend so long immersed in a story. Did all authors experience the exhilaration she'd felt while scribbling the story of Roland? Writing had brought him back, unearthed so many moments she'd forgotten. An intoxicating experience, reliving those days and nights, remembering the risks they'd taken. There were moments she hadn't dared write about. The sharpest memories were pure sensation: waiting for his train to arrive, keeping an unopened letter hidden until she could read it alone. She had been deeply in love with Roland. There would never be anyone as important to her. For years she'd been sure his loss was a kind of inoculation against dread. The sudden disappearance of Piers Le Gris proved otherwise.

Sometime in the early hours of morning, Piers let himself in. The light was still on in the sitting room, Nelly asleep in her reading chair. He left a newspaper on the hall table as a sign of his return, and tiptoed upstairs. His room smelled of invasion. Someone had replaced the cap on his pen, moved his passport. Kicking off his boots, he set them down quietly, collapsed on the bed and fell asleep.

Nelly was making tea when he came downstairs. She took a minute to compose herself before heading for the dining room with the breakfast tray. He had a nasty bruise on the side of his face, which she pretended not to notice, at least until Magali arrived.

"What happened to your eye?" she blurted out. "Where have you been? We were worried silly! Why didn't you call?"

He stammered unconvincingly about a research trip to Marseille, the setting of his novel-in-progress. Nelly put the teapot down and listened intently. He said he'd tripped on a chink in the pavement, hence the wound. No mention of why he limped or wore a thick brace around his ribs, visible under his sweater.

"What happened to you and Mouloud?" Magali was about to fire more questions when Nelly shot her a silencing look. Piers slipped further into the newspaper, obviously relieved.

When she and Nelly were alone in the kitchen, Magali asked pointedly whether he'd said anything about the wounds. She assumed Nelly knew more than she was saying.

"Monsieur Le Gris is in the final throes of his novel," she declared, meaning, soft-soled slippers, whispers in the hallway and no more questions.

Passing by his door that night, Nelly stopped to listen. All was silent. No fingers pounding on the keyboard. His espresso machine was dormant, lights out well before midnight.

SIXTEEN

WHEN ANAÏS NIN'S diaries first appeared in the late sixties, her doe-eyed profile was in all the magazines. Nelly read the tales of a free-spirited Bohemian life in Paris and New York with relish and resolved to keep a journal herself. But she got no further than a few scribbles on a blank page, judged ridiculous the next day. After the unreadable Marquis de Sade and Lawrence, the hysterical Englishman with his fascination for peasants, finding Nin's *Vénus Erotica* among the eminent professor's bequest to St. Anne's was a pleasant surprise. A somewhat obscure work, albeit a signed first edition, it was a collection of short stories commissioned by a wealthy patron who paid one American dollar per page, a considerable sum at the time.

Opening the book at random, she fell upon the story of Linda, who was past thirty and concerned with her age, yet *no less loved for being old*. In fact she was more loved than ever, especially by young men eager to learn the secrets of lovemaking, men who (according to the author) felt no attraction to girls their own age, judging them "backward, inno-cent, inexperienced, and still possessed by their families." Linda, happily married to a handsome rake, had love and leisure time to spare.

One day, when her husband was away, she re-ceived an invitation to a masked party hosted by a sociable painter. She embraced transformation wholeheartedly, choosing a heavy satin gown that outlined her body like a glove. No underwear, no jewellery by which she might be recognized, her pale blonde hair tinted blue-black and styled as a spec-tacular pompadour. The image in the mirror was startling. That evening was the beginning of many athletic adventures, leading to page after page of tit-illating incident curiously mixed with bits of advice. According to her hairdresser, who kept his little moustache pointed and glazed, every woman should, at one time or another, perform the services of a whore. "It is the best way to retain a sense of being female."

A spurious idea, she thought. Surely Nin was writing to please the patron, who no doubt em-ployed whores and liked to think they enjoyed their work. The only whores she knew of were two who'd come up from Marseille after the Germans occupied most of the Vaucluse in 1944. Tough-look-ing gals with wiry red hair and a disparaging attitude to life, they worked from a café frequented by soldiers. She'd walked past one day when they were sitting on the terrace, and tried not to look. One of them jeered at her to come and sit down. "Take a fag and talk to us. You might learn some-thing, silly virgin."

She'd hurried away, embarrassed, but the words stung. Part of her had wanted to turn back and hear what they had to say. Virginity was a burden, but then everything was a burden in those days, it was the age of making do, a daily scramble. Food, pri-vacy, petrol, even sex was in short supply, at least for some. Roland had insisted they wait. He said it was awful for a man, almost impossible. He taught her what to do so there would be no risk. Not a hint of awkwardness in his embrace, only urgent desire and a strange wave of sadness when she brought him to release. He was always grateful and tender. She won-dered if he'd even noticed the thrill she felt while touching him. She wondered if he visited the whores.

When the Allies came, any woman who'd had anything to do with German soldiers suffered hu-miliation or worse. The two she'd seen had had their heads shaved and were paraded through the streets naked. No, she thought, all women do not want to be whores. The destiny of a whore or who-rish type of woman is to grow old without a shred of dignity. After youth is gone, dignity is a woman's most precious possession.

And yet, a phrase in the story lingered: *the sense of being female.* She'd seen enough of prison life to know how thoroughly being deprived of sex robbed men of their maleness, reduced them to weak imi-tations of themselves. But women are different. It isn't sex that saves them, it's the gaze of desire. The look in a man's eyes when he sees a woman he wants. For a woman, the worst of being old is the awful invisibility. Along the way, you disappear.

One by one, Magali discarded the spoils of defiance. Chalky lipstick, unreadable books and jewellery she couldn't bring herself to wear, thrown out; perfume flushed down the toilet; pens with thick nibs, left in the library. Nothing stolen held its value. The thrill was gone. She lost interest in the secret ways a per-son can redress a private wrong. Reading Nelly's diary had brought on a new compulsion, more ex-citing and potentially more dangerous than the first. In a family so thoroughly civil that no one revealed anything of importance, the diary told the truth about wrong turns taken, decisions and regrets. It confirmed a pattern: her parent's bad marriage, the accident of her conception. Mistakes were piling up. This was a family with no history of love. Even Mouloud, who claimed he loved her, flung the word around carelessly, sprinkling it in his poems, peppering his threats and pleas with love. But did he know what it meant? Maybe love was a precious, chance encounter that happens rarely, and not to everybody.

Thinking through people she knew, how they lived, she decided there was only one true love story in the family, and it had ended tragically. Nelly's story. Marc said she was a born spinster whose brief marriage had come and gone with hardly a trace. What else did he know? Obviously, nothing of Roland, or he would have told her. Only two people knew the truth, and they were very hard to question.

The logic was thrilling. If Léonce had come home to marry Nelly, she mused, the dark-haired beauty in the flowered dress would be our grandmother. Or, there would be no us. At least we would have other names and bodies. She spent hours imagining Murielle and Roland and the life they might have lived. They would have gone to Paris after the war, she was sure. Everything would be different.

Léonce found a parking spot outside the university gate and settled back to wait for Magali. A rare cloudy day, it suited his mood. Hoping for a weather report, he turned on the radio and found a panel of professors discussing the meaning of time, yet another pointless analysis of the end of the millennium, less than six weeks away. He let them drone on for a few moments before switching it off.

The Twentieth Century: whenever he heard the phrase, he pictured the words chiselled into a tombstone. What was a century, anyway? An arbitrary span of time outside the memory of a single individual, yet bound to inspire abstraction, an abundance of pointless generalizations. For those who had experienced it, History rang false: everything he'd read and heard about events he knew first-hand was wrong. Over the years, he'd watched the Resistance waft in and out of fashion. At the time, it had been a desperate dream binding a few strangers together. Most of the people he knew had been all too willing to kiss Nazi ass, though most of them complained, of course.

As soon as the Allies moved in, the rush was on for membership in the Resistance. Suddenly, a mythical nation of silent, stealthy heroes rose up out of nowhere, as if everyone had been involved. Then along came the rebels of '68, who cut the hoard of heroes down to a ragtag bundle of ineffectual bandits. Eventually, the intellectuals settled somewhere in the middle, and nostalgia took over. At least once a month, another shaky-voiced combatant turns up on the radio to recount the glory years of clandestine activity, backed up by the sonorous strains of Charles Trenet or Fernandel. If he didn't turn the radio off immediately, the tune would ring in his head for days. Nobody knew anything, he concluded. And those who did were too tired to talk.

Looking through his pile of CDs, he pulled out his current favourite, Lynda Lemay, and slipped it into the player. She's better than Piaf, he thought. He loved the way she hurled tragic lyrics into the air with innocent gusto. The contradiction thrilled him. The music of his youth bored him. Is there something wrong with me, he sometimes wondered? For years he'd been too busy to follow trends. But lately a string of young singers, most of them women, were coming out with clever, tuneful torch songs. A little wicked and never sentimental, they knew how to lift him out of a blue mood. He was grateful and hardly ever longed for another kind of company.

Finally Magali appeared, and they drove off. Listening to Lemay in her presence embarrassed him. He was glad when she suggested changing the CD, even if her choice was an excruciating foreign band he would classify as noise. As they headed out of the city, he made an effort to hide his annoyance.

A feeble late-November sun burned the night

frost from the air. Wisps of cloud circled Mont Ventoux. Some of the vineyards had already been pruned back, revealing stark rows of gnarled trunks, like exotic dancers caught in a difficult pose. The woods were green and gold, a welcoming sign of winter in abeyance. As Magali chattered on about her classes, end of term assignments and new friends she'd made, he waited for the right moment to mention a touchy subject. He wanted to get it over with before they reached their destination.

"Magali, you know I don't like to pry, but Mouloud Mourabed ..."

What was there to say? He's a dangerous character? Ahmed's mood as they'd driven back to Les Hirondelles after a fruitless search had been grim. Whatever he knew, he wasn't telling. He wanted to caution Magali, but had no idea how to do so without sounding like a meddlesome old fool. He was loath to disturb the easy camaraderie between them.

"I guess I should ask you: what's happening to him? He isn't studying in Toulouse. His father's concerned, naturally."

"I know," she said, sinking back into the seat. She reached up and turned off the music, for which he was grateful.

"Are you and Mouloud ...?" But he was already in too deep.

She finished the sentence. "Do you mean, in love?"

Not quite. But to keep things simple, he said, "Yes."

"I don't know what the word means," she sighed. "I don't think he does either, though he uses it all the time. 'If you loved me, then ...' Stuff like that. I can't stand it, he's so ... Ah!"

As they drove in silence, Léonce squeezed his thoughts for a sensible remark. "I just hope you'll be careful," he waffled. "People in love can do strange things."

She shot him a sideways glance and smiled.

As warnings go, he was sure his rated low on the scale of usefulness. Be careful of what? Of a crazed Arab who squandered his time playing guitar and smoking dope? Ahmed's leniency angered him. Understandably, he was still reeling from his wife's death. But why waste a life's savings on trying to educate a layabout? If the Mourabeds had unrealistic ideas about the boy's future, they had Brigitte to blame. She'd filled Fatiha's mind with illusions. Send a kid like that to university? A spell in the Foreign Legion was what he needed, Léonce fumed. He blamed himself for not keeping Magali away from the boy, though in truth, he'd never made the slightest effort to dictate her behaviour. He would not have known how to begin.

As they climbed a winding road in full view of the jagged Dentelles mountain range, past one picturesque town after another, Magali admired the scenery.

"Where are you taking me?" she asked. He refused to answer, finally stopping in a parking lot at the foot of a medieval jewel perched on a hill, the village of Le Barroux.

Pointing at a high row of cypress trees across the road, he said, "That's Prince Charles' family estate, you know. Or one of the Royals. You can see it from the castle, if kings and queens are interesting to your generation. Your grandmother gave a very generous donation to the restoration of the castle I'm about to show you, in hopes of getting to meet Prince Charles, or the little princes."

"Really? Did she meet them?"

"Oh yes. Didn't she tell you? At a party held in the castle. Charles said — and I quote — 'I'm pleased to meet you, Maw-dom.' It was one of her most memorable experiences."

"Grandpa! You're fibbing!"

"She bought gloves especially for the occasion. Never wore them again, that I recall."

In Magali's recollection of the day, the sun shone brightly. Lunch with her grandfather at the Geraniums was an experience she would remember always. The terrace was closed for the season so they ate in a cosy room overlooking sloped vineyards and the Dentelles. But first they took a stroll through the narrow streets of Le Barroux, climbing past dozens of gated yards and shuttered windows, each house different from the next and lovingly restored, fitted out with pottery and flowerboxes, most of them closed up for the winter.

Their destination was a mammoth fortification perched on the highest point of the mountain, dating from the Middle Ages. "The castle was occupied by the Germans in the war," he explained. "Before retreating, they blew it up. The renovations are quite impressive. I thought it might be interesting, for a budding historian."

The main doors were open on stacks of new stone and scaffolding, evidence of construction in the courtyard, though the building seemed empty. They entered a cavernous room on the ground floor. Originally a chapel, rough stone walls had been cleaned up for an exhibition of black-and-white photographs, including some showing the castle in ruins. Mounds of guns, tarps, ammunition boxes and spare uniforms worn by the Nazis offered evidence of what went on behind the walls when the fortress became a military headquarters.

Watching him study the photographs, she knew his thoughts were back there, in the world of Nelly's diary, and that she was in the presence of a hero. As they left the exhibition, her heart beat so quickly she could hardly keep up with his pace. The birds-eye view of the Royal *mas* paled next to the revelation of a secret world. She could hear his memories roar, and struggled for a question or comment that would take her inside his head. As he started down the grassy slope on the other side of the castle, it seemed the moment would slip away.

She stopped, and called out, "Grandpa, wait for me, please."

He turned around. She was standing on a pile of rubble. He offered his hand, intending to help her back onto solid ground. Instead, she blurted out a question:

"Were you really Roland?"

He stood staring at her, speechless. She reached for his hand, and stepping over a pile of gravel, took him by the arm.

"So, who told you?" he said, finally. "I guess it must have been Nelly."

"No, I mean, not really. She didn't exactly tell me."

"How did you find out?"

"Never mind questions, Grandpa. Please, answers. Were you a Resistance fighter? Did you jump out of an airplane and land in a field one night?"

He stopped walking, eyes fixed on a point on the sky.

"Yes."

"Why don't you ever talk about it?"

He laughed. "Well, no one ever asks."

"Oh! How could we know to ask? You're so secretive. All these years …"

"That was a long time ago," he continued, leading the way down toward the restaurant. "I guess I've just never had the occasion to recall certain events. At the time, it was important to be discreet. Maybe secrecy becomes a habit. There wasn't much to tell, really. A lot of rushing around, precious little heroism."

"No, don't think you can get off so easily! I want to know everything that happened from the moment you joined the movement."

"I had a friend who had connections. An older guy, his father was in the army."

By the time they reached the restaurant, he'd warmed to the subject, though he spoke in terse sentences, as if every word were costly. She tried to resist letting details from the diary slip into her questions, thinking that if only he told her the same story, she just might get away with the act of theft, and no one ever need know.

When he came to the harrowing escape from La Roque du Buis, where his band of Resistance fighters in hiding were hunted down by the Germans, his hands were shaking. He told how he ran for hours, stopping only to scoop up the odd handful of snow from the evergreen branches, in lieu of water. About the sweet warmth of the farmhouse where he'd stopped for a rest. How good the sight of a bed by a fire had looked, though he'd insisted on staying in the barn. Discovery would have meant certain death for the people who hid him. How he made it all the way to Carpentras without being noticed, only to come face to face with the SS officer in charge of the search mission. Then a train straight to Nuremberg, and a German work camp.

"After that, it was all a matter of waiting."

The story over, he tucked into his plate of *confit de canard* as if it were the first good meal he'd had in ages.

What about Murielle? The note you left for her under the rock? Did you write her from prison? The obvious questions could not be asked. "What about Aunt Nelly?" she ventured, cautiously. "Was she in the Resistance too?"

He looked up from the plate, catching her eye for the first time. "I'm sure she must have stories to tell," he said.

For a moment she wondered if he might be asking her for information. But how far could she go without becoming hopelessly tangled in things she had no right to know?

"Everyone has such a different version of history," she said, calmly.

He smiled, nodded. "The historian speaks. Yes, I guess everyone does."

History. The word was a mistake. She knew he would use it to slip back into generalities, lecture her on grand themes, and the only story that mattered would be gone with very little chance of ever coming back. Leaning forward on her elbows, she summoned her courage and said, in a low voice, "Grandpa, why didn't you come back to Murielle, like you promised?"

He was holding his knife and fork, ready to cut a piece of meat, and stopped, as if suddenly he'd forgotten what the business of eating was all about.

"I did," he said.

A wry smile floated across his eyes. He knew Nelly's side of the story was out on the table, brought there by an emissary who had thus far been an ally. But he wasn't about to give up more information easily. She wasn't prepared to be silenced either.

"You did? But what happened?"

"She'd gone with someone else."

"You mean, she'd fallen in love with someone else?"

"Something like that," he said, dismissively. "That's what her mother told me."

"Her mother! But you didn't ask Nelly? You didn't see her?"

"She'd moved to Carpentras."

"Grandpa! It's a thirty-minute drive away."

"Not in those days," he protested. "Carpentras was ..."

As she laced the new details into Nelly's story, it seemed more horrible by the minute. So her mother sabotaged the reunion? Did Nelly know? Did she fail to mention the real reason she lost Roland?

"What happened to this other person Nelly went off with?"

"I have no idea," he snapped. She could tell by his tone that the time for questions was over.

A few terse details dropped into a Sunday lunch, and a story she'd so recently thought of as deeply romantic, even tragic, suddenly seemed crazy, silly, awful, so unfair! Why didn't they call, or take the bus, or even send a telegram? So it wasn't because of deep dark secrets that nobody in the family talked about important things. The secrets were a result of how they acted. Or more precisely, how they did not act. Grandpa, she wanted to shout, how could you? By the faraway look on his sad, grey face, she knew he was back there, wandering around Ste. Cécile les Vignes, feeling bad about bad news. She could have slapped him. But of course it was far too late now, even though Nelly was still alive and could answer all of his questions. If she wanted to answer. Probably not. It was too late for anything but truth. And who cared about that? What good would it do?

SEVENTEEN

AS A CHILD MAGALI feared the moment of falling asleep, as though falling out of watchfulness, she would fall forever. The minute she closed her eyes the room whirled. Her father bought fluorescent stars and pasted them to the ceiling, telling her not to think about sleep, just keep looking at the night sky. From then on she woke up believing she hadn't slept at all. It was ages before she started to remember her dreams.

Waking up under a dim November sky, she had a rush of the old anxiety in reverse, a feeling that some fine, important dream had been interrupted by the waking world, that she should have remained asleep until the end. Reaching for her watch on the floor beside the mattress, she saw it was not quite five o'clock. The house was dark and silent as she tiptoed toward the WC at the end of the hall. When she came back, the door was half open. She tried to remember whether she'd closed it or not, anxiety crystallizing around the idea that someone was there, or had been and had just left. Nothing seemed out of place and there was no place to hide, only a thin armoire hardly big enough for a person. She checked anyway. The sensation persisted even as she crawled into bed and pulled the duvet over her head. Finally, she had to get up and turn on a light, which is when she noticed a postcard propped up against the desk lamp, addressed to her in familiar handwriting. On one side was an intricate pattern of mosaics in neon colours, on the other, an invitation to a concert with the time, date and place in Arabic and French. Scanning the list of performers, she found Mouloud's name.

The streets were all but empty, no one up yet but a sullen sweeper, as she hurried along the narrow sidewalks that led to the other side of town. At the door to his building, she kept jabbing the button beside his name again and again until finally he appeared at the bottom of the stairs, groggy.

"Why do you do this?" she demanded.

"What?"

She waved the invitation in his face. "This."

"What do you mean?"

"Invade my life! You're a sneak. Why? What have I done to deserve this? Tell me, now long is it going to last? Where will it end?"

He stared at her, mystified.

"Why won't you answer me?"

He shrugged, leaned against the door case, as if he hardly had the strength to stand.

"It doesn't matter," he said, flatly. "Everything that's going to happen is already known. It has already happened."

"What is that supposed to mean?"

A look of deep sadness melted her anger into desperation. "Mouloud," she pleaded. "Please tell me what I can say or do to make you understand and leave me alone."

As if he had suddenly woken up, words tumbled out: "I thought you might be interested. That's all. It isn't only me, it's a big concert. The others are good musicians, professionals. I thought you— never mind!" He snatched the card out of her hand, and headed back upstairs. She followed.

"Why didn't you just ask me? Phone, or whatever? Why break into my home to tell me something simple? It wasn't necessary."

He turned around, barring her way. "What are you talking about?"

"You came into my room while I was sleeping. Why? It's creepy." She shouted. "You're trying to prove something, aren't you? This is self-destructive, you know. It hurts you more than me. Tell me why

I should tolerate someone invading my life? Why, why would I?"

"I sent you an invitation, that's all," he murmured. He handed the card back to her. Turning it over, she saw her name and address, and for the first time, a postal imprint. When she'd seen the letter on her desk, she'd been sure he had put there, in defiance of Nelly's rule.

"You sent this through the mail? … The stamp must have fallen off. Oh dear."

He headed up the stairs, this time doing nothing to stop her as she followed down a dimly lit hallway smelling of stale grease and old shoes.

"Wait, I'm sorry," she said. "I didn't realize you …"

He stopped outside a door with the number six scrawled loosely in black marker.

"May I come in?"

He shook his head.

"Please."

"You won't like what you see," he said.

There it was again, the strange, disturbing mixture of fragility and menace. She always suspected the worst of Mouloud. Every encounter left her stomach in knots, and yet he had a way of drawing her back, especially when he didn't try, like now. He was sending her away, but she couldn't go.

"What is it?" she said.

"Nothing important. But ..."

"Let me have a look."

"As long as you don't blame me, or tell any-body."

"I won't."

"Promise?"

"Of course. I promise," she sighed.

"Say it."

"I promise I won't blame you or tell anyone. I keep my promises, you know?"

As soon as the words were out, she knew she'd made a mistake. But it was too late.

"Don't think it means anything," he added.

"Okay."

He opened the door on a small room, a dirty yellow, barely enough space for a single bed, a sink and table covered by a rich embroidered cloth, a shrine for his precious laptop, the treasure chest of everything and everyone he knew in the wide world outside Ste. Cécile les Vignes. Beside the bed was a straw mat, two pairs of shoes leaning neatly against the wall. A red curtain hung over the tiny window. When she stepped over the threshold, he closed the door and turned on the light. The wall behind his bed was completely covered with a bold mural in black and red, a giant portrait of her face, cheeks, wild eyes and hair filling most of the wall. Lodged between the carefully etched details were tiny bits of limbs, bones and organs splashed in red, super-imposed with her features at odd angles. Her mouth was open, as if in a shout. A small foot dangled from the lips.

She groaned, and sat down on the bed, turning her back on the mural. Even so, she could feel the image glowering. It gave her the creeps.

"I warned you. Don't take it the wrong way," he said. "It doesn't mean anything."

"Sit beside me," she whispered. When he sat down, she reached out and took his hand. She bit the inside of her lips hard, but tears came flooding out anyway.

"Don't worry," he said. "I'm going away. I've got work in Marseille. You'll see. Everything'll be fine. You won't have to think about me again. I promise."

She put her arms around him, drawing him down on the bed. He seemed to collapse into her embrace. He was so thin, she was afraid he might break. Next to the wafer lightness of his frame, she felt robust, bursting with blood. She rubbed his arms and back as if to warm a corpse. He made no effort to hold her, though she could sense his breathing relax. Folding his head into the crux of her neck, she ran her fingers through his soft hair, smoothed it with her hand.

"Mouloud, Mouloud," she murmured. "Believe me, there is nothing about you I will ever, ever forget. Everything that happened to us will stay inside me forever, because … of what happened. You'll see, in years to come, you'll still be with me, everything, in me, somehow I know that. So I want you to know. There is love in me for you. I can't say more. I can't stay with you or anything like that. Don't ask me to stay, but take my love, Mouloud, Mouloud. Are you listening? Please listen to me, take my love and feel good about it. Take what I can give you and be strong, please."

When he didn't answer, she moved his head away from her shoulder and looked into his eyes. His expression was blank. She couldn't tell whether he'd understood, whether what she'd said had soothed his rage, or whether he was only feigning calm. They lay silent for a few moments, Mouloud staring at the wall. She could tell his thoughts were faraway. As she pulled out of the embrace and covered him with a blanket, he kept on staring at nothingness. She kissed his cheek and ran her hands over his hair, then covered him with a blanket and left the tiny airless room behind.

Walking back to rue des Griffons, she wondered whether she'd even meant what she said about giving him her love. In the presence of torment spread over the walls, a room dripping in the memory of a bad time they'd gone through together, she'd been overcome by a wave of tenderness. Her whole body ached with sympathy. Maybe it was only pity, she thought, looking back. But at the time, warm feelings had poured out of her needing words and the only word big enough was love. Now facing daylight, she was dizzy, empty, as though she'd left the word and her love behind.

When Magali had gone, Mouloud splashed his face with cold water and sat down at his computer. He took a book of poetry from the shelf fixed to the wall, selections from the *Canzoniere* by Francesco Petrarca. Opening at random, he read for a few moments, then closed the book and typed one word.
    She—
    The first lines came easily, until a church bell distracted him. He waited for the bells to finish chiming the hour. It was the hour of prayer. Looking down at the straw prayer mat, he remembered she'd walked on it with shoes that had trod the streets of Avignon, dog shit and piss and spit, who knows what else. It was time. He knew he should take the prayerful position, but was sure he could smell shit from her shoes on the mat. A sob rose in his throat. He crawled onto the bed and cried until he slept.

EIGHTEEN

PIERS FIRST CAME upon Avignon's most celebrated Brotherhood by way of a footnote to a treatise on monastic life in eighteenth-century France. For a while, he was sure he'd found a way through the labyrinth he'd been caught up in for years, and set out to learn everything about the movement.

Founded as a lay order in 1586, the Pénitents Noirs de la Miséricorde was a fraternity of professionals, artisans, landowners, with a smattering of aristocrats. Husbands, fathers, men of the world, they took as their mission the care and sustenance of criminals, notably those condemned to death. In recognition of the Order's good works and social standing, Pope Clement VIII granted the privilege of deliverance: each year, on the feast day of their patron saint, John the Baptist, one condemned prisoner of the Order's choosing would be pardoned and set free. After a ceremonial smashing of the irons, the anointed symbol of Divine mercy was crowned with an olive garland and led through the streets of Avignon by a procession of black-robed Penitents, their faces covered in cone-shaped hoods. Past throngs of the faithful and the curious, their destination was a Gothic chapel on rue Banisterie where choirs of young girls waited, waving floral wreaths and singing hallelujahs. The Day of Deliverance ended in a night of celebration to which the entire city was invited.

A powerful Order whose prestige rested on a single act of mercy, it had flourished for three centuries but dwindled in the early 1900s and finally disbanded completely after the Second World War. Today the Order's only surviving testament is a chapel nestled against the wall of St. Anne's prison. Still reflecting the design and décor created by a prominent local architect in the eighteenth century, the chapel is elegant and worldly, closer to a miniature palace than a place of worship. Images of the Order's patron saint are the dominant motif, echoed in stone sculptures and oil paintings: the severed head of John the Baptist on a platter borne by infant angel faces without bodies.

Piers had been caught up in research for weeks. Finally venturing outside the archives to visit the chapel, he discovered it had fallen into the hands of a right-wing sect. He didn't like their politics; more specifically, he didn't like the hold they had on a great tradition, but he was curious just the same. A certain Père Absalom was in charge. Piers made enquiries and found out Absalom had written a series of articles condemning certain tenets of Islam and how they were being played out in French society. He spent weeks assembling a bibliography for the poor misguided cleric, solid proof that there was less difference between monotheistic brands than its various sectarians were prepared to believe. What irritated him most was that Absalom inevitably greeted every opportunity for discussion as a sign that he was drawing the foreigner closer to the fold. Still, he found the call to debate irresistible.

Mouloud followed Piers at dusk, skirting parked cars and couples walking arm in arm, staying in the shadows as he made his way toward the centre of town. He watched him enter the brightly lit Café Forum, order a coffee at the bar and flip through a newspaper, barely glancing at the contents. Piers looked at his watch. A reflex, Mouloud checked his too, for the hundredth time that day.

A vigil begun at dawn, he'd hung around the open end of rue des Griffons all day, a murderously boring vigil. Finally Piers appeared carrying a briefcase and strode resolutely toward the post office, a brief stop to let go of a parcel, then on to Place d'Horloge and the Forum, apparently his destination. But as the bar began to fill up, the cacophony of joviality seemed to grate on his nerves. He kept looking around, as if he were waiting for someone, or suspected he was being followed.

Mouloud had kept his head down since Magali had come at him with a blast of accusations. By the time she left, he was numb, exhausted by her words. He'd fallen into a stupor and slept all day. After that, his rhythms stayed nocturnal. He could sleep twelve hours at a stretch and still wake up tired, but as soon as darkness fell he was full of nervous energy and couldn't stop walking. Solitary night thoughts preyed on his mind and crowded his dreams until there was no difference, day and night a seamless howl in his head.

Tracking Piers restored his energy, but his thoughts stayed muddled. On the side of relief: at least Magali had admitted her mistake. Selim too. He'd paid a visit with a happy purpose to tell Mouloud he was off the hook. My mistake, he'd said. His exact words: Don't worry. An easy miscalculation in the contents of the package, you were not to blame. Marco tried to screw me, Mouloud protested. But what happened that night, outside your place? Who threw the stone? Remy's friend is dead. Did you throw the stone? Did you? No. Was it you? No! Was it? NO. Who then? I don't know. You know. I don't. He was wearing leather gloves. Selim squeezed his fingers like a spider's legs, demanding to know who threw the stone that finished Remy's friend. Because if it wasn't you, he said, it was somebody else, and somebody had to pay. There was somebody with you, wasn't there? Selim demanded a name, an address. Over and over, beating him down with words. You're not to blame, he kept saying. But tell me who is. So Mouloud told him. Selim wrote it down and was happy after that, as if nothing at all had happened to turn their friendship upside-down, or disrupt their plans. I want you to pay close attention, Selim said, with the same voice he used at first, full of promise. Watch me, watch how easy it is to do an enemy in. Pay attention, you'll learn something valuable. You hear me? Hear me? Speak up!

I don't want to learn how to kill, Mouloud had wanted to shout. But he said nothing. Selim took out his pocket agenda and picked a day. This was the day, and it was turning into night. Nothing had happened yet but there was still time. Selim worked best at night.

As if time had suddenly run out, Piers folded his newspaper and left the café, walking quickly. Mouloud thought, he knows something's up. He turned down a narrow cobblestone alley into the walkway that led through Pope Urban V's orchard, Mouloud following at a respectable distance. There was a line-up for the six o'clock movie at Cinema Utopia but Piers swung right, dropping into the alley below. It wasn't far from Mouloud's room, but he'd never gone home this way.

Finally they turned into a tiny square with a church built into a high stone wall. An ornate facade with high wooden doors, the doors were open. There were lights on inside. An elderly man was standing on the steps, his back to the doors, smoking a cigarette. He nodded at Piers on the way in, and scowled at Mouloud, as if to say, you have no business being here. Mouloud ignored the look and walked calmly after Piers.

The first room was a small antechamber with wooden benches, empty. Double doors led to a larger room. On rows of benches facing a stage sat a dozen or so people, most of them old and sad or young and alone. The air smelled of burnt spices and dust. A small man in a long green cape was standing at the front, facing a table crammed with ornaments, flowers, candles; he was chanting in a strange language. Mouloud glanced around at the walls and ceiling, taking in garish paintings of chunky women holding babies and pale men with long hair dressed in pastel robes. A severed head on a platter, a naked body pinned to a cross, obviously dead. He'd seen it before, the Christian god of love and peace, murdered of course. The place gave him the creeps.

As if on cue, everyone stood up, including Piers who had taken a seat at the side. He went along with the crowd, stood when they stood, pretended to read from a black book he found on his seat, moved his lips to the incomprehensible muttering, nodded off during a long monotone monologue. Finally they broke formation and headed towards the stage, where they ate and drank from a cup passed to them by the man in green. Piers stayed immobile, eyes fixed straight ahead, as if he was staring into dead air. A few more prayers followed and the crowd began to disperse, except Piers, who followed the man in green through a door behind the stage, into another room. Mouloud waited till the room was empty then shot forward, stopping on the threshold to listen. Behind the door, an argument, though he couldn't make out the issue. At first Piers was doing most of the talking. His voice was a low hum with spaces between the words but gradually the other man chimed in and the volume rose, sentences overlapped till it was impossible to understand.

While they were still shouting, the door opened and Piers shot out, practically landing in Mouloud's arms.

"What are you doing here?" he barked, still in the mood of the interview.

Before Mouloud could answer, the other man appeared. He was dressed in a long black robe, carrying keys which he jangled angrily in one hand, a briefcase in the other. He asked them both to leave the building, polite words but clearly an order, assuming they were together. He waited till they'd left the building, then locked the doors and got into the only car left in the parking lot, a new Mercedes. Piers watched him drive away, and cursed softly, as though he were standing alone. He began to walk. Mouloud followed.

"That guy you hit with a stone …" he began.

"What about him?" Piers threw the words on the street.

"He works for somebody I know. They're trying to find you."

Piers quickened his pace, ignoring him.

"They're looking for you."

"Are they?" he stopped and glared. "Well, that's nice. I'll say hello on your behalf."

Mouloud followed for a while in silence. He couldn't think of what to say, how to phrase a warning that didn't sound crazy. His mouth was dry. Piers began humming through his teeth, a quick staccato melody in time with his stride. When they drew close to rue des Griffons, Mouloud stopped. Piers kept on walking, waved goodbye without looking back and went inside the house.

Magali was standing in the doorway to the rose room, half-hidden, swinging the door back and forth, about to ask if she could come in for a chat, but he slipped by with a nod and closed his door. Her heart beat as though the exchange had been momentous. Something about him had changed. He had a strange expression, as if his thoughts were far-away. He must be working on a new book, she thought.

She listened for sounds of activity in the avocado room, expecting water, typing, but heard nothing, only the occasional thud of his boots hitting the tiles. A few moments later, his voice. She moved closer to the wall to catch the drift. It was a one-sided conversation, low and warm, in English. She could not understand a word.

Chanelle Lambert recognized Piers' number when it came up on her phone, and picked up on the last ring. She didn't want to sound eager.

"Are you alone?" he asked, in English.

The language caught her off guard. Whenever she'd tried to coax him into speaking English, he'd refused.

"Yes, I'm alone," she said, choosing her words carefully. The tone sounded more inviting than she'd intended, no hint of the anger aroused by their last meeting when he'd stood her up, then dragged her into a congested city for a glass of rough wine at the Bar Américain followed by the insult of watching his attention leap like a hungry lion from her to a girl standing outside the window.

"How are you?" he asked, softly.

"I'm good," she replied, thinking immediately she should have said, I am well. If he noticed the mistake and teased her, she'd be furious, but he didn't. He sounded relaxed. She pictured him standing by a window, an airy white room furnished sparsely, a glass-topped desk and couple of simple Italian chairs. Shoulders slightly stooped from hours of typing, he would be holding a Scotch in one hand (as she was holding a Scotch), and staring out on a sweeping view of the Papal Palace. The writer at work, taking a break to call her. Nothing like their Tuesday afternoons, a routine launched by brute necessity. Surprised by evidence of her husband Frédéric's infidelity, she had responded according to convention with shouts, threats, tears. A lurid few days of noisy uncertainty, then the classic riposte carried out with dignity: she'd placed a classified ad in the newspaper, fielded a handful of calls, and was soon on her way to Porte St. Michel for the inaugural rendezvous with the lover she deserved.

Time passed, they fell into a routine, drifted. Meanwhile, Frédéric had a heart attack, and in the flush of recovery, proposed a trip to America. By the time Chanelle fell upon a dog-eared copy of *The Faithful Husband* in a New Orleans hotel lobby, she had no need for a lover. But an Author, that was another matter.

"I was wondering if you'd like to have dinner," he said.

His voice, as if from the bottom of a well, aroused her as it never had in person. Weeks of silence since their last disastrous rendezvous, and then out of the blue, a proper date. She held back. If their affair was about to resume, then every move would need to be considered. He was calling for a reason. He would be making calculations. Who had called it off, anyway? She couldn't remember, it had just seemed to dwindle away. She hadn't wanted a fiery ending, didn't need the bother. But she did want to know a writer. Sleep with him, maybe, most of all befriend him, draw him into her circle. The idea was thrilling, presenting Piers Le Gris: *mon très cher ami*, The American Writer.

"Why didn't you tell me you are famous?" she

said, banking on a flirtatious tone to mask inquisition.

"I'm not," he said.

"You are! I would very much like to talk about your work."

"I don't talk about my work."

"Oh, come on! Yes, all writers do. They go on television. They love it."

"Not me."

"I know you much better from reading your books."

"No, you don't. I'm not in the books."

She laughed. "Oh, you are, you just don't see it. You are always the bad guy. He's always wearing your clothes. Even when you change his name, the bad guy resembles you."

He answered with a tight, dry chuckle confirming she was right. She had many more questions, but hesitated. How famous was he? Difficult to tell, the world of the thriller was vast and lucrative. He would be wealthy, of course. He would have houses in other countries.

"I need to see you again," he said. "Is it possible?"

The urgency in his voice was thrilling. "Of course," she cooed. "I'd like you to meet some people."

"I don't like meeting people. Let's have dinner."

"Oh but you will like them," she said. "Saturday night. Don't worry, I'll drive. Meet me at eight o'clock in the usual place."

"Chanelle!"

"And please, *chéri*, write it down. *Au revoir. Bisou.*" She hung up before he had a chance to reconsider.

Over breakfast, Magali told Piers about Mouloud's concert, and asked if he'd like to go. She waited till Nelly had gone to the kitchen for more coffee, giving the invitation a hint of complicity. "It's in a disco hall somewhere outside the walls," she said, sliding the envelope across the table. Saturday, I'll meet you there."

"Be careful with Mouloud," he said.

She nodded, a faint grimace passing over her face, as though she'd heard the same thing a thousand times before.

This time the warning went both ways. A few weeks ago, he'd feared for her safety. Now he wondered which one faced greater danger, blind beauty or the fragile psyche under beauty's spell.

NINETEEN

....

THE BACK COVER of Putterly Inc.'s popular line of erotic thrillers has a photo of a man wearing a substantial black hat tilted to cover his eyes, leaving a firm jaw line in shadow. Piers kept the hat in a suitcase.

By the time he had reason to dig out the hat, his room was as spare and clean as a monk's cell. Several metres of bookshelves had been trimmed down to a few volumes: *Ekhardt*, the *King James (New and Old)*, the *Apocrypha*, *The Divine Comedy* and a slim volume of verse inscribed to a woman named Ann. The armoire was almost empty, the coffee pot stiff from lack of use. An unfinished manuscript sat on one side of the bare table, next to an unopened box of A4 bond 100 gsm, a high-quality paper meant for final drafts. In spite of everything, he had not lost hope in *The Lethal Guitar*.

It was dusk by the time Chanelle wheeled her silver Peugeot into the familiar parking lot. Piers was standing by a cement pillar. He was wearing a new black trench coat, clutching a bundle of roses in one hand, a briefcase in the other. At the sight of the black hat, familiar from his book covers, her heart leapt.

He slid into the passenger's seat, leaned over for a kiss. The brush of his newly shaven jaw against her skin was thrilling.

"You're early," she said.

"So are you."

He smelled of olive soap and something else, indefinably sweet and dusty, incense.

As the car pulled onto the highway that circled the ramparts, she asked if he knew Isle sur la Sorgue.

"Yes, well, somewhat. Chanelle, I don't feel much like meeting people tonight. In any case, I have to be back in Avignon by eleven. I'm sorry, it's unavoidable. I should have cancelled—"

"Shhh. Never mind," she cooed, shooting him a grin full of promise.

She was wearing a jersey cocktail dress that clung to her hips, an elaborate chain necklace, and leather pumps with stiletto heels. She'd had her hair cut and tinted a quiet shade of red. At the last minute, she had reached for a spray balm of *Je reviens*. A soft old-fashioned scent, it lacked the audacity of newer perfumes, but she was not in the mood for bold strikes.

They stopped at a red light. Piers reached over and placed his hand on hers, which was resting on the stickshift.

"Chanelle," he said, firmly. "Let's go somewhere for a quiet dinner, alone."

The light changed to green. She shifted into first and the vehicle lurched forward.

"Oh, there'll be plenty of food at the party. And excellent wines, I can promise. It's the last meeting of our wine-tasting circle before the holidays. You'll meet some very interesting people. In fact, you're going to meet my husband. He's bringing a 1992 Chateau—"

"What?!"

They had entered a narrow stretch of highway joining one suburban centre with the next. A fat minivan barrelled down the middle of the road.

"*Calme-toi, chéri.* He knows. He's cool."

"Stop the car!"

Piers reached for the steering wheel. She did her best to keep the vehicle from veering off but the interference was distracting. Her foot bore down on the accelerator involuntarily. She swerved to make room and just in time, the minivan roared past, barely avoiding collision. Piers let go of the wheel and covered his eyes. In the excitement she braked and the car jerked, drawing a sharp blast from the vehicle behind.

Finally, they reached a patch of countryside. Voice shaking, Piers said he needed to get out, get some air. He pointed to a laneway ahead and she turned off onto a grassy field. Without waiting for the engine to stop, he leapt out.

"You almost caused an accident," she said, slamming the door as she followed him. "What's the matter?"

He was staring at the horizon, gripping his brief-case, the hat jammed awkwardly on the back of his head. Initially mysterious, it now looked comical. She made an effort not to laugh.

"Relax, *chéri*," she sighed, her voice strangely calm. "I'm a very good driver."

He was taking great gulps of air and had gone completely pale. It was the first time she'd ever seen him upset, possibly furious. She opened his trench coat, slipped her arms around his waist but his spine stayed rigid.

She noticed he was wearing the mauve silk shirt she had given him ages ago. He must have opened it especially for this evening. The packaging creases still left ridges. As she ran her fingers along the folds she thought of *The Faithful Husband*, the myriad of details he'd absorbed from their encounters, while she'd only floated on the surface, caught up in the moment. Her memories of their Tuesday afternoons all blurred into one, and even the one was brief.

Nothing like the version he'd summoned for his books. She nuzzled his neck and whispered his name. He set the briefcase down and kissed her lightly on the lips. She responded, enveloping him in a snug embrace, her stiletto heels sinking into the damp grass.

"Why don't we go somewhere?" he murmured. "I want to be with you."

"We could."

"Give me the keys. I'll drive."

She laughed. "You don't need to drive. I'm perfectly capable."

"I know, but I like driving."

"No you don't. And you don't know where we're going."

He ignored her, got into the driver's seat, adjusted it to give his long legs more room and twisted the rearview mirror upwards. Then he stared blankly at the complex dashboard of dials and buttons, and it struck her that he had no idea how to operate her precious Peugeot.

"Really, I'd prefer to drive," she said.

He turned the key. The motor roared. The car lurched backwards and stalled.

"Piers, please." Her tone was not endearing. She opened his door. He got out.

Resting a hand on her shoulder, he said, calmly, "I'd like to make love to you."

The sun was setting behind a clump of cypress trees. They were stopped on the edge of a minor hayfield, rural but hardly private. A few metres ahead was a bungalow with a two-car garage and line of laundry stretching out over a child's sand pile. The jingle of a popular television series floated through the evening air, reminding Chanelle of the hour. She glanced at her watch, then at the car, which was resting at an odd angle.

"Oh no," she groaned. "Look. I've got a flat tire. *Merde!* "

Hélène and François Garçin's villa in Isle sur la Sorgue had a generous garden full of shrubs and trees that stayed lush well into late fall. It was surrounded by a fence and hedge, with a high iron gate and plenty of parking along the sidewalk outside. Still, Chanelle had to comb the side streets before finding a spot within walking distance of the door. She hadn't been to a wine-tasting evening in ages. Amid the static generated by her husband's affair, she had insisted on separate social lives, partly as punishment, but also as a test of what divorce might hold in store. Now that she'd made a new friend worth showing off, she was eager to reconnect with a circle of well-heeled professionals who might appreciate her find. While not exactly literary types, most of them were better conversationalists than

Frédéric, a podiatrist, who had trouble looking people in the eye. Tonight's hosts were partners in dentistry but they owned an apartment in Vienna, an inheritance from a distant cousin, a count, so they claimed.

As she rang the bell Chanelle leaned close to Piers and, squeezing his hand, promised, "Twenty minutes to say hello and we'll leave. The rest of the night will be ours."

Hélène opened the door, releasing a tumultuous wave of music. One look at the split-level living room behind and Chanelle realized why parking had been so difficult. The scene inside was closer to a downtown discotheque than the demure evenings she'd attended a year ago. People were crammed shoulder to shoulder in the main room, leaning over the railing of the second floor galleria, sitting on the stairs, huddled in corners. Some even tried dancing to a throbbing rock beat emanating from a powerful sound system.

"Darling, great to see you, finally!" Hélène gushed above the din. She was wearing a filmy transparent blouse over a black push-up bra and tight jeans. Her eyes were glassy.

"Where have you been? Ouch! Who is this luscious man you've brought us? You do like surprises, wonderful!"

Before Chanelle had a chance to reply, Piers was dragged ahead into a murky cloud of marijuana and tobacco smoke. When she started after them, a bearish man she recognized as her accountant blocked the path. He was wearing a boldly striped tie, the knot loosened. He bellowed her name and, leaning down, dropped a sloppy kiss on her neck, slipped his arm around her waist and pulled her into the throng. She snarled at him to let go but he seemed not to hear. Before she could get his attention they were standing at the bar, where two young men with white t-shirts stretched over taut chests were serving drinks. The atmosphere was frenzied, confusing. There were many people she didn't know, most of them middle-aged, but a few were young and decidedly not the kind of people she and Fred knew. Three men in leather pants and vests with prominent tattoos and multiple piercings were hovering over a lightly packaged girl whose ensemble included feathers. A woman with a beaked nose slouched on the sofa, her skirt hoisted up, revealing black stockings held up by garters. She had her hand in a man's crotch. Looking closer, Chanelle saw the man was her husband.

"Frédéric!" she shouted. Neither of them seemed to hear. When the woman leaned over and slipped her tongue into his mouth, Chanelle kicked him in

the shins. He bit down hard, the woman screeched
and slapped his face.

Glancing up, Frédéric said hello, his face twisted
in an uneasy mixture of bemusement and shock. A
small man with short legs and the beginnings of a
belly, he had to boost himself with both hands to
get off the low sofa. As he staggered to his feet,
Chanelle grabbed his neck and pulled his ear toward her mouth. He smelled of liquor and someone
else's perfume.

"What the fuck is this?" she shouted over the din.

He nodded, as if it was all quite simple and, taking her arm, wedged them both through the crowd
toward the kitchen.

"Did you bring your friend?" he panted, when
they'd cleared the throng.

"Would you mind telling me what's going on?"
she fumed.

He pointed to his ear, shook his head, implying
either that it was still too noisy to talk or he couldn't
think of an acceptable answer, she wasn't sure
which. Even the kitchen was crowded. The accountant was making his way toward them. She ignored
his grin and turned back to Frédéric, who was
looked longingly at the living room.

They were standing beside a door. She tried the
handle. It opened. She stepped inside, pulling him

with her, and swung the door shut, felt along the wall for a light switch but couldn't find one. As her eyes adjusted, she saw they were in the laundry room. Frédéric murmured her name. Just as she was about to tear into him, she heard sounds coming from behind a white curtain that hung ceiling-to-floor next to the washing machine. Groans, pants, the unmistakeable rhythmic noises of two people in an embrace.

A hazy smile spread over her husband's face. He leaned toward her and ran his tongue along her lips. The couple next to them were so close Chanelle was sure she could smell the heat from writhing bodies. Her spine tingled with embarrassment. She was about to whisper, let's go, but he reached up under her skirt and tugged at her panties, pressing his groin forward until she could feel his hard sex against her stomach. He kept looking at her, rocking forward gently, half smiling but expecting nothing. For the first time in months, maybe longer, his attention was riveted entirely on her. A hungry, craving look with a hint of resignation, as if he was sure she wouldn't dare act on what he so obviously and urgently wanted. The sounds beside them grew more intense. She reached back, put her hands on the washing machine and lifted herself up until she was sitting, perfectly poised to slide down on top of him. They were soon too engrossed to notice the couple behind the white curtain slip out of the laundry room. Chanelle barely heard the woman's giggle or the man's low chortle as he closed the door behind them.

Later, as she made her way through the crowd alone, the whole dizzy spectacle came into focus. Her husband's sudden enthusiasm for fine wines, the interest he'd shown in meeting the Author. Of course, he'd been coming here for months, while she'd had Tuesday afternoons with Piers.

Consequences? So far, the best sex they'd had in years. As far as she could see there wasn't an ounce of jealousy in the whole gigantic indoor pool of adult entertainment, no apathy either. Groping couples, singles locked in anxious negotiation, a room full of hunger, it was thrilling and scary. Her head was clear. She felt better than she'd felt in years. Her thighs ached. She was famished.

She looked around for Piers, sure he'd be ready to leave. *I want to make love to you.* His words echoed. Thinking back on the drive out, she decided she'd been harsh. She'd have to tell him she was sorry. *I'd love to have dinner somewhere quiet, where we can talk. I want to make love to you too.* She said it under her breath. The party was winding down, people were leaving, the music was a maudlin torch song. She spied Hélène slumped in a chair, nursing a cognac. She asked for Piers. Hélène shrugged and pointed at the door.

Stepping out onto the terrace, Chanelle hoped Piers would be waiting, but he wasn't and she stared at the steps, as if staring would make him appear. The night air was crisp. The walkway was a bed of fine round stones. She could feel the stones pressing up against thin soles, and it struck her that if the road were covered in stones she would be able to run. Suddenly it seemed important to connect with Piers Le Gris.

By the time she located her car, the wild joy of moments ago was fading. The flush of triumph, mutual conquest, for once, absolute power over a situation, yet the feeling didn't last. On the back seat lay the bundle of roses and his briefcase. The shadow of his presence sent her spirit plunging. She drove around the block twice, hoping he might have stepped out for fresh air, considered going back inside in case they'd just missed each other. The problem was Frédéric, she dreaded having to face him again. She headed for the car.

Making her way slowly back to Avignon, she watched the side of the road, in case Piers had set out walking. She'd begun to suspect he'd left with someone else. By the time she reached the Rhone, his absence had filled her completely. She doubted she would ever see him again. A forlorn certainty, the worst of it, a terrible sense of betrayal. Why, she wondered? What have I done? Made love to my husband. Floating up out of a sea of unconsciousness, guilt, remorse, all very illogical, yet as true and powerful as any feeling she had ever known.

She parked behind the gate at Les Angles and retrieved the roses. The briefcase was unlocked. Suddenly frantic for a morsel of his existence, she looked inside. It was empty except for a box of chocolates. She leaned against the car door and sobbed.

TWENTY

IN THE MID-1960S Alonzo Martin and his brother Victor inherited a stony farm in the Luberon from a bachelor uncle, a house and barns in various stages of decay, the miniscule arable surface consisting of a few scraggly apricot trees. Most of the property was a steep incline choked with thorny brush, the perfect grazing ground for goats, but otherwise quite worthless except for the view, which was breathtaking. Victor settled in Cavillon, where he married, prospered and dropped dead at sixty, leaving three daughters to inherit his share. Alonzo had no wife, no children, no reason to die young. In old age he was land-rich and friendless.

As he made his way along a deserted country road on a brisk November night, he was thinking of a woman who'd knocked on his door that morning. She claimed she was from the government, come to clean his floors. He'd seen right through that ploy, as he'd seen through all the others. Three greedy nieces bent on proving him insane — what more did an old man need to keep him on his toes? Luckily, he had a spare set of keys for his dilapidated 2CV, otherwise they'd have taken that too. Those girls had a hundred devious ways of robbing an old man. They claimed he was blind. They hinted he was senile. Insane, am I? he fumed. Because you're driving me insane!

The car had holes in the floorboard and issues with the finer gears, but once he got her rolling, she hummed along like a sardine tin on wheels. Whenever he was feeling edgy he'd load his hunting dogs into the back seat and drive. Sometimes he drove all night. It was so peaceful after midnight. Driving calmed his nerves, gave him a sense of purpose. He hummed under his breath to keep himself awake, occasionally blurting the odd phrase out loud, something he'd said or should have said, a few salient bits from the never-ending flow of thoughts uninterrupted by conversation, eruptions from the deep. By the time he came upon a tall man on the side of the road, he'd given the cleaning woman a piece of his mind. Laurent and Julia were used to their master's arguments. When he slowed down for the man in black, they went right on sleeping, but the smell put them both on alert.

"Shhh! Shut your traps, curs," Alonzo growled

back. "Don't pay any attention, monsieur. They're useless beasts. I'd shoot them both, put them out of their misery, but my nieces! Ho! Let me tell you about those bitches. They're after a man day and night. Where're you going? Just name your destination. I'd be happy to drop you off. Avignon? Oh, that's not far at all. Be glad to oblige. Yer car break down? I can go back and take a look. No? No car? All right then, Avignon it is. Get in. Let me move the gun. There you go. Duck down now, mind yer hat. And we're off."

Though hardly twenty kilometres as the crow flies, the highway between Isle sur la Sorgue and Avignon is a twisty marathon, a complex network of traffic circles and diversions through connecting towns, a route dating back centuries. After an obligatory exchange of names, Alonzo settled back to enjoy the trip and the sound of his own voice.

"You know, in Petrarch's time, the trip took a day or more, depending upon the mode of transport. Sometimes walking was quicker in the end than counting on beasts of burden, considering the feeding, watering, ailments and delays. People didn't zip back and forth between towns in those days, no sir. They set out on carefully planned journeys, often taking every stick of furniture they owned. Those popes and cardinals, they summered in the countryside, built castles. Petrarch himself spent most of his time in Fontaine de Vaucluse, which is a short distance from Isle sur la Sorgue, the fountain in question being the one that feeds the river Sorgue. Take a look at Petrarch's book about his walk up the Mount Ventoux and you'll see he never got to the top at all, his philosophical musings refer to a similar trip taken by someone else, most likely his brother." The last word slipped out. Once he'd said it, Alonzo couldn't remember whether it was Petrarch's brother or Victor who'd taken the trip, or rather taken the credit for taking the trip. He personally, Alonzo Martin, definitely had walked up Mount Ventoux, years ago. Or at least up Mount St. Victoire, which amounts to the same thing, as far as foreigners go.

Anyway, Victor told stories about it for years. Victor claimed they'd both gone, which was transparent bullshit. Victor never walked anywhere, but he had a real knack for fabricating details. "It's a shame to criticize the dead. The truth of the matter is I never had the slightest reason to rebuke a brother. We hardly ever saw each other, which might have given cause for rebuke, had one of us been that kind of man, but we wasn't. We made our beds and were prepared to lie in it." Another slip. He hadn't meant to bring Victor into the conversation at all but it was late and the stranger was interested, at least he seemed to be, or wasn't in a talking mood. Anyway, the 1900-plus-metre journey up Mount Ventoux was a considerable distance in those days. Still is! He burst into laughter.

Julia and Laurent hated laughter. It was a noise Alonzo only made when strangers were around, and strangers made their teeth hurt. A horse woman who owned their mother had given them pretentious human names and then given them to Alonzo, who was too true or too dumb to think of better. Two lean hounds, their glory years behind, they refused to close an eyelid after Piers Le Gris climbed into the car. The drone of the master's voice was reassuring. Better steady conversation than explosions from solitary thought. But they didn't like the smell of the passenger at all. He reeked of women, their soapy, pungent skin and natural secretions that made men's mouths water. Better women steeped in kitchen smells, fried fat and onions. The lick of a kitchen woman's hands was a far distant memory, as faint as mother's milk. Still, they sat up on their haunches, paying strict attention, heads bobbing in the night like oversized car ornaments, which is what they felt like most of the time, forced to jiggle along bumpy country roads full of rain ruts and quick turns. Inevitably, Alonzo had insisted on a shortcut (or a scenic route or a treacherous farmer's trail he imagined would take him past some long-forgotten landmark) but as usual the detour soon petered out and forced them to turn back on themselves. They weren't surprised. Laurent was fairly sure they had nothing to fear from the man in the hat. He favoured settling back to sleep but Julia was on edge, so they rode like that, bobbing along a moonless country road, oblivious to most of what was going on, except that Alonzo was babbling and lost and the stranger was anxious. They could smell his anxiety. He wanted to be somewhere else.

"Avignon," he murmured. "I must get you to Avignon!"

The driver roared laughing, and began to sing. "*On y danse, on y danse, sur le pont de Avignooooonnn.*" His singing voice reminded the dogs of warm gravy. Laurent licked his lips; Julia whimpered painfully. It was years since they'd had a drop of gravy, or anything prepared by women's hands. They hoped the man would lead them to a kitchen fire. Julia pressed her wet snout against his shoulder but to no avail. On and on Alonzo droned and bellowed. Finally, the jalopy wheeled into a parking lot and stopped. Both men got out and slammed their doors.

The Café Bar Meridian is attached to a small

hotel and stays open after midnight, when the owner, Marcel, feels inclined. Even in winter there are people who need rooms suddenly and sometimes late. Marcel had cleaned down the counter and mopped the floor when the travellers walked in.

"I hope you're looking for a room," he said to the two who stepped over his slop pail. "Otherwise I'm closed."

"Two whiskeys," Alonzo roared. "I'm paying. He's lost his briefcase. Can you believe it! That's a good one. Where is it, *mon vieux*?"

The passenger slid his hat onto the bar, took a seat and muttered a terse reply. Alonzo burst out laughing.

"HAHAHAHA! He says he must 'a left it at the orgy'!"

Warmed by laughter, Marcel set three glasses on the bar and settled in for a rousing bit of chat.

When they'd gone he wondered who they were. He imagined they had come from far and would still be travelling when dawn broke. Two men on a long journey, one of them was completely mad, the other forgot his hat.

After dropping his passenger at the Porte St. Lazare, Alonzo wheeled out into the wide boulevard that circles the city.

"Might as well take time to see the sights," he shouted over his shoulder. Julia and Laurent whimpered acquiescence. As he drove, he hummed an old familiar tune. It began to rain. The words came back and he belted out the melody, keeping time with the windshield wipers. A hit from his father's time, it was a love song by Trenet, full of joy and yearning, a memory of a memory. He envied the stranger, a man in his prime, rushing to appointments, facing situations. Though the cause of his mad dash back to town, he'd been reluctant to divulge. Naturally a man of his sort would be discreet. There was about him a generous, enveloping spirit. Yes, he decided, an aura. In spite of his obsessions, a man of depth and soul.

"Imagine, leaving a briefcase at an orgy!" he exclaimed out loud. (Convinced they were being spoken to, Julia and Laurent barked agreement.) All very well and good, he thought, but a man like that is facing ordeals. Mustn't let nostalgia have a go. No, it wouldn't do to pine after a life like that.

Then, out of nowhere, a thought hit him broadside. As clear and sharp as stone, it woke him up and stung. He pulled the car over on a grassy knoll, with a view of some distant town, and got out.

What if those bitches are right? What if I am going daft?

As soon as the pebble thought hit, another followed. As soft and kind as a blanket, it spoke directly to him: "If you think you might be going mad — then — definitely you are not — yet."

He laughed out loud. Then, so that anyone who cared could hear, he shouted, *Yes, I am on my way mad-crazy-senile-gaga! But not quite there yet!*

Looking up at the starlit sky, he vowed to remember the moment forever.

TWENTY-ONE

NELLY WAS READING by the fire when the doorbell rang. Three urgent bursts, and before she could reach the vestibule, a long blast. Expecting Magali who routinely forgot her keys, she flung open the door, ready with a stiff reproof. It was Piers, cheeks flushed, eyes ablaze as though he'd been running. His long black coat was soaked, rivulets of rain streaming down his face. Without a word, he brushed past and raced up the stairs, taking two at a time.

She called after him, asking if he wanted tea, but he was already out of sight. Moments later he came rushing back down, this time dressed in a leather jacket.

"I forgot this!" he said, waving an envelope. Her response was to hand him an umbrella. He kissed her three times on the cheeks, uttering a hoarse *bonsoir madame*, and disappeared into the rain.

The night air whirled around her ankles as she peered into the empty street. What was he up to, turning up after midnight like an empty-handed beggar, rushing off again when he should have been settling down to work? She'd thought he was working in his room. In a doorway across the street, she saw the shadow of something moving, a beggar seeking refuge from a wild November night. She closed the door and turned the lock.

The sitting room was stifling. A large log piled on olive-wood coals had finally caught, sending off gusts of heat. She opened the window for a breath of air. Two green eyes peered at her from across the street. It could be that wolf, she thought. A rabid beast had entered the city by mistake, and slaughtered several cats, including the pregnant mother of Caesar, or so her neighbour claimed. Reaching for the phone to summon police, she heard a familiar bark and looked closer, recognized the eyes.

"*Mon Dieu!* What are you doing over there?" she scolded. At the sound of her voice, The General let out a meek growl, as if to say it's not my fault, and stumbled toward the front door, wagging his tail furiously.

She ordered him to go around to the back door. Keeping his head down, he shifted direction and padded toward an alley at the end of the block that led round to the garden gate. She was waiting, and marched him into the kitchen, ready with a lecture, until she noticed he was favouring his left front leg. A gash on his snout was caked with blood.

"Where have you been, eh? How did you get out? You're far too old for the night life, *mon Général*. Stay home at night! Listen to me," she said softly, massaging his wet fur with a towel. After devouring a slice of ham with a clump of bread soaked in warm water, he headed for his bed beneath the table, tired but unrepentant.

Her hands smelled of dog, a pungent mixture of old hair and fresh sweat, evidence of a scuffle in a back alley somewhere. She'd thought he was beyond the game of growls and snaps. So you've still got your manhood, even into old age, she mused. If his dreams were still of battle, ancient victories and future threats, then there was no use scolding. What did the other combatant look like? she wondered. A snappy little cur with hound's-tooth prints along its bony haunch? The pulse of life, the thought pleased her.

The fire had settled down to a steady blaze. She closed the window and retrieved her book, the last in a stack that had taken her weeks to go through. Not exactly great literature, she concluded, but nothing that would harm a weary lot of caged men either. Her written report would say so, and leave it at that. If Hervé Brunet ventured to ask (she suspected he would not), she would say that all of the books donated by the famous professor, at least those she'd been asked to read, were about sex — a common human impulse, therefore deserving a place in literature. Few were content to mention the act. They inevitably tried to recreate its effect, somehow capture in words the clouds of lust and emotion around the act. Most often they failed. Accounts of fictional characters' sexual experiences on the page seemed no more real or tangible to her than descriptions of flora and fauna in Madagascar. Or maybe I'm too old to judge, she thought. Those days are over.

One book remained. Nothing like the others, it was the most beautiful volume in the pile, a hardcover, the spine bound in red leather with gold lettering, and yet described as a manual of instruction. When she opened it, a waft of attic mildew escaped from pages turned the colour of desert sand. The full title was *The Perfumed Garden, A Manual of Arab Erotology*. Written by Sheikh Nefzaoui in the sixteenth century, it was a reprint of the first translation made by an unnamed captain in the French army, 1850. A bestseller since it first appeared, the book she held in her hands was published by Les Editions Georges-Anquetil in 1927. Glancing first at the index, she saw the twenty chapters covered almost every imaginable aspect of "things relating to the act of generation": attractive qualities of men and women, causes of enjoyment; the sexuality of animals; treatments for sterility, impotence, small members, body odours; commentary on virtue, deceit and pregnancy. A virtual manual of desire, a practical book. No story to tell, no erotic agenda.

From the moment she began to read, a booming voice rose up from the page. Standing over her shoulder was Sheikh Nefzaoui himself, a large, lusty man from another world, spilling out his joyful harangue as if to an innocent reader who had everything to learn. His words, elegant and completely exotic, gushy by turns, then blunt and practical, sometimes both in the same passage, a dizzy mixture. Most surprising of all, Sheikh Nefzaoui knew things about women she had never seen in print before.

Praise be given to God, who has placed man's greatest pleasure in the natural parts of woman, and has destined the natural parts of man to afford the greatest enjoyment to woman. He has not endowed the parts of woman with any pleasurable or satisfactory feeling until the same have been penetrated by the instrument of the male; and likewise the sexual or-

gans of man know neither rest nor quietness until they have entered those of the female. Hence the mutual operation. There takes place between the two actors wrestling, intertwinings, a kind of animated conflict. Owing to the contact of the lower parts of the two bellies, the enjoyment soon comes to pass. The man is at work with a pestle, while the woman seconds him by lascivious movements; finally comes the ejaculation.

God also it is who has embellished the chest of the woman with breasts, has furnished her with a double chin, and has given brilliant colours to her cheeks. He has also gifted her with eyes that inspire love, and with eyelashes like polished blades. He has furnished her with a rounded belly and a beautiful navel, and with a majestic rump, and all these wonders are borne up by the thighs. It is between these latter that God has placed the arena of the combat; when the same is provided with ample flesh, it resembles the head of a lion. It is called the vulva. Oh! How many men's deaths lie at her door? Amongst them, how many heroes!

Passages of advice were mixed with stories supposedly illustrating the facts. Delicious tales, they were all about journeys with only one destination. The speaker, a cross between a mad professor and a

Provençal rustic whose knowledge sprang from barnyard lore and blood sport. Or a clownish priest of sex who saw no gap between particular experience (his) and the eternal. When she wasn't helpless with laughter, she was tempted to interrupt by pointing out that much of what he offered as fact was superstition or science that had long since been contradicted. And by praising Allah/God as the source of libido, did he not effectively rule out any hope of morality? But there was no arguing with a sage who rolled out advice with the speed and authority of Zeus.

The Master of the Universe has bestowed upon women the empire of seduction; all men, weak or strong, are subjected to a weakness for the love of woman. Through woman we have society or dispersion, sojourn or emigration. I, servant of God, am thankful to him that no one can help falling in love with beautiful women, and that no one can escape the desire to possess them, neither by change, nor flight, nor separation.

Fire consumed the olive log and died, but Nelly didn't notice.

TWENTY-TWO

A FEW FLAKES. No more than a shake or two of ground pepper on his tongue, but the effect was instant. As if a wire had fallen from heaven and fastened itself to the top of his head and was now pulling up, Mouloud's feet hardly touched the pavement. He was light-headed at first, then light all over. His mouth tasted chalky, like during Ramadan. Fatiha always insisted he fast. He resisted at first and cheated behind her back, but soon fell into the rhythm and began to look forward to the half-hour before sunset when hunger, like a fist, gripped his insides and twisted. Finally he began to see what fasting was all about: insulation against pain. It makes you strong. Everything looked sharp and clear, his eyes seemed to penetrate the night. A few seconds or half an hour, he couldn't tell the difference.

But this feeling was different. Nothing to do with pain, it was a gift. The first time, he'd been walking along the street one night and there was Selim, coming toward him, smiling like a long-lost brother, as if nothing had happened. Not a word about Remy or who would have to pay for what happened. "Enjoy," he'd said, slipping him the treat. "Take it from me, here, take it. Never mind the money. It's on me, *cheb*. Hey, I hear you're part of the rave at the Lion d'Or. The Troubadours. Awesome! I'll be there. We'll talk. Look out for me."

Selim disappeared. Mouloud stood in front of the merry go round in Place de l'Horloge, staring at the curves and colours and gold trim, mesmerized by the beauty of a giant toy, wondering if he'd been dreaming. But the gift was real. Now it all made sense. Trailing Piers Le Gris had been a waste of time. Nobody appeared out of the dark to grab him and make him pay. Selim had a lot on the go. He didn't have time to worry about chaff. He knew everybody, even the people behind the concert. He knew their two-bit garage band was called the Troubadours, meaning he'd made a point of finding out. In the days that followed, the sick fear that had hung over him since the fight outside his room had lifted, and he'd started to think that maybe the move to Marseille would happen after all. Selim had said let's talk, which was another way of saying, I've got a job, I need you.

It was a forty-minute walk from his room to the concert venue outside the walls, a cavernous warehouse with high ceilings and a vast parking lot. The event was bigger than he had expected. He'd had to use a map and set out early so as not to be late. Now there was time to kill after the sound-check which was supposed to happen at seven. The other band members had come by car, and turned up twenty minutes late but nobody seemed to notice. Everything was running behind.

Waiting around unnerved Mouloud. He'd been sure the others wouldn't show. In the end, there wasn't much to do after the stage manager told them where to come on. They were about to head for a smoke behind the lead guitar player's van when the manager called Mouloud back and said there'd been a change in the schedule. The Troubadours had been moved to the second half of the show. At the last minute, he muttered something like, "If there's time."

The other band members didn't like the sound of it. Mouloud told them not to worry, but he had a sinking feeling they'd never get a chance to play. The rest of the line-up consisted of established names. The other musicians all seemed to know each other and be friends of the people running the event. The Troubadours had been offered the gig on the basis of a sketchy demo and a quick conversation with a guy Mouloud had met in a bar. It all seemed too good to be true.

By nine, people started trickling into the hall. A

disco CD throbbed over the sound system, but he couldn't get into the mood, decided to take a walk, heading out through the open gate of a high iron fence decorated by a gigantic painting of a lion. He kept his head down, eyes on the pavement. From behind, someone shouted his name, slapped him on the back. It was Selim, come to wish him luck. He handed him a tiny folded paper containing grains of magic. Mouloud slipped it into his jeans pocket. He knew he should wait until after the concert, but halfway round the block he swallowed the whole thing. After that, putting in time was easy.

At midnight the hall was packed. He couldn't believe there were so many people. Where had they all come from? The streets had looked empty. After a couple of warm-up acts, a rai band came on and the crowd woke up. Disco Maghreb, direct from Oran, slick, totally derivative, not a nanosecond of originality between them, which is why they were so big, he decided. They'd stolen every note and move. Worse still, their claim to being Moroccan was just as faint. As the lead bellowed out a bad imitation of Sting, Mouloud abandoned his corner of privacy backstage and plunged into the crowd, a few hundred gyrating fans in a wide pit below the stage.

He could feel himself sinking back to earth, and was glad of it. If he flew too high, he might not be able to play. He picked his way through a sea of strangers, eyes focused straight ahead, as though he had serious business on the other side of the room. The crowd pressed in, choking him. He wished he'd stayed on the sidelines. A question, seriously buried until now, drifted to the surface of his mind: where was she? He'd vowed not to care whether she turned up or not, but sober reality triggered an over-powering reversal. Now catching sight of her was all he cared about.

After a few false starts Magali found the venue on a side street off the Route de Tarascon, a part of the city she didn't know. She'd taken the wrong bus and had to double back, fighting rain. Following the music, she came to a high iron fence with an over-sized lion's face on the gate below a sign, Club Privé. Bouncers guarded the doors. She'd given Piers her invitation, and had to buy a ticket. She wished she'd asked him to come with her, but at the time had been reluctant to disturb his routine. The whole point of inviting Piers had been to avoid wandering around alone, feeling out of place in a strange envi-ronment, which was exactly what was happening. Bad planning, she thought. If she hadn't said she'd meet him, she'd have turned around and headed home.

None of her friends had even heard about the concert, and nobody wanted to come along. Probably one of those government-sponsored events meant to convince immigrants their culture matters, they said. Expect speeches, amateur acts, belly dancing. But it wasn't that at all. The band was pumping out a disco beat and there was a dance floor near the stage. The crowd was young, mostly guys dressed in tight pants and big belts. Some of the women wore headscarves but they also had on high heels and makeup. A clutch of older men gathered at the entrance in serious discussion, as if they had come to do business and it wasn't music.

The scene reminded her of Spain, a trip she'd taken with her parents two years earlier. They'd gone to a bullfight, and her father wanted her to turn away for the bloody finale. She'd refused, of course, but the animal's death wasn't what she remembered. It was the atmosphere before, the certainty that something awful was about to happen, and everybody knew. A few weeks later, she was told they were getting a divorce. Looking back on the trip, their last as a family, she figured they must have known then. The terrible news had been hanging in the air around them, like death. The time in Spain and what happened after had folded into a single bad memory. Maybe it's only because everybody here has dark hair, she thought.

She stood at the side of the hall, looking for a familiar face. Two guys nearby were talking and looking her way, on the verge of striking up a conversation, so she started walking, skirting the edge of the room, looking for Piers. Twenty minutes felt like hours. The band changed. This time the lead singer was a woman with a tambourine. The music was still electronic but the song was in Arabic, a simple refrain repeated over and over. People started clapping in time and chanting. She wondered if she was scared because she was alone and it all seemed so foreign. Or was there good reason to be afraid? The looks she got were somewhere between leers and curiosity; so far nobody had spoken to her.

Then she saw Mouloud. He seemed to emerge from the tight centre of the crowd, as if he were coming out of a dark pool, eyes straight ahead, looking for someone. For her, she hoped. She shouted his name and waved but he didn't seem to notice, and veered off. She caught up to him, grabbed his shirt. When he wheeled around and saw her, his face hardly changed, as if he didn't recognize her.

"Sorry I'm late. Have you been on yet?" she shouted, leaning close so he could hear. When he shook his head, she said, "Great! The best is always last." He smiled, but only with his eyes. His lips barely curled at the edges. He reached out and put his arm around her shoulders and she was glad she'd found him.

"Who's that singer?"

"That's Assia," he said, cocking his head to the stage. "Trance music. You have to let yourself go, get into it. Takes time. You want something to drink?"

She nodded. He pulled her by the hand into the crowd, toward the other side of the room. When they reached the bar he let go and turned to get the barman's attention. Behind them, the singer's spot came to an end. The crowd cheered wildly, shouts of bravo, feet stamping. The star dove into her encore.

Holding two bottles by the neck above his head, Mouloud nodded at Magali to follow, and led her through a side door. The crisp outside air was a relief. They leaned against the wall, sipping cold Cokes. She was about to ask about his music, but another thought popped into her mind, and she said, "Have you seen anything of Piers Le Gris?" A simple question, but Mouloud heard something else. He seemed to wake up, as if his face had come unfrozen.

The centre of the crowd was a pulsating vortex as Mouloud fought his way to the edge like a swimmer in over his head. He was coming down from the high fast, spent a few minutes at ground zero and kept on sinking. By the time he reached the edge of the crowd, he was sure the only way out was to keep on walking, forget about the Troubadours. Just go back to the city, his room. It wasn't meant to be. His head was pounding. He couldn't see straight. The skin on his face was stretched so tight it felt like it was about to crack. He was still swimming and half-blind when Magali came up to him. He didn't believe she was real until he put his arm around her, felt solid flesh. Then he heard himself babbling on about trance music and they were heading toward the bar. By the time they got outside his head had started to clear. A cold blast of night air, a swig of sweet liquid and he was back to the surface again, and grateful to be back. They were standing under a canopy roof outside the hall, a shelter between a wild night inside and the downpour. She was wearing a white sweater under her jacket, a gold chain around her neck. He slipped his arm around her shoulder. Her hair smelled sweet. She was so beautiful, soft and pure. Suddenly the night was alive again. The urge to run had gone. Of course he would play and sing the songs he'd written for her, because she was there to hear them.

"Have you seen anything of Piers Le Gris?"

Her question came from nowhere. At first he didn't understand. She said she'd invited him but he might not show up. He was interested in music.

Her eyes darted as she spoke, looking for someone through the rain. Piers.

"Are you fucking him?"

"No! Why would you ask a thing like that?"

"You are, aren't you?"

"Mouloud, don't be crazy. I said I'm not."

She glared at him, half laughing, half furious.

"I know you want to, and you will," he said
calmly.

She stepped out into the rain as if to run, then
suddenly wheeled around and slapped him, hard.
Surprised, he reeled back, landing against the wall.
The sting of her hand on his cheek acted like an
elixir. It made everything clear again and he wanted
to take it all back. Who cares?

"Okay, forget about it," he said with a shrug,
and looked away. But of course she wouldn't. She
kept on talking, telling him how wrong he was, insisting he was wrong. He was always wrong. You
promised me, you promised, promised, over and
over, like the wail of a siren, you promised. His head
was pounding. So he walked off, left her standing
under a tin roof with the rain tapping like finger-
nails. What's the use, he thought. When he heard
her shout his name into the darkness, the real reason
for running away caught up with him, causing a
choking pain in his chest, then tears.

TWENTY-THREE

THE ONLY WAY OUT to the street was through the concert hall. Magali went back inside and plunged in,
keeping her head down, the energy of anger cutting
a path through the crowd. As she reached the main
doors, prepared to run for the bus, she felt a hand on
her arm and turned around. It was Piers Le Gris.

"Sorry, I'm late," he said. "Have you been waiting long?"

"No," she answered weakly. A lie from the
depths of confusion, she'd been waiting for ages and
struggled to swallow a sob.

"Oh dear," he said. "What happened?"

"Nothing, I'm all right." Determined not to give
him an opening for more questions, she wiped her
eyes and looked away.

"Has Mouloud been on yet?"

"Not yet. I don't really — I mean, I don't care.
He's ..."

She hadn't meant to babble, yet dreaded running

into Mouloud again, especially if he found her with
Piers. He'd looked crazy, definitely on something. It
might be best to keep out of his way.

Piers seemed to catch her drift. "Do you want to
go? I'll call for a taxi if you like."

She shrugged, thinking how disappointed
Mouloud would be when he found out later she
hadn't bothered to stay for his set.

"Let's wait," she said. "That's what we came
for."

Piers reached down and took her by the hand.
"Come on. We can wait at the bar."

It felt strange being led, as if she were a child
crossing a busy street and she might step out in front
of a car. Eyes darting over the crowd, he seemed to
be on the lookout, hardly aware of her at all. They
wedged their way into a spot at the bar. Beads of
sweat had formed on his forehead. His face was
flushed. When the waiter turned away to get their
drinks, she noticed his hand resting on the counter
was shaking. She laced her fingers through his. He
looked down, then at her. Mouloud had been right
all along, he hasn't come for the concert, she
thought. He came here for me. So they would drink
a glass of wine or two, listen to music, then go back
to rue des Griffons, to his dingy green room that
smelled of old newspapers and fake cigarettes,

where they'd stayed up most of one night, and she'd heard his strange story. She would ask all of the questions she'd wanted to ask. But first she reached up and slid her hand around his neck, pulled him down and kissed him, no more than a quick brush on the lips, but enough to determine how this night would end.

By the time Mouloud heard his named called once, then twice, he had collapsed behind a sheaf of black tarp that served as a curtain. The stage manager pulled him up by the collar and shouted, "Hey kid. That means you. Come on, your band's up there, waiting." Thrusting a bottle of water at him, he said, "Let's go."

Mouloud took a long gulp and splashed the rest on his face. Picking up his oud, he staggered toward the stage. The light stung his eyes. Suddenly somebody shoved him and he was staring into the centre of a powerful spotlight. From the dark pit below came weak applause and cheers. His arms hung loose at his sides. He reached for the strings but his hands were a dead weight, impossible to move. Out of the darkness somebody hollered, "Let's go man." The room was alive. He spoke the first words, low and deliberate.

I find no peace, I am not at war,
I find not peace, I am not at war,
I have no peace, I am not war.
I fear and hope and burn and I am ice.

His hands came unlocked, he found the strings, played the first line, played it again and sang the words exactly as he had taken them from Petrarch. Finally he was alone and lost in the light. His fingers seemed to leave his body. He played only every other line and slapped his hips in between.

One keeps me jailed who neither locks nor
   opens,
Nor keeps me for her own, nor frees the noose;
Love does not kill, nor does he loose my chains;
He wants me lifeless but won't loosen me.

The pit began to breathe with his rhythm. He could see eyes, faces, bodies swaying, and the clutch of people gathered in front of the stage began to merge into one being. He held his breath, counted back from ten, then began again.

I see with no eyes, shout without a tongue;
I yearn to perish, and I beg for help;
I hate myself and love someone else.

He sang the verse twice, more melodiously the second time, lifted his hands from the oud into the air above his head and spoke softly, his voice full of anguish and anger.

I thrive on pain and laugh with all my tears;
I dislike death as much as I do life:
Because of you, lady, I am this way.

Dropping his arms to his sides, he bowed his head, turned and walked offstage. The crowd broke into wild applause and the band picked up his tune.

The rain stopped. As the taxi headed up rue de la République, Piers told the driver to let them out at the corner of Henri Fabre. He hadn't said a word since they left the concert. Afraid she would say something silly and regret it immediately, Magali had stayed quiet too. Silence in a small space was intense. The driver had a strange impenetrable accent and kept shouting into his cell phone in a language she didn't recognize. She was glad when they got out. Piers slipped his arm through hers and led her towards Place St. Didier, chattering on about the driver. Had she noticed the scar running down the side of his cheek and the weird wood carving hanging from his rearview mirror? She began to think the heaviness she'd felt as they rode must have been her imagination.

Suddenly he stopped in front of a gate on rue du Roi René, the entrance to a popular theatre. In an ironic tone, as if he'd suddenly turned tour guide, he said, "And on your right is the Chapel of Ste. Claire, where Petrarch first saw Laura, in 1327. She was fourteen. I think. Not much older." He paused, as if expecting a comment. "Did you know that?"

She shook her head.

"Petrarch, the famous Italian poet, who lived in Avignon. Really, you should read the history of this place, my dear. It's extensive, and important."

She wanted to say, I know who Petrarch is, but he didn't wait for an answer, took her hand and led the way to rue des Griffons.

At the door, he stopped again and said, "No, no, no, she was older. I must be thinking of Juliet. Definitely, Laura was married with children when Frank clamped eyes on her. Imagine, cruising a married woman in church! That's the Italians for you."

When she laughed he put his finger to her lips, and they tiptoed after that, taking special care to pass the dining room quietly.

TWENTY-FOUR

AT THE SOUND OF VOICES in the vestibule, Nelly turned off the lamp and stood up quickly. The book fell to the floor. From the hallway came a ripple of Magali's laughter, and footsteps on the staircase. The sudden darkness left an afterglow, an undulating motion like a floating carpet bed before her eyes. The image made her head swim. She sat down, felt for the book at her feet. Opening it in the dark, she was startled by a waft of scent rising from the pages, the stale smell of old paper, but something else. Burying her face in the fold, she inhaled a waft of sweet, dusty air, a mixture of dried flowers and archaic words, sumptuous, mysterious, monastic, a strange elixir, it made her head light. She turned on the lamp, sat down and resumed reading.

The kiss is assumed to be an integral part of coition. The best kiss is the one impressed on humid lips combined with the suction of the lips and tongue, which latter particularly provokes the flow of sweet and fresh saliva. It is for the man to bring this about by slightly and softly nibbling his partner's tongue, when her saliva will flow sweet and exquisite, more pleasant than refined honey, and which will not mix with the saliva of her mouth. This manoeuvre will give the man a trembling sensation, which will run all through his body, and is more intoxicating than wine drunk to excess. A poet has said:

> *In kissing her, I have drunk from her mouth*
> *Like a camel that drinks from the redir;*
> *Her embrace and the freshness of her mouth*
> *Give me a languor that goes to my marrow.*

A vulgar proverb says:

> *A moist kiss*
> *Is better than a hurried coitus.*

Sundry Positions for the Coitus: The ways of doing it to women are numerous and variable. And now is the time to make known to you the different positions which are usual. God, the magnificent, has said: "Women are your field. Go upon your field as you like."

Finding Piers in the chaos of Mouloud's crazy concert, Magali had felt a sudden rush of delicious familiarity, as if they were on a crowded island together. Standing in his room with the door closed, the feeling crystallized: how totally inevitable, this night. Piers Le Gris, telling stories, humming softly, lighting candles. When his back was turned, she slipped out of her t-shirt and bra and stood leaning against the door, hands tucked into her jeans.

He turned around, and sighed, "You are a beautiful woman."

"Thank you," she said, trying not to sound self-conscious.

"No, no. It's got nothing to do with me. Or you, either, for that matter. I don't mean to flatter. You just are beautiful. You will do what beauty does."

"What's that?"

He was looking at her intensely, it made her squirm.

"Break hearts, launch ships, that sort of thing. Take off your jeans, please."

She laughed, and thinking following orders wasn't very romantic, strode across the room and sat down in his writing chair.

"You wouldn't have a glass of Scotch?"

"I think you've had enough for one night," he said, in his scolding voice.

"Well, I'd like one."

He splashed a few tablespoonsful into a cup and handed it to her, put the top back on the bottle and set it on the table next to a pile of books. Then, as if he was getting ready for an ordinary night's sleep, he took off his clothes, hung up the trousers, tossed the shirt and socks in a pile, and poured himself a glass of water.

"You've cleaned up your room," she said. "It looks like you're leaving. Are you?"

"After tonight, I would say, yes." He took a sip of water.

She was surprised to see him wandering around the room naked except for skimpy briefs and totally at ease, as though he was wearing a silk smoking jacket, dangling a cigarillo from his lips. She'd thought he was more of a prude. Watching him, she decided he was faking. There must be a huge gap between the person he showed to the world and the true one underneath. He was far more complicated than she'd imagined. So perfectly relaxed, he made her feel quite naked. The oddest part was his surprising lack of eagerness. Almost fatalistic, as though he'd already been accused of something and pronounced guilty, waiting for the sentence. The room wasn't warm, but the candles made it seem so. She could feel goosebumps forming on her arms, yet her cheeks were flushed. She was on edge and yet totally open to the moment. Anything could happen.

"I want to make love to you," she said, setting her cup down beside the chair.

He let slip a nervous laugh. It restored her confidence, so she went over and put her arms around him. He took her head in his hands, and whispering her name, kissed her, and the amazing nonchalance dissolved. Maybe it was only a pose, she thought. She could feel his whole body tremble as he kissed her forehead, eyes, cheeks, neck, again the lips, slowly and with deliberation, as though staking a claim to different parts of her body. She threw her arms around him, he lifted her up and carried her to the bed, and stopping at the edge, twirled once around. A sudden joyous turn, like falling in love, it made her laugh. He laid her down on the bed, and running his fingers down the bone between her breasts, continued kissing her, nothing like the frantic pace she was used to from guys her own age, nervous preludes to the main thing. His kisses were like sips of great wine, all the nerves belonged to her. He kept his eyes open, watching. Every move was smooth and calm except his gaze, which was a wild fiery look that seemed to flow right through her and made her feel so young and powerless. Pulling back from his embrace, she slid her leg over his torso, made him roll onto his back and then she bent down to kiss him, her hair draped over his face, pinning him down, hips swaying in the air, breasts sliding across his chest until he groaned and reached for the zipper of her jeans.

Somewhere in the distance, she heard a sound.

Pick ... pick ... pick ... pick ... pebbles hitting glass. A soft spray of hail on the windowpane. She knew instantly who it was: Mouloud, in the garden, looking up at the window.

"Wait a moment," she whispered. "I'll close the curtains."

Sundry Names Given to the Sexual Parts of Man
Know, O Vizir (to whom God be good!) that man's member bears different names, as:
El dekeur, the virile
El air, the member for generation
El ablil, the liberator
El nasse, the sleeper

Nelly thought of Olivier Fare, then of other men she'd known, and laughed out loud till tears ran down her cheeks.

El zodamme, the crowbar
El hamama, the dove
El molki, the duellist
El aouasa, the vast one
El aride, the large one
Abou belaoum, the glutton
El mokaour, the bottomless
El bazzaz, the restless

El mezour, the deep one
El zeunbur, the wasp
El ladid, the delicious one

Following on the lexicon of excitable parts was a
passage that struck her as cruel, or at least, mis-
placed: a description of how the member appears in
dreams, and what it means. With the confidence of
a sorcerer, the Sheikh left no doubt that a man's
power and glory lies in his loins, his frailty too. The
news of dreams is often bad.

Demons and desire enter by one door: the mind.

As regards the names kamera and dekeur, their
meaning is plain. Dekeur is a word which signified
the male of all creatures, and is also used in the sense
of "mention" or "memory." When a man dies, they
say, "His member has been cut off," meaning, "His
memory is departed from the world."

Hard-soled boots with heavy heels, the girlish sprint
gave her away. Nelly knew without looking that the
footsteps on the staircase were Magali's. She heard
the front door open, waited for the second set.
Surely Piers would follow her. But he didn't.

There was a draft in the hall, the front door carelessly left ajar. Turning the deadbolt, she slid the

chain lock into place, thinking: this is no time to take chances with so much rushing about. If she plans on returning before dawn, I'll have to come down and let her in.

TWENTY-FIVE

CAESAR WAS HUDDLED on the doorstep as Magali stepped into the night. One whiff of her presence and he cried out.

"What are you doing here?" she whispered, scooping him up. "You're supposed to sleep in your basket, little one. Who let you out? Oh, you're shivering. Come on, crawl inside my jacket. That's good. Stay close to me. I'm glad you're here. Don't be afraid. I'm not afraid. There, there, calmly, little one. Close your eyes and be safe."

Mouloud was standing inside the gate. He heard her voice, the soft cooing sound. It was not for him.

When she saw him, said his name, he stepped back into the shadows, fists clutched in his pockets. Nothing there but a handful of stones. He backed away, she followed, whispered his name.

"You lied," he said. "It is him, isn't it? All along you've been—"

"That's none of your—"

"Liar!"

The angry mood terrified Caesar. He struggled to get out from her grasp. Magali unzipped her jacket and stroked his head.

"You know who this is?" she said softly, in a voice she hoped would calm him down. "It's Caesar. Look how cute he is. A little baby kitten. His mum died in a bloody mess. They say it was a wolf that did it, but that's hard to believe. Anyway, we nursed him back to life, didn't we? His mummy and his brothers and sisters all died too. It took hours and hours of feeding him, one drop of milk at a time. But he's fine now."

Her words were a lullaby full of warmth and love, but Mouloud felt accusation in her look, accusing and pushing him away. He wanted desperately to be the kitten, and not the object of her steely gaze. But it was no use wanting. The sadness choked him. He leaned against the garden gate, dry sobs rising from the bottom of his heart. Caesar sniffed despair and let out a sudden, terrified screech. His limbs stiffened. He started clawing at her chest and, with one powerful leap that sent Magali reeling, sprinted into the night.

It scared her, and stopped Mouloud's sobs.

"Caesar, come back!" she called. But he was already out of sight. "He's not coming back," she murmured. "He's gone."

"I'm sorry," Mouloud said.

"It's not your fault," she sighed.

Mouloud wheeled round and strode off. The sight of his thin frame, the familiar slump as he followed the path the kitten had taken filled her with sadness. Suddenly it seemed important that he not go off like that, with the heaviness of a few ill-chosen words ringing in his ears. It all happened so quickly. The scratches on her breast were bleeding, a thin line of red staining her t-shirt. She went after him, calling his name, but he didn't stop. He started walking faster. She caught up and grabbed his jacket sleeve, slipped her arm though his and walked with him until their steps fell into time. Under the alien lights of a town she'd never wanted to know, she wished time would roll back, and instead of the lazy Rhone, they were in Paris, somewhere near the Seine, making friends and full of plans. She wished Caesar hadn't run away, she needed to hold him in her arms like a baby and sing him asleep. When they reached Mouloud's front door, he pulled free and said, "Go back home."

"I have no home," she said.

"Go to Piers Le Gris, then," he said.

"Mouloud …"

"I accept my destiny."

"What do you mean?"

"I love you, that's all," he said, his voice flat. "Don't be afraid. I would never, ever harm you."

She believed him. Every fibre of her body knew his word was good. She leaned over, kissed him gently on the neck. He stared at her, impassive.

"Do you want me to come upstairs with you?"

He shrugged.

"Mouloud, listen to me: I haven't made love to—to anybody, not Piers Le Gris, or anybody else, since you. I don't know what that means. Probably nothing. But it's true. Are you listening to me? Okay, yes, I would have done it with him, but you threw stones at the window and called me and so now here I am."

He stared at her, then turned and headed up the stairs. She followed. When they were in his room, he leaned against the wall, a familiar pose, as though he needed the wall to keep standing. She pressed her body against his, touched his sex. He was aroused.

"Crazy, crazy, Mouloud," she murmured.

She pulled him down onto the bed and kissed him till he unthawed and wrapped his arms around her. They were like two playful kittens who had been away from each other far too long. She was glad she had chosen to be with this sweet grateful friend who loved her in his bones.

When she'd gone, Mouloud turned on the light and downed a full bottle of water. His lips were sore. Sitting on the side of the bed, he felt a terrible emptiness settling in. Not the feeling he'd imagined would follow making love to Magali. He'd thought of nothing while they did it. Finally, he'd been able to stop thinking and let go. The act had cleared his head, brought her down to earth. He thought of his vow; he'd sworn to keep it no matter what. It didn't trouble him at all. The vow gave meaning to all he'd said and done till now. Made the moment pure. The future, easy. He threw on his jacket and headed out into the street.

Only when she'd bolted the door did Nelly realize how cold the house had grown. A sudden drop in the temperature made the ancient radiators creek. She headed upstairs. Piers' door was ajar, from the room behind a strange golden light. He must have turned on the small gas heater she'd given him to take off a chill. She knocked, intending to remind him not to fall asleep before turning it off. When he didn't answer, she peeked in. The light came from a dozen candles placed at various levels, on the empty bookcases, the nightstand, both windowsills. There was an open bottle of liquor on the table, Magali's sweater and bra lay in a heap on the floor. Piers was stretched out on the bed, asleep. At least the rhythm of his breathing suggested sleep.

Why would Magali run off? she wondered. Had he said something to frighten her? Or sent her away? That hardly seemed possible, and yet he was by all indications asleep, or lost in a dream state. Drugged, maybe, or terribly drunk. His mouth was open in the careless slack-jawed position of a sleeper, one leg raised slightly in a bend, the other straight. The back of one hand was resting on his forehead, his arm twisted in an uncomfortable gesture suggesting guilt or pain; the other lay limply on his chest. He was breathing through his nose, the heavy sighs of dark thoughts. His sex was firm. Names came into her head: the pigeon, the tinker, the liberator, the sleeper ...

The thunder of the Sheikh's ribald litany made her smile. He might have been standing nearby. His hectoring tone seemed to fill the room, giving the moment a strange air of unreality so that she wasn't alone with a sleeping man but somehow wide awake with a powerful one whose voice rendered all thoughts naked and alive. As if hearing the booming voice in her head, his member moved. She couldn't take her eyes away. Resting one knee on the side of the bed, she leaned over, took it in her hand. Piers stirred, his torso rising gently. Without

opening his eyes he slid his arm away from his forehead and reached out. She inched forward onto the
bed. It was an easy distance to kneel over him.
Taking the member in both hands, she began to
stroke slowly, then more quickly, finally bending
down to kiss. He tasted like the sea, soft at first,
then hard as an eel. All those careful nights with
Roland had taught her how to touch a man stealth-
ily, silently, with a minimum of fury, stroking,
kissing, licking until he grew into the rhythm of her
movements. A powerful experience, pleasurable and
familiar, her open thighs pressed against the taut
muscles of his legs, moving to the beat of his breathing, sharing the ascent, her thoughts in perfect
harmony, as if his desire was also hers.

Suddenly he pulled away, and reaching for her
hips, swung her around until she was lying on her
back. Sliding his hands under her nightgown, he
began a long, slow caress of ribs and breasts, reaching around to her back until he was holding her,
lifting her, suspended. She felt weightless, overpow-
ered, brittle, as though her body might break in two.
A terrifying charge as he entered, rough at first, and
painful. She cried out. His heart pounded against her
head, thrusts growing stronger, more insistent, then
a rush, he groaned, collapsed. She was overwhelmed
with a desire to cry, a strange mixture of relief and

sadness. Her chest hurt from holding back. As if sensing the swell of emotion, he cradled her head in one hand and pressed her body into him with the other. She could taste the salty warmth of his chest. The familiar scent of his ritual morning kisses was deeper, more intense. Hardly daring to breathe, she lay still for what seemed like a long time, wondering how she could escape. Every muscle remained taut, his mind whirling. She counted slowly to ten, shifted position. His grip loosened and she was able to slip out, pull the rumpled nightgown down past her waist and head for the door. She looked back, a glance only. He was watching.

TWENTY-SIX

LÉONCE WAS SITTING at his desk when the telephone rang. Piles of ledgers and stacks of bills covered a wide table facing a window that looked onto vineyards and distant mountains. A routine dating from a time when his weekdays had been busy, he counted on Sunday to catch up on his paperwork. Lately, though, he tended to spend the morning gazing out the window or reading. Hours passed without the sound of a human voice.

The clang of the telephone caught him in deep reverie. Expecting a stranger, he answered with a brisk *bonjour*. Nelly's voice was a shock, as if she'd suddenly come into the room and laid a hand on his shoulder. Her presence always affected him. Once their eyes met, he was fine. The ritual smile, an old code of indifference carried him along. But hearing his name spoken with urgency took him back decades, to a time he had learned to forget.

"Léonce ... I'm afraid it's bad news." Followed by silence, as she waited for him to speak.

"What is it? ... Is it Magali?"

"No, the Moroccan boy. He's had an accident. At least it seems so. The police wouldn't say much. Something about an attack of wild dogs. Monsieur Le Gris has gone to the hospital. He's going to phone. You'll have to contact your man, bring him down right away. He doesn't drive, does he?"

"No, Ahmed doesn't drive."

A deluge of information, shock then relief, the final note made him angry. He hated the way people of a certain generation referred to immigrants as Your Man, The Moroccan, as if they were personal possessions. Typical bourgeoisie who lived in big houses and towns, read *Le Figaro* and rarely spoke with anyone who didn't share their own shallow anxieties. He was reluctant to count Nelly among them, though the temptation restored distance, provided the jolt he needed to take charge.

"But you're saying Mouloud is all right?"

"I wouldn't know. They plucked him out of the Rhone, of all places. If he didn't drown, he may be poisoned. That water is rank. He was carrying a note addressed to Magali, with her phone number. Imagine! She's hysterical. Oh Léonce, I don't know what to do. I suppose it's my fault. I'd no idea — a girl her age. It's awful, just awful. What will Paul say? Oh dear, I don't know—"

"Nelly, Nelly, don't think so far ahead. I'll call on his father, we'll leave immediately. Where is Mouloud? Which hospital?"

Ahmed heard the knock on his door through a cloud of sleep. Thinking it might be a dream, he lay still. The second knock told him months of worry had come to a head. He was silent on the drive to Avignon. Worry beads wrapped around one hand, he hadn't the strength to move his fingers as he prayed.

Piers Le Gris was sitting in the hospital corridor beside a rotund little man. "This is the man who saved Mouloud," he said, introducing his companion. "Indirectly, that is. His dogs pulled him from the river. They saw him fall from the St. Bénézet Bridge and went in after him."

Fall from the bridge. Ahmed heard the words and cried out in Arabic, a grief-stricken wail. The little man clutched his arm. "It's all right, *monsieur*. Your boy'll be fine. Don't let them put down my dogs, please. They saved his skin. He jumped off that bridge and I sent the dogs after him. I don't want my dogs blamed for nothing they didn't do. I'm not asking for a reward or anything. Don't get me wrong. But if it wasn't for my Laurent and Julia—"

Piers nudged him and whispered, "Shhh. I told you, let him see Mouloud first."

A nurse appeared and took Ahmed off to Intensive Care. When they were out of earshot, Alonzo started up again about the dogs, and Piers said, "Monsieur Martel, would you be kind enough to make a call on behalf of my friend? Actually, I can vouch for the dogs in question. They wouldn't hurt anybody."

"I saw the boy jump," the man huffed, his eyes bulging. "We were walking near the bridge. He was bent on doing himself in. I sent them after him. If there's flesh wounds, I'll swear the lad fought back. But he's alive, you can see for yourself. If I hadn't put my dogs at risk, that kid'd be dead by now, by his own doing. It's not right, making the dogs pay."

Léonce looked at Piers, then at the stranger who seemed ready to explode. "All right, give me the details. I'll look into it."

Piers took out a cell phone, fed in a number and handed it to Léonce. A few seconds into conversation with the police department receptionist and it was clear a personal appearance would be required. Piers agreed to wait with Ahmed while the stranger took Léonce to rescue the dogs.

Ahmed went limp at the knees when he found Mouloud stretched out on the hospital bed, eyes closed, tubes stuck into his nose and arms, forehead and limbs bound in white gauze. He had a nasty bruise on his cheek. He was so thin his body left the impression of a child under the white sheet. At Ahmed's greeting he opened his eyes and closed them again, either too weak to concentrate or fearful of the lecture he knew was sure to follow. Standing by the side of his son's bed, Ahmed looked down as if looking into a coffin, and recited his thoughts in a low murmur. The nurses, who didn't understand Arabic, assumed he was praying and tiptoed out of sight to leave the two in peace.

His words were not a prayer, they were the summation of all that he had learned during thirty years in France, the essence of his grief following the loss of Fatiha, his resolutions, the hard residue of many long nights when he had lain awake wondering where his beloved youngest son could be, what dark alleys his soul would find on its journey through a hostile land. His words had the soothing cadence of a litany, though the import was hard. Mouloud listened with his eyes closed. As his father spoke, the darkness deepened. He felt a heavy weight pressing on his chest. But midway through the talk, he remembered the light he'd seen as he stood on the edge of the bridge, his back to the water, a few seconds after he'd let go and was falling into the Rhone. A glimpse of stars, and then the light, a reminder of the lights his mother must have seen in the last seconds of her life. The light filled him with hope.

"My son," Ahmed began, "you have done a terrible thing. Brought disgrace to our family, but it is nothing next to the danger to your soul. The twenty-ninth line of the Nisa verse of the glorious Qur'an clearly forbids the taking of one's life. Had you succeeded you would be damned forever, lost to our family and all time. Someone or some force intervened and so you were saved. Praise Allah, you were saved for greater things. Even had you died, my beloved son, I would not have despised you. These past few weeks I have prayed incessantly for your salvation. What this French woman has done to you is terrible. Tonight you have been saved from a danger as great as the French girl. Now you must be rescued once again. You do not belong here in this decadent place. You are weak. You do not know how to gird yourself against the infidels. But you can learn, I am sure, and you must learn. I will make arrangements for you to study and train. You will go back home to a school in the countryside, where you will learn many things: a true and profound understanding of the sacred scriptures. How to be strong of mind and body in the light of Allah. Your teachers will know how to put your talents to use. When you return to your family, you will not be the weak child I see stretched out before me. You will be a man, able to defend yourself, your family, your faith, the word of Allah. Sleep now my son, a miracle has redeemed you. Your father, Ahmed Mourabed, honours all those who have brought us to this moment of salvation. Allah is great, Allah is good."

Mouloud opened his eyes and stared at his father. A wrinkled old man, worn down by hard labour, eyes ablaze. The darkness had lifted, the fierce light was gone. He saw the room in shades of grey, his future, stretched out like a line in the desert sand. When Ahmed had gone, he sank back into sleep, hoping to be rescued by dreams.

By the time he'd extricated himself from the drama of hound incarceration, Léonce had heard a good part of Alonzo's life story, including the saga of his wicked nieces and how the pair of sibling curs had come into his custody. He was tempted to ask about Piers Le Gris, who was the fellow, really? He tried to imagine the circumstances under which he and this strange peasant had come to know each other. He wanted to ask, but the fellow's monologue was seamless. He'd have had to grab him by the shoulders and fire a question, and was sure such a blatant show of curiosity would soon get back to Le Gris.

Instead, he helped the trio into the ancient 2CV
and shoved a handful of cash at the little man.
Alonzo refused at first until Léonce insisted Monsieur
Mourabed would be insulted if the dogs didn't get a
few good meals for their trouble. Suicide is a mortal
sin for an Arab, he explained. "You didn't just save
his life, you saved his soul. And the family's honour."
Alonzo nodded and the two dogs whimpered, as
though they'd understood completely.

TWENTY-SEVEN

IT WAS LATE AFTERNOON by the time Léonce returned to rue des Griffons. Nelly assured him Mouloud was out of danger. Following her into the kitchen for a fresh pot of coffee, he asked how Magali was taking it all.

"Not well," she sighed. "She cried most of the morning. I had the doctor come around and give her a sedative. She's sleeping. She seems to think it's all her fault. Apparently the boy had made some kind of vow, and he was carrying it out against himself. I don't understand at all. A crazy Arab boy, he's been lurking around here for months. I told her—"

"Nelly, Mouloud was born in France. He's in love with her."

"Well, I suppose that explains everything," she answered coldly.

"Yes, in a sense it does," he said.

She'd been busy with the coffee pot and only half watching him. But the sadness in his voice caught her attention. When she turned around he was standing at the end of the table, his face was drawn, dark blue eyes gazing at her from a mass of lines. He looked frail, as if life had given him a good hard beating, and he was grateful just to be alive. Gratitude was not a state Nelly associated with Léonce Martel. She was tempted to feel sorry for him, but just then the coffee bubbled up. She poured two cups and took them into the sitting room. He followed.

They had just sat down when Piers arrived back from the hospital. He said Mouloud was resting comfortably and would be kept in overnight. Ahmed would spend the night in town with his sister and brother-in-law. Nelly offered coffee, but in the melee of handshakes and exchange of important facts they somehow ended up drinking from a large bottle of Scotch he brought down from his room. At least the men drank; she took a small glass of homemade nut wine.

As she watched and listened, a passive observer to an ancient ritual, she thought how naturally men rule the world. Once something happens to galvanize their attention — a crisis will do — emotion doesn't stand in the way. After a single stilted dinner at the Grand Café, the conversation hummed along like a good car on a freshly paved motorway. They hardly gave her a second glance.

The moment Piers Le Gris sat down, Léonce noticed the atmosphere change, the familiar haze of intimacy, calling her *Madame Reboul*, an unconvincing politesse laid on for the benefit of an interloper. He decided they were lovers. He kept up a rousing conversation with Le Gris but watched her every move, looking for confirmation.

Had Piers been alone with Nelly, he would have found the encounter awkward. The presence of Léonce handed him a lifeline. He was grateful for an opportunity to be sociable and generous with his Scotch, a chance to watch her out of the corner of his eye without having to face her gaze. They carried on as if nothing had changed. If he drank a little too much, or too quickly, it was pure carelessness and not a contest. A diligent drinker, Léonce had a precise understanding of his own tolerance and monitored his intake. As the evening wore on and evolved into dinner, hastily prepared by Nelly, he made an effort to draw her into the conversation. He was determined to demonstrate indifference.

Later, thinking through the evening, Piers would marvel at how adroitly the old man had played the scene. He ignored Nelly for long stretches, then out of the blue he'd turn to her and say something, recall a distant detail about some person or trivial event in their past, and his attention covered her like a cloak.

She was helpless in such moments, totally drawn in by his gaze. An outsider felt invisible. By the end of the evening Piers wondered whether he might have dreamed the previous night. Had she really come into his candle-lit room? Was that her waiflike body he'd held in his arms? The fragile embrace into which he'd poured months if not years of desire? He was thinking these thoughts, reliving a dreamlike night that had delivered him into a state of grace, a new world in which miracles do happen and the future is assured without anxious mortal intervention, when he was seized by an involuntary urge to yawn.

Nelly stopped talking in midsentence. "*Monsieur Le Gris!* Oh dear, listen to us going on and on about people and things you've never heard of. Please excuse us!"

There was no avoiding the cue. He apologized for yawning and excused himself for the night. She followed him to the bottom of the stairs.

"Please speak to Magali," she whispered. "She needs to talk about today. I'm sure she would want to see you." Her motherly advice surprised him. So that's the way it is now, he thought. I'm being handed over to the girl, told to keep her company while an important house guest finishes what he came for. Her tone was almost patronizing, the edge of jealousy he'd felt for months was gone. Trudging up the stairs, he suddenly felt exhausted. There was no light in Magali's room, so he went on by and collapsed noiselessly on the bed.

"I'm quite incapable of driving," Léonce announced, as Nelly came back into the room. She noticed he'd tossed a large log on the fire.

"Your boarder is generous with his Scotch," he added.

Nelly said, "I'll make coffee."

"Oh no, I can't take coffee after dinner. I'd be up all night. Maybe I should look for a hotel."

"You're perfectly welcome to stay here," she said curtly.

The nearly empty bottle of single malt was sitting on the coffee table. Léonce reached over and poured a splash into his glass and offered it to Nelly. She declined.

"You're looking well," he said, leaning back in the chair. The new log had caught on and the room took on a friendly glow.

"As are you," she replied. "The last time I saw you, you looked drawn."

"Did I? At the restaurant?"

"No, I was thinking of before. After Brigitte's illness, you were worn out."

"Oh yes, the funeral. I was tired." He swirled the

drink around in the bottom of the glass and took a sip. "So, you take in boarders? Why?"

"For the company. I don't like living alone in such a large house."

"Nor do I. But you— that surprises me. I've always thought of you as someone who's quite happy to be on her own."

She looked over at him, slumped in her reading chair, feet crossed and resting comfortably on the needlepoint footstool. He had no idea of who she was, how she'd managed all those years. It occurred to her that she could agree, claim she'd preferred being alone to marriage, that it had broken her heart to leave Ste. Anne's for the privilege of changing her name, and although Alphonse had been a devoted husband, an excellent provider and a saint on his deathbed, she didn't miss him much at all. But that wasn't quite the truth.

Instead, she sighed and looked at her shoes, handmade Italian pumps worn with sheer stockings, a trim grey suit and pearls. An outfit chosen with him in mind.

She was sitting in a straight-backed chair, legs crossed at the knees, hands resting in her lap, holding a tiny glass of homemade wine. An elegant bird, Léonce was thinking. It had always surprised him how thoroughly urban Nelly had become. The word *bourgeois* came to mind, her opinions as well as her wardrobe. Buxom Brigitte fit in easily with village life and motherhood, but Nelly had left it all behind. A touch eccentric, a true original. Without the galvanizing presence of her boarder, he found it difficult to think of something to say.

Interpreting his silence, she said, "You must be tired. Let me show you to your room."

They tiptoed up the stairs in darkness and turned into a narrow hall. He was surprised, the house seemed much bigger from the outside. The entrance, formal front rooms and vast marble staircase suggested grandeur, but the living space was relatively insignificant. Nelly pointed out the WC as they passed, and led him on to a room at the end of the hall, no bigger than an oversized closet. As if reading his thoughts, she whispered, "I'm afraid this room is quite small."

The bed reminded him of an army cot, and looked about as comfortable. When he sat down, the springs sank. The dressing table was crowded with perfume and cosmetic bottles, a cotton nightdress draped over a chair. Yet even without these signs, the room's aroma would have told him it was hers: flowers laced with something faintly medicinal, camphor or pine, he wasn't sure which, but the effect was potent, confusing. She had taken him to her bedroom. Now she was standing over him, rambling on about finding a pair of pyjamas.

"Don't bother," he said. "Is that your husband?"

He nodded at a photograph hanging over the bed, though he wasn't looking at it, he was looking straight at her. He'd noticed the photo as soon as he entered the room, the shadowy back of a man's head and a full-on shot of the great statesman himself.

"Yes, that's Alphonse getting his medal from the General," she said, a touch stiffly.

"I recognized de Gaulle," he said. Then, thinking the remark might have sounded sarcastic, he said, "What was the medal meant to commemorate?"

Nelly detected accusation in his tone. She sat down on the dressing table chair. "He was wounded at Ardennes."

"Alphonse Reboul fought at the Battle of the Bulge?!" The decisive victory in the Liberation of France? How had a minor military pawn made it that far? Had he escaped the Occupation and fought on the front? Incredulous, Léonce turned to look again at the late hero, searching for signs that it could be true.

"Oh no," she said. "It was May of 1940 ..."

"Ah!" The fall of France. So the talk had been true: Reboul had missed the action, packed it in early with a minor medal. He kicked off his shoes.

"I have a better picture of him here," she said, opening a drawer in the dressing table. She handed him a yellowed photograph. This time Alphonse was alone, staring straight at the camera, with a medal pinned to his chest. A broad reliable face without a spark of intelligence, Léonce decided. No sign of de Gaulle either.

"I have others," she sputtered. Rummaging through an old chocolate box, she described the events that had led to his medal, but Léonce wasn't listening, he was removing his socks, pants and shirt and slipping under the covers. When she turned around he was lying in her bed, covered with a blanket she had kept since the war.

Confident that comparison with the shadowy hero of a lost battle would stand him in good stead, he said, "Turn out the light, my darling, Lie down beside me and fall asleep in my arms."

The command struck her as bold and arrogant. He hasn't changed at all, she thought. The rumours had flown around Ste. Cécile of his many affairs, and none too discreet. Observing Brigitte's marriage from a distance, she'd had ample evidence that destiny had dealt her the better fate, a consolation that held up on a day-to-day basis, even if memories of Roland still had their power. He really is another man, she thought, casting a glance at the sleeping figure reflected in her dressing-table mirror. He's changed completely. Nothing at all like Roland.

His eyes were half closed, he was watching, waiting. He'd been around enough women to know there comes a moment in seduction when a man can lose everything with one wrong word. There's no way of knowing what that word might be. No point taking the risk.

Bubbling contempt kept Nelly rigid. Every fibre of her body wanted to know if he smelled and tasted like Roland, but the distance between yearning and fear, between the dressing table and the bed, was great. It angered her how he'd slipped into bed behind her back, expecting she'd peel off her clothes in front of him. Even if she could forget the past, the thought of standing naked, of revealing what time had done to flesh, would have stopped her. Where was the hectoring Sheikh Nefzaoui when she needed him? His thundering commands, pure Eros, an irresistible aphrodisiac for the mind had been banished by the presence of real time, too much history, too many solitary nights, too many reasons to stay fixed, staring into the mirror.

What finally made her turn around was a thought evoked by what he'd said, or so she'd heard him say.

Lie in my arms.

The words made her think of Piers, the impulsive almost brutal skirmish that had left them both embarrassed. Not the act itself, a blurry, unexpected invasion. But the way he'd held her when it was over, the feel of his hand on the back of her head, the other firmly around her spine, pressing her against his body. At the time, all she could think of was how to escape. But now the memory of his embrace burned. She wanted that feeling back, the sensation of being held by a man, in a man's arms. Days, weeks, years later, it wouldn't matter that she had been thinking of Piers Le Gris as she turned off the lamp, slipped out of her clothes and climbed into bed, into his embrace. Léonce would never know, and in any case, he wouldn't have cared. In due time, Nelly herself would hardly remember thinking of Piers Le Gris in the dark. The reunion of a dead hero and a weary survivor would leave no room.

TWENTY-EIGHT

MORNING OF THE WINTER SOLSTICE, Nelly and Magali left for Ste. Cécile in the blue Mercedes. Caesar travelled up front in his cat basket, The General ensconced in the back seat, his head resting on Magali's lap as she stroked his neck and drank in the small talk of lovers. They were making an effort to pretend nothing had changed, but of course everything had. Even without the advantage of knowing who they'd been during the war, Magali was sure she would have noticed the difference. Their words had turned from grey to blue and gold, colours that proved love was possible, which was all she needed to know.

Mouloud, too. His name was no longer green with rage, it was the red and orange of sunsets over the sea. As promised, his father had sent him straight back to Tangiers and she'd already received a postcard. She answered straightaway, assuring him she'd gone back to his room on rue de la Palapharnerie

and rescued the poems just in time, before the land-
lady tossed them into the garbage with the rest of
his belongings. I'm keeping them till you come to
your senses, she wrote, and meant it.

Walking back to rue des Griffons with the bundle
of papers in her arms, she'd seen Piers Le Gris standing on a street corner, staring off as if his thoughts
were an ocean away. He already looked like someone she'd known a long time ago. Maybe a trick of
light, but the air around him seemed to glow. She
would have gone over and spoken, but the bundle
was heavy and Nelly needed help. A great burst of
cooking had settled the question of what they would
eat for the *réveillon*.

Evening. Solitude has returned to rue des Griffons.
In the absence of familiar voices, the house has
given up on grandeur, let shabbiness reign. The only
sound, a printer churning out the final chapters of
The Lethal Guitar. Piers is stretched out in the
horsehair recliner, eyes closed, mind's eye lingering
on the story's last scene: the usual carnage followed
by the flourish of a door slammed shut, his personal
contribution to the trademark.

In a far corner of the avocado room, a door
slides open. Sounds of laboured breathing, the creak
of ancient joints willed into movement, the slow

scrape of clunky soles dragged across terracotta tiles, muffled by the chug-chug-chug of pages piling up. An odour of stale coffee masks a cloud of incense hovering around a tiny wizened creature now making his way across the room. Hardly human — a description he would not dispute.

Mindful of the half-sleeping man, he plants himself behind the recliner, out of sight so as not to risk surprise, and waits. A cord holds his hopsack robe at the waist. He unties the knot, ties it again, considering his next move. A minute passes, two, five. He's stalling. This has happened to him before. In the penultimate moment of a mission, he falls into a kind of stupor and the message, even the sense of himself as a messenger, seems to dissolve. He has already missed the moment once. A draughty café on rue de la République, a morning spent reading old newspapers, consuming one cup of coffee after another. (His eyelids twitched for weeks.) As the hour approached, he'd lost his nerve and fled. They met again in the dark night of a serious injury when Piers lay close to death. It was Gabriel who'd kept him talking while others took care of his wounds and it saved him. So much for the body, what about the soul?

A tickle rises in his throat. He coughs. Piers leaps out of the chair, startling them both, and glances around the room. He senses someone there but sees nothing, and reassured, draws a glass of water from the tap, stands staring at the wall. He is thinking of the womblike room on the other side, and the girl, how her presence tortured and delighted, woke him from a dreary sleep and led him to new place. He is sorry they never made love but, at the same time, deeply relieved.

Heartened to know Piers' thoughts have drifted toward the past, the messenger steps forward. An aura of reverie provides a perfect opening; it will make what he has to say easier. If only Piers would sit down. A hand on the shoulder is always a strong beginning. Words whispered in the ear are credible. Not like the old times, when a burning bush, a thunderbolt would do. These days revelation must travel by stealth.

But Piers does not sit down. He reaches for a small cloth-bound volume on his writing table, and opens it at random. *The Courtesan's Prayer Book*, a Christmas gift from Nelly. As soon as she left the house, he had ripped off the wrapping paper and read from beginning to end. He is still mesmerized by her story, by knowing she wrote it under this same roof while he typed for money and let himself be tortured by old demons. He looks at the pages, but he isn't reading, he is studying the handwriting, a neat feminine script, the style all French girls were taught before the war.

Suddenly, as if he'd heard his name called, he stands up, and sliding the book into his pocket, heads for the door.

Gabriel follows him down the dimly lit hall, their footsteps keeping time. What a picture they make: a tall man wearing a bathrobe and slippers and a tiny hooded creature in a monk's robe and sandals. At the end of the hall, a room smelling of perfume and the occasional cigarette. Piers turns on the lamp. He has never seen this room before and yet it is painfully familiar, a minute shrine to an intimate life. He sits down on the cot.

Gabriel is standing on the threshold. Their eyes meet. He steps back, ready for the shock of recognition but Piers looks straight through him, as though the intensity of the moment has rendered him blind. The messenger cringes, offers a cracked smile exposing misshapen teeth, a sight he himself could not face in a mirror. But Piers keeps on staring at nothingness until Gabriel is forced to recognize a new truth, yet another sign of how the times have changed, shrunk.

I am invisible.

Before he has a chance to digest the news, Piers slips off the cot and onto his knees, a melting motion as if some force other than will has moved him. Reaching under the pillow, he pulls the duvet back on sheets as white as skin that never sees the sun and bends over, sinks into the sheets and inhales, filling his lungs with the scent of her dreams. A second breath, shameless, as if the scent were his to take.

Gabriel leans against the door frame, watching. The shock of invisibility has unhinged him. Reality has never been something he could count on, but this is new. Sadness, envy, confusion and so many other disguised forces well up until his eyes leak acrid juices, and he gives into a human weakness. Later the Lord's Messenger will tell himself and anyone who wants to know that he wept for a god-less time, a time full of gods. It hardly matters. Inflation is as bad as extinction. The truth is, he cried for himself, for his whole redundant tribe left hanging at the end of a millennium. Irony, a curse: the revelation is all his. Angels are futile, so sayeth the man who goes down on his knees in homage to a human conceit. Something to do with procreation, giving rise to taboo and often tears.

Desire.

The spasms Gabriel witnessed in the avocado room, an old woman and this sorry man wrestling with their lust, strange to behold and vaguely violent. Afterwards, the two of them could hardly look each other in the eye, yet everything had changed. Their sense of time, knocked askew. Years, gone. Hope, like a familiar tune hummed unconsciously, no longer a delusion. Since that night they have acted from confidence, acted on their true desires.

Nelly will never admit she was wrong to have turned her attention away from waiting for Roland, that the tragedy of their separation was not all his fault. But she will not run away either.

Piers will never abandon his monkish ways. In a world bereft of mystery, his hunger for the sacred can never be sated. But he will reach out to the child-girl, the product of his desire, love her and let her love him back. His mission, like a river diverted, will find a way: if not a Holy Father, at least an inadvertent saint, a man who leaves a trail of redemption behind him.

What's left for the messenger to say? The feeling in the lavender room is the feeling he was sent to deliver. The purpose of his message. A state of grace.

Unmindful of the need for silence, he thunders along the freezing hallway, making mental notes for the inevitable report. A task accomplished will surely be commended. So why is he forlorn?

He stops by the avocado room just long enough to help himself to a finger of Scotch and continues on downstairs, out into rue des Griffons. Snow is falling on the streets of Avignon. The old stones are covered with an uncommon air of purity. His footsteps are mute.

— The End —

Acknowledgements

MANY MANY FRIENDS were pressed into service during the years I worked on this book. Sincere thanks to all of you, including Mark Czarnecki, Sheila Fischman, Isabel Huggan, Linda Leith, Elise Moser, Mélanie Grondin, Mark Abley, Ian McGillis, Kim McArthur, Pamela Erlichman and no doubt others who are not mentioned. Thank you to my excellent agents Carolyn Forde and Bruce Westwood, the team at McArthur & Co, Devon, Kendra, Kim and the book's designer Tania Craan. This story would not exist without our friends in Provence, especially Monsieur Bault, Jacques Lagarde, Eliane Grimaud and Nini Albertini, Mohammed, Rana and Rachid. And as always, profound appreciation to my patient husband, Gwyn.